life is

but a

dream

Brian James

FEIWEL AND FRIENDS

NEW YORK

for all the dreamers

A FEIWEL AND FRIENDS BOOK
An Imprint of Macmillan

Library of Congress Cataloging-in-Publication Data

James, Brian,
   Life is but a dream / Brian James. — 1st ed.
      p. cm.
   Summary: When fifteen-year-old Sabrina meets Alec at the Wellness Center where she is being treated for schizophrenia, he tries to persuade her that it is the world that is crazy, not them, and she should defy her doctors rather than lose what makes her creative and special.
   ISBN: 978-0-312-61004-3 (hardback)
   [1. Schizophrenia—Fiction.   2. Psychiatric hospitals—Fiction.   3. Creative ability—Fiction.   4. Mental illness—Fiction.]   I. Title.
   PZ7.J153585Lif 2012
   [Fic]—dc23

                                                                    2011036131

Book design by Barbara Grzeslo

Feiwel and Friends logo designed by Filomena Tuosto

First Edition: 2012

10 9 8 7 6 5 4 3 2 1

macteenbooks.com

Is all our life, then, but a dream
Seen faintly in the golden gleam . . .

—*Lewis Carroll*

Something is wrong with the sky. Thinner and nearly see-through, the sky is like a worn bedsheet tacked loosely over the sun, which blazes brightly on the other side. I stop for a second to watch and the other kids hurry past.

I breathe in and the blue fades out. I exhale swirling colors that streak across the clouds like rainbows on soapy water. I reach upward with my free hand. The evening sunlight touches my skin like golden water and I feel safe—almost like heaven is falling from the sky to protect me. It should be confusing but somehow it all makes sense to me. It makes sense the way a dream makes sense. The only difference is, I'm awake.

I see the cars out on the freeway. Their lights blink like shooting stars. I start to walk toward them when a cold hand touches my shoulder. The air rushes out of me in a gasp. My heart flutters against my ribs and for an instant, I cease to exist.

—Sabrina? Aren't you coming?— Kayliegh says. She looks beautiful in her slim black dress—the skirt shorter than any my mom would ever let me wear. Her hair is pulled up so only a few strands hang down around her ears. The hair spray must have glitter in it or something because the blond strands sparkle when the sunlight hits them just right.

—I was just . . .— I start to say, but I don't know how to finish. Instead, I point to the sky. There are faces in the clouds and I wave. They flutter like angels for a second before evaporating. Kayliegh doesn't see them. She laughs and locks elbows with mine, pulling me along with her.

The ground shifts under my feet as I walk. Concrete turns to sand and my toes sink in. The world is trying to swallow me, but Kayliegh keeps me from sinking. She keeps me moving forward. Our friends are ahead of us. They head into the lobby of the hotel, excited for the Freshman Dance to begin and the school year to end.

The banner over the entrance greets us with the theme our class has chosen. It reads *Live Forever* in bright neon letters. We walk under it and I sense the world crumbling behind us. Everything that once was there fades and now there is only what's ahead—the dizzy sound of music like a gathering storm. For a brief moment I'm in between where there is nothing.

As soon as we step inside, the music washes over me. The throbbing from the speakers weakens my legs. I feel unsteady and hold tighter to Kayliegh. It's mostly dark except for the spinning lights cutting through the crowd like swords. The music is so loud the glasses of soda scattered around the tables vibrate and everyone is screaming to be heard over it.

The conversations all blend together. They get lost in the music and form a cloud that hangs over me. It's trying to tell me something. It screams with a thundering voice as it calls out my name. *Sabrina* is the sound hiding behind everything and I feel myself slipping away. It terrifies me.

—Not now— I whisper. *—Not here.—*

I close my eyes, press my fingers against my temples, and try to massage away the drifting feeling that threatens to overtake me.

When I open my eyes again, the lights appear as flashes of lightning in a storm.

—*You okay?*— Kayliegh asks.

—*Fine*— I lie to her. —*Just excited.*—

—*Me too*— she shouts, and rushes into the crowd.

The music is a magnet pulling bodies together. Kayliegh is pulled into the middle of the room, swollen with people. She disappears and the noise grows louder. It's too much to fight it and I let it pass through me. Like falling backward into a swimming pool, trusting the arms of the water to hold me, I give in—wondering if I'm going to disappear, too.

ONE

I've always been different from other kids my age—from everyone, really. Special is one way to put it. The word is attached to me like a shadow. It's a halo hovering over me as I sit in class or walk through the halls at school. My parents always said that I was special too. Special in a good way, like I was delicate or rare—not special like something's wrong with me. Not before. Not like now.

Maybe everyone has an adjective attached to them—one they don't get to choose. A second name that other people know them by.

My dad is *successful*.

My mom is *bright*.

The man who works at the gas station convenience store is young and missing teeth. He smiles sideways and winks at me in the summer when I come in wearing flip-flops and a bathing suit under a towel. He is *creepy*.

Thomas Merker lives down the street from me. Since sixth grade, all the kids I know say he's *cool*. Sometimes he's also *funny*. He's lucky to have two words that anyone would want even if I don't believe they really belong to him.

Special has always been my word. It's not so much anymore—at least not in the same way. Now everybody thinks I'm sick. That's why

I was sent here to the Wellness Center whose name is like my adjective. It means something other than how it sounds. *Wellness Center* is just a nicer way of saying loony bin.

I'm here because I'm special. I see things others don't see.

I see the sky change colors when I wave my hand. I smear sunlight like finger paints and trace the clouds, giving them a soft glow of rainbows. I see dim halos hiding inside the most imperfect stones and I collect them. I keep them in my pocket, in my palm until all the sharp edges are worn down. Once they're smooth they glow through my fingers.

I feel things differently too.

The wind doesn't just touch against me, but blows through me—through my bones and through my soul like the fiery wave from an atomic blast.

My mom used to say I had an overactive imagination. *—You don't really* see *those things, Sabrina—* she would tell me. *—It's just how you picture them. There's a difference.—*

My response was always the same. I would tell her *—I see what I see. I don't know how there could be a difference.—*

I see the sky wrinkled like faded paper. The sunlight is ink spilling all the way to its edges. I see the swirling lines left behind in the path of birds as they dip and dive. I see the branches of trees dance a ballet in the background.

Kayliegh loves all of the things I see—or she did anyway. *—You have a gift—* she would say before asking me to draw her a picture. I'm good at that—at drawing the things I see. Once, Kayliegh thought they were beautiful. But she stopped asking for my drawings a long time ago.

It feels like forever since we were close, but maybe it doesn't seem so long to her. Time is always out of order for me. My memories are like a shuffled deck of cards, each one coming up at random. Every time one of her is dealt, it hurts a little.

I remember the last time we had fun together as clear as today. We were sitting on her front lawn after school, staring at the reflection of our bare feet in the shiny rims of her older brother's car. He had just washed it even though there were water restrictions due to the never-ending drought. Kayliegh kept reminding him about it. Not so much that she cared, more just to see him get bothered. —*Screw that, there's always a drought*— her brother Eric said with the hose on full force. —*It's okay for me to go halfway down 101 and pay some car wash to do it, but I can't do it myself? That's a load of crap.*—

He stomped around with angry steps. We laughed, because without his shirt on, he moved like a skinny gorilla. Kayliegh pointed at the hair around his nipples and made me look even though I didn't like to. I thought they looked like pink spiders and Kayliegh made me say it out loud until we both cracked up so bad that her brother turned the hose on us. Then we sat there smiling with water spray on our arms, glittering in the golden sun of a southern California drought.

That was all before.

Kayliegh doesn't want to know what I see anymore. —*Sabrina, that stuff is kind of kiddish*— she told me last summer. —*I mean, it was fine before, but come on . . . we're almost fifteen, going on sixteen. We're too old for pretend.*— Everyone else seemed to agree with her too.

Last year when my grades started to slip and my teachers complained that I didn't pay attention, my parents got angry. —*You're a better student than this!*— my mom shouted until her face turned red. —*Your grades are important, Sabrina. College is only a few years away.*—

—*How you do this year is crucial*— my dad said. —*College is going to be here before you know it. It's time to grow up and stop daydreaming all of the time.*—

When I was little, they encouraged me to use my imagination. They bought me posters of unicorns and fairies. Everything I had, from my little girl makeup to my glittery pink sneakers, was bathed in make-believe and came from a place where every girl could become a princess. I guess I never knew I was supposed to stop believing. The other girls were able to turn off their dreams in junior high. Puberty flicked a switch inside of them and dreams were replaced by hormones and college prep courses and varsity sports while I continued to look for fairies in the woods behind my house.

For a while it wasn't such a big deal. I was labeled immature, but that was fine with me. Then kids at school started to say there was something off about me. I was too much of a dreamer for them. They began saying I was mental.

—*I don't care*—I told my parents. —*I like the world in my dreams. It's a happier place than here.*—

Everyone else in the world is missing so much and they don't even know it. They're in such a rush that they blaze past all of the secrets there are to see. If they just paid attention, I'm sure they'd see what I do. They'd understand how the subtle changes in the sky can slow time. Or how the sound of ghosts is trapped in old records, whispering confessions about things they've learned since being carried off to heaven. Nobody else hears anything.

They are blinded by distractions. But I can tune out all of the noise that fills the world like so much screaming in the sky. I know how to stand still even when the Earth spins faster and faster than it ever did before. The rest of them try to keep up with the rhythm until it makes them dizzy. And with dizzy eyes, they stare at me and say I'm crazy.

Sometimes I like being alone in the truth.

Sometimes, though, I just feel lonely.

It's lonely here in the hospital, but things move slower here. It's not as loud and rushed. I don't feel so confused.

Here, I can walk for hours along the paths that carve up the grounds around the large brick buildings. Not red brick—gray bricks that make it feel like an old church or a boarding school like the ones in black-and-white movies set in England. I like that about it. The buildings feel out of time and I feel that way too.

From three in the afternoon until six in the afternoon, I'm allowed to shuffle barefoot over the lawn and through the gardens within the surrounding walls of the hospital. Sometimes I keep my head down, looking for stones with a hidden glow. When I find one, I pick it up and put it in the pocket of my sweatshirt because the nurses don't like me to collect them.

Other times, like today, I prefer to stay in one place, staring up at the sky and waiting for it to change. Here, it doesn't change as much as it used to. I still need to watch, though. I need to make sure those perfect moments don't go away forever.

―――――――――――

There's a boy in the common room who I haven't seen in here before. He stays apart from everyone else the way all new patients do. His body sinks so low that he becomes part of the cushions. He's almost flat, fading into the furniture like a small beetle trying for invisibility. His hair ruins the illusion though. It's so bright and clear, as if part of the world has been bleached out of existence.

I don't notice people most of the time. They pass by in a blur and it's rare when anyone stands out—especially here in the hospital where the nurses are all in uniform and all of the patients try so hard not to be seen. None of them have strong outlines to bring them into focus the way he does.

A soft glow surrounds this boy, whoever he is. It makes me want

9

to memorize the shape of his face and collect it like all the little stones I keep in my pocket.

I've been sitting silently and staring at him since he came in. That's allowed in the common room. This is the room where all of us are free to play games, read, or do nothing at all while we sit and stare. It's a kind of indoor recess. Sometimes I draw, but not recently. Nothing quite looks right anymore. Everything stays the same color from one minute to the next and the scenery is as steady as a photograph. Dr. Richards says that's part of getting better. She says I'm better when things are plain and not worth putting on paper for saving or sharing. She's a doctor, so I guess she's right. But I'm glad the boy isn't so dull as everything else around me. I'm glad that I have something interesting to watch.

He's watching me too.

Every minute or so, he lifts his head. His eyes search the room with a strange light. His eyes have the green glow of a radiated cat under a full moon. Darting here and there and into every corner, they search. But they always settle in the same place. They always end up on me.

He smiles every time.

Strangers make me shy. Usually their smiles make me turn away, but he isn't like other strangers. He's a familiar stranger. I've seen him before in a dream. I believe sometimes my dreams are of memories from the future. Sometimes they are about places I will go someday or people who I'm going to know but don't know yet.

It drives my parents crazy whenever I try to explain this idea to them.

—*Sabrina, dreams are just that . . . they're dreams*— my dad always says. —*You can't believe what a dream tells you.*— He believes dreams are only your brain scattering your thoughts while you're asleep. But mine aren't like that. Mine stay around even when I'm awake. They are everywhere around me, shadows that I see out of the corners of my eyes. Sometimes they are more than shadows. Sometimes they are real enough for me to see and hear, even touch. Those dreams aren't dreams at all but windows into other places. Those special dreams exist in the small places where two worlds rub up against each other.

The longer I stare at the boy from across the room, the more I remember that we've met.

When I close my eyes I see him dressed only in the sunshine. The clouds above him are in the shape of stick-figure ballerinas with rabbit ears made out of paper. They dance in the sky, high above us as we sit on a tire swing, swaying back and forth. Our thumbs are looped together around the frayed rope suspending us both above the ground. I can remember the way his fingers feel on my wrist and the sound of his voice even though we've never spoken.

When he looks at me, I wonder if he sees it too.

Is it possible the dream was his to begin with? Maybe I just wandered into it? Dreams can work like that. As long as we're the same, they can—as long as he's special like me.

I get caught in another one of his glances, another smile, and this time I smile back. When he stands up, the light catches his eyes. They shine brighter than the sun when you stare directly into it.

My blue eyes are shimmering stones just below the surface of clear water when I stare at him. Once his eyes and mine meet, the two colors make a halo around us the way clouds can sometimes make a ring around a bright moon.

There is a split second before he speaks when his mouth rests open in the shape of a pink oval. I see not only words waiting to come out but also the entire story of his life wanting to be woven together with mine. As he exhales, I hold my breath.

—*Hi*— he says, saying that one word as if he's said the same thing to me every morning of every day he's ever lived. —*I'm Alec.*—

I know he's waiting for me to talk and it makes me smile. He can't see it though. I've brought my hand up to my mouth and placed the sleeve of my sweatshirt neatly between my lips. Then, slowly, the purple fabric falls from my mouth and I tell him —*I'm Sabrina.*—

He makes a quick movement. Flicks the ends of his hair before he speaks again. —*I've sort of noticed you staring at me. Thought I'd come over and make sure you weren't a psycho or anything.*—

My eyes grow bigger and I shake my head nervously.

—*Sorry. Bad joke*— he says.

—*Oh*— I say, letting my breath out quickly. —*I guess . . . I didn't get it, that's all.*—

—*Forget it. It was dumb*— he says, tilting his head up toward the ceiling. —*It's just that I was watching and you don't seem like the others. You don't seem crazy. That's all I was trying to say.*—

—*I'm not*— I say. —*At least . . . I don't think I am anyway.*—

—*Yeah, I don't think you are either*— Alec says.

—*How can you tell?*— I ask him.

—*Because you actually understand the words coming out of my mouth. Most of the kids here . . . it's like they're from another planet. I've tried talking to some of them, but I don't get very far.*— He raises his eyebrows and looks from side to side as he says it, but none of the kids nearby return his glance.

—*Oh . . . yeah*— I say softly, sadly. I know the ones he's talking about. Ones like the girl at the table next to me with heavy circles under her eyes like she's been awake for days. Her mouth is always moving. Talking to someone who isn't there. There are a lot of kids like her here. They scare me a little. That's why most of the time I try not to talk to anybody.

They don't scare Alec though. From the way he looks at them, I get the feeling they simply frustrate him.

—*Mind if I sit down?*— he asks, kicking gently at the empty chair across from where I am. —*I won't bite, I swear. The medicine I'm on makes sure of that. Or, so they tell me.*—

This time I know he's kidding and I nearly laugh except that it seems so out of place in this room. I cover it quietly with a cough instead. He covers his with the sound of the chair's metal legs scratching over the floorboards.

Once he's sitting down, he is just as I remember. The bend of his elbow on the table is familiar. So is the way his chin rests in his palm. The bright morning light shining in from the window to touch his face at just the right angle is exactly how it was on the tire swing when the sky changed colors each time we pumped our legs to go higher. The memory sends shivers through me.

—*So, how long have you been here?*— he asks.

—*I'm not really sure*— I say. —*Sometime after the start of the school year, I know that. Sometimes it feels like a long time ago and other times it seems like it just happened. I lose track of time easily. It's part of why I'm here, I guess.*—

—*Consider yourself lucky. I've only been here a few days and it drags . . . so . . . slow*— he says, spacing out his words. —*All these stupid tests they're giving me, it's like spending three straight days at the dentist, you know what I mean?*—

—*The tests stop*— I say. —*I mean, once they know what's wrong.*—

Alec rolls his eyes. —*You know what the real problem is?*— he says. —*Maybe there's nothing wrong to begin with.*—

—*They say . . . that I live in my own thoughts too much*— I say, putting it as gently as I can. I'm still not comfortable with the word they use—with saying I'm schizophrenic. I'm not even sure it's true.

—*What does that mean? You daydream?*— he asks.

—*Sometimes*— I say.

—*Me too*— he says. —*Sometimes, I just think up stories and get lost in them. Beats being stuck listening to some teacher talk about algebra.*—

—*Yeah*— I say. —*They say I do it too much though . . . and too often.*—

—*You know what? I bet if you told them it was because you wanted to be an actress, like every other girl within a hundred miles of L.A., they'd encourage you. The problem is that you're probably different from those girls and that's what bothers them. I bet they put you here for the same reason I'm here . . . because you aren't exactly like all the other brain-dead teenagers walking through the malls. Am I right?*—

I shrug one shoulder and look away.

—*I've never really been like everybody else*— I admit.

—*Thank God for that, right!*— he says, tapping his fingers on the table in applause. It startles the whispering girl at the next table. She stops mumbling for a second, twists her hair tightly around her finger too, but Alec never looks over at her. His eyes never stray from mine and it's like we're the only two people in the world for him. —*I mean, why would anyone ever want to be like everybody else? But you see, that's what places like this are all about. Robot factories. All of the defect models are sent here for new programming until they get everybody thinking the same way and sharing the same opinions. You know what I mean?*—

—*I've never thought about it*— I say. —*Not like that.*—

—*Maybe you should start*— he says. —*They'll zap away those daydreams of yours, just watch.*—

—*Do you think they can?*— I ask, suddenly alarmed.

—Only if you let them— he says. —They won't change me though. Know why?—

—Why?—

—Because I know what they're up to, and like they say, knowing is half the battle.— He pauses then and smiles. —Also, I have super-powers.—

I bite my lip for a second because I know a boy in my group session who believes he can blink people into and out of paintings and he seems crazy to me. But then Alec raises his eyebrows twice and winks. —You're kidding?— I say, and we both laugh.

—Of course— he says. —But I wish I did. I could straighten some things out in this world if I did, that's for sure.—

When he's finished talking, his eyes flash in annoyance as he nods in the direction of the door. I turn my head and see one of the nurses standing there. Her blue scrubs make her look like a crayon. Her white sneakers are like clouds squashed under her. I don't recognize her. She's not one of the nurses who come for me. Nurse Abrams says I won't ever know all of the nurses because they have different units working different shifts to cover the patients who all have very different needs. That was her word. Needs. But I know it's like so many other words here that are used instead of saying sick.

—Alec? It's time— the nurse says, and I wish I could wave my hand to make the words vanish.

Alec blows his breath out slow and angry. —Got to go— he says, pushing the chair away as he stands up. —Can't wait to see what they have lined up for me today. A little shock therapy, maybe? Or worse, they'll probably just talk me to death like usual.—

—Wait— I whisper desperately because I don't want him to go. There are so many things I want to ask him.

His hand is still flat on the table and I cover it with my palm.

15

His skin is warm and mine is ice—they meet with electricity.

He looks at me curiously, but doesn't pull away. His fingers yield to mine and I squeeze his hand. Our eyes meet and hold their glances. When he smiles, I have all the answers I need. Alec is the same as me—special like me.

The nurse grows impatient and clears her throat. She clicks her fingernails against the open door and calls for him again because everything here runs on a schedule.

Alec takes a sideways step away from me and bows his head slightly. —*Nice meeting you, Sabrina*— he says, slipping his hand free. —*I'll see you again soon.*—

Leaving the room, he half turns and waves at me.

I wave back, but he's already looking away.

In a few minutes a nurse will come to take me to my meeting with Dr. Richards. Until then, I pull my knees up to my chest, hold them close, and feel different than I've ever felt before because Alec really believes me when I say that I'm not crazy.

TWO

The next time I see Alec, he is sitting in the hallway outside my room. His knees are pulled up into his chest. I can't see his face because he's not looking anywhere but at the floor in front of him. But I know it's him. I've memorized the shape of his body.

Amanda is with me. She's one of the few girls here that I talk to. Or, well, we don't exactly talk. She's real quiet and so am I. I guess we just like to be quiet together. We always walk together after our group session because her room is near mine and she doesn't like to be alone. I don't know if that makes us friends or not. Things like friendship are harder to understand here.

When I see Alec, I'm happy. There's something about him that makes me want to talk and sing and be noisy—something about him that makes me feel real, like the person I am in my dreams.

Amanda doesn't like when things don't happen exactly the same way every time. The nurses say that's part of what's wrong with her.

—*What's that boy doing there?*— she asks me.

—*It's okay*— I tell her. —*That's Alec. I know him.*—

He looks up when he hears my voice and I see him smile. I see his eyes light up behind his hair, shining on me like spotlights. I'm not surprised to see he came for me. He will always come for me. That's what it means to know each other in a dream before ever being awake. I can't explain how I know, but I do—like something my heart whispers to me.

—Hey— he says, pushing with his legs so that his back slides up the wall until we are face-to-face. His hands are nervous bundles in front of his pockets until he hides them away and raises his shoulders. —I stole a look at the nurses' schedules and kind of figured out where your room was. Hope you don't mind me waiting here for you. It's just, you're kind of the only one here I know . . . so, I thought maybe . . . —

I'm grinning as I shake my head. —I don't mind— I say, feeling my skin turning pink.

Amanda is biting her nails and fidgeting with her hair. When Alec holds his hand out for her, she jumps back a step. —I'm going to go, okay, Sabrina?— she says like she's asking permission, but she doesn't even wait for me to say good-bye before slipping around Alec and disappearing into her room three doors away.

—She's real friendly— Alec says, raising his eyebrows.

—She's just . . . shy— I tell him. —She doesn't know you.—

Alec shuffles his feet. He lowers his head but never takes his eyes off of mine. —I didn't mean to intrude or anything. Do you want me to go?—

I shake my head. I don't want to be with anyone but him. As soon as I saw him, it was as if the walls of the hospital evaporated and there was only us.

—Alright, cool. You want to go for a walk or something?— he asks.

I nod. I have free time between now and when I meet with Dr. Richards. —Let's go outside— I say. —I can show you around.—

—Show me around what?— Alec says. —Is there really anything to see?—

—*Sure there is*— I say. —*There's the lawn and then behind it are the trees. There's even a little path so that it's kind of like being in the woods.*—

—*That doesn't seem like much*— Alec says, grinning.

—*It's not*— I say softly, tracing my lips with my fingers and turning away. —*But if you look at it the right way . . . it's really kind of perfect. I can't really explain it.*— When I turn back, I'm worried he won't understand. I'm afraid he'll look at me with strange eyes the way Kayliegh sometimes does when I say things that are different. He's not though. The way he stares at me lets me know that he does understand.

—*Sounds okay to me*— he says. —*Let's make a deal. You show me what you see and I tell you what I see. Deal?*—

Once we step into the fresh air, I feel free—better than I've felt in a long time. I rush out onto the grass, smiling up at the sky. I don't look behind me. I know he's following me.

I run until I reach the little tree that isn't much more than a sapling. Still, it's taller than me and I wrap my hand around the skinny trunk, spinning around to face Alec. The tree's branches reach down and tickle my hair and I laugh just once before letting go to join him on our walk.

I have more energy than I really know what to do with so I start to wrap the string of my sweatshirt hood around my wrist, only to unwrap it and start over again. I keep forgetting he's new here—that he hasn't been here the whole time I have and isn't used to anything yet.

—*Have they started your routine yet?*— I ask him.

—*I guess. I mean, they have me scheduled for things all day*— he says. —*I still don't understand the point of any of it though. I don't belong here, so I don't know what it's supposed to do for me. Whatever. It's all a waste of time.*—

—*Why?*— I ask, because sometimes I wonder the same thing.

—Because there's nothing wrong with me— Alec says. —You know what it is? Our society is so screwed up, from top to bottom, everything about it, that it's become impossible to fix. It's easier to change people and make them fit into something that's broken. Know what I mean?—

I've seen cracks in the sky and people swallowed up inside of them.

I've seen computers steal souls a little bit at a time.

—Yeah, I think I do— I say. —I think I know exactly what you mean.—

—And it's insane, right?— Alec says. —But the worst part about it is that they try to convince us that we're the defects. We're not defects. It's the whole world that's gone off the rails. We're just victims of the Modern Age and being in here is our punishment.—

—It's not so bad— I say. —I don't mind it here most of the time.—

—But you'd rather not be here, right?— he asks. —I bet you got like a million friends or whatever. I'm sure you'd rather be with them. Unless of course you have the wrong kind of friends and that's why you're in a place like this?—

I place the end of my sleeve in my mouth and keep it there for a second before shaking my head. —Not really. I mean, I don't really have a ton of friends. Not swarms of them anyway.—

—Yeah? Why not?—

—I don't know— I say. —I have some friends. I never had to walk to class by myself or sit alone at lunch or anything like that. I was just never popular because to be like that you have to be a girl who doesn't draw fairies on the outside of book covers.—

—Do you really draw fairies on your books?— he asks, and I nod shyly. —Fairies can be kind of wicked and evil. They're pretty awesome.—

—My friends think they're for little kids— I say.

—What do they know? They're probably all into vampires— Alec says, shaking his head. *—Isn't it stupid how one thing can be cool and the other isn't just because the Pop Culture Police say so? I never did understand that. But I guess that's why you have to be a bit brain-dead to be popular.—*

—Being popular doesn't matter that much to me— I say.

—Me either— Alec says. *—I went to this private school and it's all these kids from Brentwood or wherever. I didn't want to be part of that crowd. It's all about money and name-dropping famous people and getting into the right parties with the right people. I guess being who I am was always more important.—*

—That must be why we belong together— I blurt out.

Alec smiles. *—You think we belong together?—*

—I know it— I say, and then I race ahead a few steps and turn around to face him. When I do, my hands are on my knees and I'm laughing. As I watch him look at me like I'm special, it's so easy to forget about the way all the kids at school looked at me once their hellos in the hall were replaced with whispers. It was like all of a sudden, nobody could see the bright side of my personality—they only saw my flaws. Alec makes me remember the better parts.

—Sabrina? Will you draw a fairy for me?— he asks.

—I'll draw you a million things— I answer, smiling.

When his hand touches my arm, I feel like I'm ready to explode. There are fireworks going off inside of me. My eyes sparkle. My heartbeat flutters like a tiny rabbit and I feel as though I never want him to let go. I wonder if this is how Kayliegh feels about Thomas? But it can't be. Not with him. Not like this. Because when she's with Thomas, she changes.

When I'm with Alec, I feel like me again.

—*You seem to be doing better today*— Dr. Richards says after we've been talking for a few minutes. Not about anything interesting, just about things like my day so far and what I had for lunch. She makes the comment about me doing better after I tell her about the tacos. Borrowing something Kayliegh always said, I told Dr. Richards how they looked like rolled-up crap but tasted like a million bucks. Then I laughed and to Dr. Richards that means I'm doing better. —*You're very talkative today.*—

Sometimes I don't feel like talking.

Sometimes I roam around the room quietly as her eyes track my every step, waiting for me to be still or to look in her direction or show any sign that I'm willing to have some sort of conversation. I always know she's watching and it makes me want to talk even less. When I'm in one of those moods, I usually stay by the shelves of stuffed animals and books meant for the younger kids here. Even if they aren't supposed to be for me, I'm allowed to pick them up whenever I want. I rarely do. I prefer to just let my fingers slide over the different textures—tracing their sewn-on smiles, brightened by sewn-on eyes.

Sometimes when I don't feel like talking, Dr. Richards doesn't care so much. On those days, she just wants me to draw pictures the same way Kayliegh used to. —*Just draw for me what you saw*— she says. Then she looks at the pictures, pointing out things here and there before asking if she can take them with her only to ask me more about them at some other session.

Today is not like any of those days.

I'm sitting across from her—looking at her without trying to hide my face. Today is one of the days I feel like talking. Meeting Alec has made me this way. In the last week, we've never been apart unless we had to be. Finding someone who accepts the way I am has made me want to not hide anymore. It's carried over into my sessions with Dr. Richards. It's like I want to make her understand about how I see the world even though I'm not sure she can. I guess I'm just getting tired of being alone in the room with her questions all the time. I want to fill it with my own words instead.

—*Nurse Abrams tells me you've been more social lately. She says she's seen you with some of the other patients. Have you made many friends?*— Dr. Richards asks.

—*Some.*—

I think about Alec and how we ate breakfast together today.

He had cereal and I had watermelon and we talked about foods we hate. He hates yogurt because he says even saying the name sounds like throwing something up. I told him that I don't like carrots because their color is too bright and they taste the same as chewing aspirin.

Thinking about him, I feel my cheeks getting redder and I look away. But Dr. Richards never misses anything or any chance for a new question. —*Is one of these friends of yours a boy?*—

—*Maybe*— I say, and she grins at me.

—*That happens quite a bit around here*— she says. Leaning forward in her chair, she acts more like an older sister home from college asking me about a new boyfriend. Not that I have an older sister or anything. It's just the way I picture it. Probably from some movie I saw once but can't remember. Or maybe it's the way Dr. Richards squints to make it look like she's super interested. Deep down, I think she's just trying to be like an older sister because she thinks it will get me to open up.

It almost works too.

I'm so close to telling her about Alec but then I pause to think about what I would say. I listen to myself in my head and wonder if she would ever believe it if I told her something from my dreams is true and real and in this very hospital.

She wouldn't.

Her job is to convince me that those things are less than what they seem. It's better not to say anything.

I can tell my newfound silence worries her. Afraid of losing me to the quiet, she drops the sister act. She straightens her posture and smoothes the hair away from her face, making herself suddenly look five or ten years older and smarter. —*There's no reason to be embarrassed. I think it's a good thing*— she says. —*Showing interest in a boy means you're making progress. It's important for you to make connections with other people. It means that the medicine is working.*—

The link between the two puzzles me and makes me talkative again.

—*How so?*—

It pleases her that I ask—that I'm showing an interest in my own well-being. I know because her eyebrows normally stay in a straight line but now one of them arches curiously upward just before she speaks. —*Well, the pills I've prescribed for you should help you communicate with others better by helping to clear your mind of all the clutter*— she says.

—*What clutter?*— I ask.

—*For example . . . the noise you've talked about.*—

During other sessions I've told her about the noise. The invisible noise that only I can hear—a noise that sounds like the mumbling of a million broken voices saying nothing at all or the hum of the wind through an open car window at seventy miles per hour. I can even see the noise sometimes. It circles above people like a clear vulture with sparks of electricity in its wings—hovering dangerously above their heads before swooping down. But that's kind of separate from the noise and also part of it at the same time. The part I can see, I call static. The noise is only the roar of its footsteps.

The static is dangerous. I don't like to think about it.

I've never told Dr. Richards about the static. She'd say I was making it up or that my mind was. She's like my mom, she thinks I imagine things that aren't there just because she can't see them.

—*Do you still hear the noise?*— Dr. Richards asks.

—*Not like before*— I admit to her for the first time. It's the truth. I haven't heard it in days. Not the way I used to. It was so loud sometimes I had to cover my ears or put headphones on full blast to make it quiet. —*Now when I do hear it, it's like it's not really there at all. Like I'm only remembering that I heard it once upon a time. Does that mean there was something wrong with me but now there's not?*—

—*It's not a matter of right and wrong*— Dr. Richards tells me. —*Your brain just makes too much of one chemical and not enough of another. That's what schizophrenia does.*— I'm tired of hearing about how my brain produces the wrong amount of certain chemicals. How do they know what's the right amount for me? Alec says as far as the hospital is concerned, a patient is well once her brain functions exactly like everybody else's. —*The fact that you don't hear the noise like you did before means the medicine is starting to create a balance and getting it under control. The way you perceive things is improving.*—

—*You mean changing*— I correct her, and she seems surprised.

—*I suppose you could look at it that way*— she says. —*But changing for the better, certainly.*—

—*But why is it so wrong for me to just perceive what I perceive?*— I ask her. —*Everyone's always said I should believe in myself. Until I stopped believing what they wanted me to . . .*—

—*You're asking me why we don't simply allow you to remain in these delusions?*— Dr. Richards grins at me. Her expression remains steady. It's as if she's been waiting for me to ask this question.

—*Yeah. I guess that's exactly what I'm asking*— I say.

—Don't you think that would be difficult for you?— she asks without skipping a beat because that's one of the things she does during our sessions. She answers my questions with questions of her own. I don't like when she does that. Somehow it feels like she's trying to confuse me by putting words in my mouth—making me say things I don't want to or don't mean.

—Not really. Other people I know do the same thing— I say. Dr. Richards can tell I'm annoyed by the sound of my voice. But even when I get angry with her, she never gets angry back. Not like my parents.

—Can you give me an example?— Dr. Richards asks.

I tuck my hair behind my ears. *—Well, how about video games? I know kids who spend hours in their fake worlds. There are games where you eat, sleep, and buy things just like in the real world. Why is that okay? Why don't the kids who play those games have to be in a place like this too?—*

—Because there are healthy ways to spend time living in your own imagination and then there are unhealthy ways— she says, leaning back in her chair. *—The trouble occurs when reality and your imagination blend together. Once that happens, you can't tell which world is which and then there's a good chance of you being harmed . . . either by others or by yourself—* she explains.

My eyes are squinting and skeptical. *—That doesn't make much sense. If you're saying what I see isn't real, how could it actually hurt me?—*

—It could cause you to be confused— she says.

I sort of roll my eyes and give a small shake of my head. *—I've been confused a million times in my life. It never hurt me.—*

Dr. Richards grins the way a teacher does when they don't like the answer I give. But like all teachers, she already has a response waiting. *—What's bothering you, Sabrina?—*

I shrug.

—*I don't know*— I say, bringing one of my hands out from my pocket and placing it near my mouth—so near that I can smell the sour stain of my breath in the fabric. —*I guess I just want to know why do we have to talk about all the stuff that happened before if the medicine is fixing things?*—

—*The medicine does only part of the work*— Dr. Richards explains. —*Your condition is more complicated than taking a pill and being all better.*— I remember her saying the same kind of thing to my parents the evening they brought me here. She told them sometimes it was hard to determine exactly what was causing symptoms like mine. That it could be any one of a whole range of social anxiety disorders. She told them it was best that I remained so they could observe and pinpoint and give me the best possible treatment. —*Even if you're doing better, it's important that you and I still talk about things*— she says to me.

—*But why?*—

I don't want to take her word for things anymore. I want to know exactly who they think I'm supposed to be before I get any closer to becoming that person.

—*The more we discuss the circumstances of your previous episodes, the more you'll fully understand the nature of your condition. It may help prevent other similar episodes in the future*— she explains with the kind of calm my father never could manage whenever he and my mom spoke about my condition. I used to sit at the top of the stairs and listen when they argued. I'd hear my dad shout and I could feel the fury in his voice directed at an invisible me who wasn't supposed to be listening from the shadows.

Some of the time I knew exactly what I'd done to upset them. Other times I wasn't so sure—or I couldn't quite remember. Well, that's not right either, because I did remember, just not in the same way they did. So whenever that happened, my dad would lecture me endlessly about there being a time for making up stories and a time for telling the truth and that at fifteen years old, I should know the difference. But I wasn't lying. They never understood that.

Seeing things others don't is what Dr. Richards calls my *episodes*. They are where her questions always lead and today is no different. I always know when Dr. Richards is going to ask a serious question. She telegraphs them by taking a deep breath through her nose just before each one. She does that now, shifting her legs around as she leans forward. All her talk about me seeming better was just her way of getting there. —*Sabrina? I would like to discuss what happened the day before you came here. Is that okay?*—

I bring my hand near my face again. This time I don't just put my sleeve close to my mouth—I place it to my lips and place my tongue against the fabric.

Dr. Richards knows my habits. She knows what they mean. —*Do you not want to talk about it?*—

—*Not really*— I mumble through my sleeve.

—*Can I ask why not?*—

—*Because*— I say, but that's not good enough. She wants to know *why*. She always wants to know why about everything. —*When I think about that day, it doesn't feel the same anymore. It all made sense then, but now . . . now it doesn't. Almost like it was a different person there instead of me. It freaks me out a little bit.*—

—*That's okay. It's part of the process*— Dr. Richards says.

—*That doesn't make sense*— I argue.

—*Why not?*—

—*Because you said things were going to get clearer. But when it comes to everything that took place before I came here, I only feel more confused.*—

—*Don't worry*— she says. —*I'm here to help you make sense of it.*—

When she smiles at me, I'm suddenly overwhelmed with a strange feeling in my stomach. It's like the first-day-of-school feeling of not knowing who to talk to or what to say. There is something about her that makes me think she's one of the people I shouldn't talk to. I don't know what it is, but I don't completely trust her. I guess I never have. I feel comfortable sharing with Alec in a way I would never feel with her. It's because he listens to me while she's always trying to change me.

Dr. Richards is trying to take away the part of me that makes me special. That is what she wants. It's what my parents want too. But it's not what I want.

I don't want to see things their way.

I don't want to look at the sky and not see the changes that come with each breath or suddenly notice that all of the light has evaporated from every stone hiding just below the dirt. The thought of a world that plain frightens me.

—*I don't really want to talk anymore.*—

—*Okay*— she says, but I can tell by the little sigh that escapes her that she doesn't really mean it. Or at least that she's disappointed. —*Do you want to talk about something else?*— she asks, sounding hopeful again. —*Maybe about your friends? What about Kayliegh?*—

—*Can't I go now? I want to go*— I say suddenly.

Dr. Richards takes another deep breath. Looking at the clock on the wall, she says —*I suppose that would be okay.*— It's what she has to say. During our first session she told me these meetings would last only as long as I wanted them to and no longer. That is our deal.

As I'm getting up to leave, Dr. Richards tells me that she thinks we're making real strides. —*I know this is hard for you sometimes. But believe me, you're doing well.*—

I don't say anything. I turn away and stare at the smiling eyes sewn onto dozens of stuffed animals and wonder what exactly it means to be doing well.

THREE

—*Go on . . . it's your turn*— Alec says, pushing the bangs away from his forehead where they are sticky with sweat. Tucking them behind his ear makes his ears stick out like mine do. He's wearing this crooked kind of smile too and I can't help but laugh a little. He's so gangly and goofy the way he's standing. The pant legs of his jeans are rolled up above his calves and his arms stick out like skinny tree limbs. He waves them around, standing under the basket as I stand by the foul line. — *What's so funny?*— he asks once he notices that I'm giggling at him.

—*Nothing . . .*— I say playfully.

—*Oh, you're laughing at something*— he says. —*And I know it's me . . . so what is it, huh? What? I got something on my face or something?*—

He starts wiping frantically at his nose and I chuckle.

—*It's nothing like that*— I say sincerely. The wind catches his hair—blows it out in all directions until it stands on end like straw and I can't keep a straight face anymore. —*You look like a scarecrow*— I tell him.

Alec looks down and sees what I see. He grins to himself and then looks back at me, holding his arms out to his side. —*It's not how you look on the court*— he jokes. —*It's all about the skills.*—

—You don't have many of them either— I tease, covering my mouth as I laugh.

—You're one to talk— he teases back. *—I at least hit the backboard.—*

—I guess you're right. We both suck— I say, and it's something neither of us can argue with.

It's my turn to shoot and I dribble the basketball twice. I like the feel of the orange rubber on my fingertips. Even when I'm not holding the ball, it almost feels like it's still there. The smell stays behind—a mild odor of dirt, sweat, and sports equipment that I find nice in small doses, sort of romantic even, but terrifies me the moment it brings back memories of first-period gym class freshman year. No matter where I am or what I'm doing, it's like I time-travel instantly back to that class—shivering in my shorts, pretending to participate in soccer or whatever as I stare at my sneakers and watch them get stained green by grass still wet from the morning dew. One stray scent can bring a memory back so completely that I actually feel an imaginary chill in the breeze.

—Enough stalling already— Alec says, and I pull a face at him— sticking my tongue out so that he laughs. *—Come on. Throw the ball up there and earn your next letter like a man . . . and by man, I mean like one of those tough girl-power kind of teen girls that are always in movies . . . you know, the kind who isn't afraid to kick someone in the balls. Not me, of course. I'd rather not get kicked in the junk if it can be helped.—*

He's trying to make me laugh so that I'll miss the shot and earn the S in our game of H-O-R-S-E. He doesn't need to though and he knows it. I'm going to miss the shot anyway. I've missed every one so far.

—Silence— I say like a queen giving her commands. *—I need to*

concentrate.— Alec obeys and I dribble twice more. I catch the ball for the last time and raise it to my chest. With both hands, I push it toward the hoop with all my strength.

Alec watches the ball sail over the backboard and over the fence behind the court. I see his eyes arch in a rainbow of amazement and surprise and I fall over laughing. He quickly joins me, holding his side and shaking his head. I can tell by his expression that it's been a long time for him, too, since he cracked up so spontaneously.

—*I guess that's game*— I say. —*It's a tie.*—

—*A tie? What are you talking about? That's S for you. I only had O. Clearly, I won.*—

—*You can't prove that*— I say. —*We didn't finish.*—

—*Oh yeah? We'll see about that*— he says. He bends down, getting on one knee, and starts to untie his shoelaces. In no time, he's holding a sneaker in each hand and racing to the basket in his socks. He grunts as he swings his arms wildly, throwing both shoes up in the air.

One falls through the net and the other falls toward his head.

Alec covers his face and pretends to yell out in pain when the shoe hits him. Then he's jumping up and down excitedly. —*The left one went in*— he shouts. —*Your turn again. Now if you miss, that's game and I win.*—

I'm sitting on the foul line, still laughing. When I don't make a move to get up, Alec comes over and stands with his arms on his hips.

—*What's the matter? Chicken?*—

—*No*— I say defiantly.

—*Well, go on. Shoe-toss time.*—

—*Fine*— and I slip off both of my shoes. I'm not wearing socks though and don't want to run over the blacktop. I take careful steps until I'm standing under the hoop. I look back over my shoulder, asking Alec with a glance if I'm in the right spot and he nods. I flip both shoes at once. Miraculously, they both go in.

My jaw drops open in surprise.

I start to jump around ecstatically, pointing at Alec as he sulks from the foul line. —*That's two for me*— I say. —*You don't win.*—

—*I'm still ahead by one letter*— he says.

—*Nope. I declare it a tie.*—

Alec smiles, his expression telling me the game isn't over yet. He picks up his shoes again and throws them up even before I've stepped away. I cover my head, expecting them to rain down on me. When they don't, I look up and see his shoes have both gotten stuck in the net. I burst into a fit of laughter. For a split second I think he might be a little upset, but then he's laughing too.

—*That's it, you've clearly lost*— I tease.

Alec tries to claim that having both shoes in means he's clearly won. When I refuse to give in to his logic, he resorts to a six-year-old boy's tactic of persuasion—he chases me across the hospital lawn.

I scream as I run and he growls.

The nurse near the door takes a nervous step until she sees we are just playing around. I can't blame her for being concerned though. Fun isn't exactly a common sight among the patients. Hiding in corners and secret whispered conversations are all very common. Not laughter.

When Alec catches up with me, we collapse onto the grass. My heart is pounding so fast I can hear it pulse in my eardrums. Part of it is just because I'm out of breath—I haven't done anything physical like running in a while. Mostly, though, it's because Alec is so close beside me—his body pressed against my side is what really makes my heart jump.

Lying on our backs, looking up at the sky, the sun dances on

Alec's skin. —*Back home on the beach, I throw a towel down and watch the sky for hours*—he says.

—*I watch the sky all of the time*— I tell him. Then I smile because that's another thing we have in common. The sky is a place we both return to.

—*Do you ever just gaze up there and imagine you can fly?*— he asks me. —*I do. When I want to get away from everything, I just close my eyes and in a minute, it's like I'm floating. Up there, I can look down on the city, see all the boredom and chaos, and it starts to seem laughable almost because it can't touch me when I'm in the sky.*—

—*That's how the sun must feel*— I tell him. —*It's like you're watching from the other side of the sun.*—

—*Yeah, I guess that's exactly what it's like*— he says.

—*It sounds perfect*— I say.

—*Let's try it together*— Alec says.

We both close our eyes and take deep breaths. I lay completely still, against Alec. The sky takes over and colors the inside of my eyelids and I feel the wind tickle my face. Soon the two of us are flying in a clearer and brighter sky than I've ever known.

The air around me is the soft breath of a billion fairies. The breeze is the flutter of their wings. The feeling is such a happy one that I can't help but smile and laugh a little.

—*Better than talking to any doctor, am I right?*— Alec says.

—*Much.*—

—*What is it? Come on. Show me*— Alec says, turning my wrist to get a look at my hand.

I pull my arm away violently.

My action is so swift and sudden that I don't even have time to think about it. I've become so good at hiding things that it's just instinct—an involuntary reaction like kicking a leg out when a doctor taps your knee with a tiny hammer. But when I stop to think about it, I realize that I do want to show him.

For the first time in months, I'm not afraid to be myself with someone else. So I roll up the cuff of my sweatshirt. —*Okay*— I say, and hold my hand out for him to take in his.

There is a birthmark on my left hand on the part between my thumb and my pointer finger. It's always been there, obviously. They're called *birth*marks for a reason. It's not real big or anything—about the size of two quarters, but no bigger than that. It's barely a shade darker than the rest of my skin and probably nobody notices it. But it's different when it's on your own skin. You stare at it every day and it stares back.

Alec caught a glimpse of it when I brushed a strand of hair away from my mouth. He wanted to look at it. I finally let him and now he's fascinated by it.

We are sitting in the brightest part of the lawn with the hospital behind us. I'm sitting in the sun. Alec is sitting in the shade of a tree. His hair is transparent even in the shadows. Mine is a lighter shade of dark in the sun.

Alec turns my hand around in his fingers.

His touch is warm but it gives me shivers.

—*I like it*— he says. —*It's a cool shape.*—

—*I used to draw around it so that it looked like a cat*— I tell him, studying the familiar outline. He smiles at me whenever I tell him the littlest things. —*I called him Fred.*—

—*Yeah, I think I see it*— he says. —*Are these the ears? And this the face?*—

—*Almost*— I say.

He takes a pen from his pocket and hands it to me.

—*Show me?*—

—*Alright*— I say.

I scoot forward into the shade where the lines are easier to see. Lately the glare from the sun is so harsh. It used to have a soft glow with dull edges like watercolor paint. Dr. Richards tells me it's because of the pills. They make my pupils dilate a little wider and make me light-sensitive. It's better in the shade next to Alec, but I miss the warmth of the sun on my skin.

I pull my legs up under me and lean against him. Once I start to draw the features in, the cat comes out easily. He's always there, even when he's not drawn in. A cat named Fred who lives under the surface, just waiting to come out.

The ears and tail emerge first. Then comes his face. I can make him smile or frown—give him open or closed eyes so he looks to be sleeping. Most of the time, he feels the way I do. That's why I draw a smile before the last step where I add whiskers. —*See? That's Fred*— I say, dropping my hand in Alec's lap.

I kind of expect him to smirk and shrug and then that'll be the end of it because that's what anyone at school would've done. Maybe they would say it was cute or something before changing the subject. Either way, it was just to let me know they thought drawing a cat on your hand was kind of strange without actually having to say it.

Alec isn't like them.

His interest in me isn't fake.

—*That's seriously awesome*— he says after tracing the lines with his fingernail.

Dr. Richards pretends everything I say is important, but I've learned that's only so she can point out all the places where I'm wrong. My parents do the same thing. They only listen for mistakes, so they never hear what I say. But not Alec—he listens because he wants to know everything about me. I can tell by his eyes. People with clear eyes are sincere. It's something I've always known as easily as a baby knows how to breathe—all people can be judged by their eyes.

—*So? What's Fred's deal?*— Alec asks me.

—*What do you mean?*—

He flings his hair away from his face so that I can see the way his eyes shine in the stray sunbeams invading our shade. And when he laughs, I can't help but laugh with him because the sound of him is contagious. Then he grabs my side, just under the ribs where it tickles, and I squirm away, laughing even harder than before. —*I know you well enough by now to know there's a story behind Fred*— he says. —*I bet Fred has a whole secret life that you thought up. So what is it? Is he like a ninja or something?*—

—*No, he's not a ninja*— I say, rolling my eyes. Then I fold my arms and hold my head up like I'm offended. But he knows I'm only kidding and it only makes us laugh again. —*Fred's peaceful*— I say. —*And educated.*—

—*Educated, huh? How so?*—

—*Well, Fred studied at Oxford before coming to live on my hand*— I tell him, remembering all the details of Fred's biography I'd invented while daydreaming in grade school.

—*I had no idea he was a world traveler*— Alec says. His laughter is a faint breeze against my neck. His fingertips are tiny antennae exploring my arm. —*I wouldn't have guessed from his size. He seems like kind of a runt.*—

—*Fred's full of surprises*— I say, teasing him.

—*Yeah? Like what else?*—

—*Well, once he wrote a children's book about himself*— I say. —*I had to draw the pictures though.*—

—*No way. Really? You really did up a whole little book?*— Alec asks excitedly. —*Do you still have it?*—

—*Sure. Somewhere*— I tell him.

—*I totally want to see that some time*— he says, and it's the first time either of us has mentioned something that will take place later—after the hospital. Even if it is just an expression, it feels new. Having something to look forward to, no matter how insignificant, is still something.

—*I'll have to see if I can find it then*— I say. —*I'm kind of a clutter bug.*—

In my mind, I start running through all the places it might be back home. I can picture the stacks of papers piled in my closet. Drawings I haven't looked at in years—bits and scraps that I scribbled on during class. Mostly though, the piles are of postcards I collected from the places we drove to on family vacations. I know somewhere there's one with the San Diego Chicken on it and one with the New York skyline, but not the real one—the one in Las Vegas. I have tons and tons of them stashed away. I always loved how the memory of a place could be captured in a picture like that.

I used to spend hours going through those piles in my closet. I'd arrange them by subject and make scrapbooks or collages for my wall. But over the past year or so, it was as if they'd vanished even as they towered around me. Now suddenly, I want nothing more than to sit for hours sifting through them.

Dr. Richards told me this would happen. She said I would slowly start to find old interests appealing again. All the things I stopped doing over the last year and a half. Things like swimming and reading and tearing pictures from magazines. I suppose Fred is one of those things too. Or something like them anyway.

Alec can see that all of this is making me happy—making me

come alive before him. —*Tell me more*— he says, not wanting the moment to fade away.

—*Okay. Um . . . oh, I know . . . Fred had his own table setting for a while*— I say, suddenly remembering a long-forgotten detail. —*I used little dishes and forks from a toy dish set. One day, I just put them out on the table. My parents thought it was so funny. But then . . .*— I shiver as a cloud rolls across my happy memory.

I stop talking and stare off at the hills in the distance. My hand is still wrapped in Alec's and he squeezes a little harder. —*But then, what?*— he asks.

I reach up with my free hand and tuck my hair away, shrugging one shoulder. —*Then . . . after a while I could sort of tell they wanted me to stop. They wouldn't actually say it, but they stopped taking an interest. It's weird though. I mean, they used to encourage me to use my imagination and then it was like all of a sudden that was a bad thing.*—

Alec shakes his head, letting his breath out with a little huff like the sound a dog would make after coming up empty when begging scraps. Nothing too angry, but enough to show displeasure. —*Parents suck*— he says without much emotion.

—*Are your parents like that?*—

—*Mine? No . . . not quite*— he says. —*Mine wouldn't notice a Fred if I drew it on my forehead.*—

—*How come?*—

Alec rolls his eyes. —*Because my parents like to think of themselves as important people. Dinner with the governor, lunch with a judge or whatever. You know the type. On top of that, they've got this expensive traveling hobby that takes them away from home a lot. They're always going off to some country or other and I don't exactly fit into their schedule*— he tells me.

—What about you? You don't go with them?—

—Never— he says. *—Not that I want to go either, their trips are so boring. It's not exactly family vacation time. It's always about work. Their careers have always been more important. I don't know why they ever had me in the first place. Probably thought it was just one of those things they were supposed to do. I think that's why most people have kids actually. They're just following this path that everybody is supposed to follow. College. Career. Marriage. Kids. Death. But if you point that out to them . . . well, you end up in a place like this. Know what I mean?—*

I think about all of the people sitting in their cars as traffic stands still on the freeway. I think about all of the fathers like mine back in Burbank, mowing their lawns every Saturday and hating every second of it. I think about the girls I was friends with in elementary school and junior high and how they now spend so much of their energy hating so many of the things we loved back then because they are afraid of liking something that makes them different. All of them are so hypnotized by the spinning of the world that they don't realize they are simply dizzy.

—It's like they're all sleepwalking— I say.

Alec glances at the sky, letting his mind wander through the idea before he nods. *—Yes. It is like they're asleep and I'm always trying to wake them up. I guess that's my problem. I can't keep my mouth shut. So suddenly I'm the one with problems. I'm the one who needs help. It makes no sense.—*

As Alec is talking, I see the nurses exit the building. A troop of them sent to gather us up like children picking flowers in a garden. I wish there was more time. I wish Alec and I could stay out here forever and talk because now I want to tell him about my dreams. I want to tell him all the things I don't want to tell Dr. Richards. I know he'll understand.

—Sabrina? Alec?— Nurse Abrams says, strolling across the lawn toward us. *—It's time to go inside now.—*

We both stand up and brush the grass from our clothes. Nurse Abrams watches us to make sure we head in the right direction because it's getting harder and harder to separate us anymore. Once we head back inside, she turns around and moves away to fetch the next patient. That's when Alec takes hold of my hand. His fingerprints press against mine for a brief moment before our fingers lock together. As we walk silently back to a schedule of meetings and activities and meals, I glance down at our arms swinging in rhythm and notice how careful he is not to cover Fred with his thumb.

FOUR

Where the bus drops me off from school, the road is a straight line. A tightrope walker could practice her balance by walking the double yellow stripes that run from one horizon to the next—a neon audience of air-conditioned strip malls looking on. Everything is so busy and loud on the main road. On my street, most of it disappears. There are only houses huddled in the shade of trees planted so many years ago that they've grown taller than the roofs and drop stray leaves and acorns over the shingles.

There are thirty-five houses between mine and the bus stop. There are more on the other side of the street because on that side there are cul-de-sacs and turnoffs onto more tree-lined roads identical to mine. I don't count the houses there. I never walk on that side.

It takes me fifteen minutes to walk home if I go slowly—five if I run from a rare rainstorm. The junior high bus stop was closer because the bus would actually turn into our development. The school board figures that by high school we should be able to walk a little farther. By the end of freshman year last spring, I had gotten used to it. I just felt bad for the kids who lived even farther, like Lillian Wagner—she lives seventy-two houses away from the bus stop.

I used to walk home with Lillian sometimes. We weren't really friends—just on the walk home. We had two classes together, so there was always something to chat about. She started softball in the spring though, and of course that meant she stayed after school and took the late bus home and probably got picked up by her dad. I didn't walk with anybody then. Not really. I sort of trailed along with Thomas and his friends. But I never talked too much. Most of the time I just listened, rolling my eyes at their rude comments and dodging their dirty suggestions about what I might do in my bedroom once I got home and what they were definitely going to do in their bedrooms when they got home.

Sometimes Thomas would get me alone—strolling several paces behind his friends. He'd always want to know about Kayliegh, because this was before they hooked up and became a couple. I only ever told him what she'd carefully instructed me to tell him, so our conversations were brief. Most of the walk I would just feel him staring at my knees or ankles, anywhere there was bare skin.

Thomas's house is twelve houses closer than mine, so I always walked the last part by myself. I loved to walk that last part with my head back watching for the changing sky and streaking rainbows.

In those minutes alone, I would set in my mind what I'd pretend to be for the next two hours before my mom got home. I would lay on my bed with the window open to the breeze, getting lost in a daydream as the afternoon surrendered into evening. My homework would sit in piles on the desk in my room or still zipped up in my backpack. I couldn't bring myself to even glance at it. All I wanted to do was lie perfectly still and drift away.

I could be anything in those hours. I just had to concentrate—think through the details before I started. If I did, I'd travel off to wherever I wanted as soon as I closed my eyes. I could be the last person on an earth lost to desert sand. I could be a fairy flying into lonely rooms at night where candles burned. I could warm my butterfly wings near the flame. Sometimes I imagined myself being pregnant—my body still thin and small except my belly, which became more swollen each time I filled my lungs. I never pictured a baby inside of me. Instead, my womb was filled with a tiny ocean teeming with all kinds of new life-forms waiting to find a way out. Whenever that was my dream, I never flushed the toilet after I peed—just in case.

Outside my window, the sky would flash with a short burst of something like lightning exploding in the sky. Only it wasn't lightning because the sun would still be yellow and shining. What I saw was bigger—everywhere at once and nowhere at all. It didn't look like lightning does, cracking the sky like broken glass. It was more like a swarm of invisible insects devouring the scenery, like static disrupting the picture on a television. That's how I gave a name to it.

Nobody else ever saw it. I could tell by the way they never flinched or stared. Everyone else went about whatever they were doing like children playing in a field, not knowing the danger of an approaching thunderstorm.

That doesn't make me crazy though. I just have a gift. I can see how the world is falling apart around us. Just because they don't see it, they say I'm wrong. But nobody can know that for sure. I think I'm lucky to see what I see.

I slowly become aware of Dr. Gysion's attention resting solely on me from across the circle of kids. Dr. Gysion is pretty easygoing about that. He lets you space out every now and then during group session. But occasionally he'll single somebody out just to make sure you stay somewhat involved.

—*I'm sorry*— I say. —*I wasn't exactly paying attention.*— Even though that's allowed, I still feel my cheeks flush and my hands get sweaty the same way I would in school if a teacher asked me something

I couldn't answer. It's a conditioned reaction learned early in elementary school. Like raising your hand or potty training. But this isn't at all like school and Dr. Gysion isn't a teacher.

—*No worries*— he says with a laugh. It's easy to feel relaxed with him. His voice is really warm. It doesn't hurt that he's handsome either and closer to our age than the other doctors. —*It happens to all of us from time to time.*—

A chorus of muffled laughter squeaks from around the room. Our circle is symbolic. It means everything that is said inside can't be repeated. It makes everyone a little more comfortable about sharing.

I look over at Dr. Gysion, uncertain of what I'm supposed to do next. —*So . . . what did you ask me?*—

—*Just if there was anything you feel now that you didn't feel when you first arrived at the hospital*— he says. It's a question he's asked before. Pretty much at the end of every week, he asks someone that question. There's a list of standard answers ranging from *bored* to *better*. Dr. Gysion accepts these one-word answers. It's another reason why I like him more than Dr. Richards. He doesn't make you explain anything if you don't want to. He's happy if we just express ourselves in front of kids our own age. One word lets everyone know the sound of your voice.

My answer is always the same.

—*Safe.*—

Dr. Gysion smiles because it pleases him to hear me say that. It's the truth. I do feel safe here. As long as I'm inside the walls of the hospital, the static can't ever find me.

Alec has group at the same time as me but in a room down the hall. He's still in that room when I reach the door. Just him. The other kids in his group have already scattered and the door has closed behind them.

I bite on my bottom lip and glance through the window. I see the back of Alec's head. The doctor that leads his session is facing the door and I duck away before she sees me. —*I wonder what they're talking about*— I say.

Amanda chews on the ends of her hair and shrugs.

I lean over and look again. I can almost hear Alec's voice even though the rooms are soundproof. Then he suddenly turns around and I see his face colored with anger. His hair is so blond and bright it turns his skin into fire. I'm almost scared, but then he sees me. He smiles and the anger fades.

Coming through the door, he glances over his shoulder and says —*What a waste of time*— loud enough for the doctor to hear. Behind him I can see the doctor begin to say something but the door slams shut on her words. Alec takes my hand and we spin away.

—*What happened?*— I ask.

—*Nothing*— he says. —*She was giving me a hard time because I said our group sessions were retarded. She kept focusing on that word, retarded, and not the big picture. So, I was just explaining how I don't see the point of group. Nobody ever says anything but her. When anyone does, it's mostly only half true. Anyone can see that. So basically, group is nothing more than another doctor talking at us for an hour.*—

Amanda shuffles her feet and frowns. —*That's not always true*— she says because she likes group. She's told me so. —*It helps us.*—

—*Not me, it doesn't*— Alec says fast as electricity, and it frightens Amanda.

—*I think I'm going to go*— she says.

—*Okay*— I say because I can't stop her or change her mind. —*I'll see you later?*—

Amanda nods silently and quickly disappears.

—*Did I do something wrong?*— Alec asks. —*I didn't mean to chase her off.*—

—*Our group doctor is nice, that's all*— I tell him. —*She just likes him.*—

—*Mine's this total hippie that thinks we should all hug and heal and be happy as long as we're together*— Alec says. —*I told her she could have fun with that, but I wanted no part of it.*—

I laugh at the way he mimics his doctor because he's right. Sometimes they are like that—like kindergarten teachers. —*What did she say?*—

—*She said I was having a hard time adjusting and I told her that's because I wasn't trying. She didn't exactly like that. So much for being honest, I guess. You know, I'm starting to hate this place more than school.*—

—*It's nothing like my school*— I say. —*People are nicer here.*—

At my school everyone started to avoid me like I was contagious. There were all kinds of rumors about me. Most of them came from Skylar Atkins. She's hated me since fourth grade when I accidentally ruined her diorama of the Redwood Forest when the bus turned too fast. I've always been afraid of her. She reminds me of a witch who eats children in fairy tales. Her shadow always seems to be cackling even if she is standing still.

Skylar liked to whisper things behind my back and whenever she caught me looking she'd ask what my problem was. —*What makes you so special?*— she would growl. There were a lot of things that made me special but I never wanted to explain.

None of that matters anymore as I squeeze Alec's hand tighter.

—You know why they sent me here?— Alec asks, and I shake my head. *—They said I couldn't relate to others and it was causing me to become emotionally cut off. Give me a break. Like I'd even want to connect with those kids. The girls are all future plastic surgery candidates with borderline eating disorders. The guys are midlife-crisis-cases-in-waiting, already busy picking out the overpriced car they're going to buy to feel better about themselves because these people only care about money and things. They're all so superficial that it's sickening. But that's the way we're supposed to be. If we're not good little consumers, then we must be mental.—*

—My dad says sort of the same thing— I say, and Alec looks surprised.

—Really?—

I nod. *—He thinks a lot of the stuff the kids at my school have is unnecessary. He says it's not healthy to make who you are about what you have.—*

—That's the complete opposite of my dad— Alec says. *—He totally buys into that crap. I think he's worried that because I won't, I'm going to turn into some kind of terrorist or something. Not that he's worried for me . . . just that it would destroy his image. I guess he figures locking me up in here will straighten me out. I think his wet dream is that I come out of here begging him to buy me a Porsche.—*

I can almost see his dad when Alec talks about him. I picture his eyes drowning in static. Because I know now that the static has been trying to trap Alec the same as it has tried with me, by changing the world into a place where we can't survive.

We have to find a place that is ours. The doctors keep trying to make us fit into this world, but they're wrong. We need a world that fits us.

—Don't worry— I say to him. *—We'll find someplace where we*

can be ourselves. Then nobody will be able to tell us what we're sup-
posed to think.—

—I like that idea— Alec says, putting his arm around my shoulders and forgetting all about the doctors and his parents and everything else as long as we're together. *—All we have to do now is*
find it.—

FIVE

—*Can't we go ask your mom to drop us off at the mall or something?*— Kayliegh asks. She's lying on my floor with her arms stretched over her head so she can reach her iPod and switch songs every twenty seconds or so. She's in one of her restless states. She always pouts and whines when she's in one of these moods. She reminds me of Lyla, the five-year-old down the street I sometimes babysit. Lyla kicks her feet when she throws a tantrum. Kayliegh moves hers slower over the carpet, but she can't quite keep them still either.

—*She already said no. Remember, I asked her earlier and she said she didn't feel like driving.*— Really it was because of the story that's been on the news the last three nights about the little girl from the next town over. She was only MISSING for a day before they found her body thrown on the side of the road. Even though she was only nine and I'm thirteen and can take care of myself better, it freaks my mom out. She doesn't want me going anywhere without her—not until the guy who did it is caught.

I don't want to tell Kayliegh because I know what she will say. She will think it is unfair. She already thinks my parents are too strict to begin with. In her current mood, this will put her over the top.

—*What are we supposed to do all night then?*— Kayliegh

complains. She pushes a button and the song switches. We've only heard snippets of the last five that have come on. It's just one of those times when she is so bored that she hates everything.

—*I don't know*— I say. There's a rare rainstorm outside, so we can't go for a walk or wander my neighborhood. My parents haven't gone to bed yet either, so we're not going downstairs. But I'm actually fine right where we are, doing what I'm doing—drawing an image of a girl leaping through a field at the edge of a road.

—*Can't we go watch a movie or something?*—

—*My parents are down there*— I say.

—*God! Why don't you have a television in your room like everyone else?*— Kayliegh moans as she sits up. —*No computer, no cell phone, no TV. What? Are your parents trying to make you Amish or something?*—

—*Ha-ha. You're soooo funny*— I tease, and Kayliegh cracks a smile for the first time in over an hour.

—*Seriously, though, what's the deal? I mean your parents seem like normal enough people on the outside. Why don't they let you be normal too?*—

I shrug as the colored pencil glides easily over the paper. —*You know why. They think people spend too much time with stuff like that.*— I turn around and roll my eyes up in my head like a zombie and hold my hands up pretending to grab for Kayliegh. —*It controls your mind and rots your brains.*— I growl and we both crack up laughing.

Kayliegh stands up and comes over to my desk. She absentmindedly sifts through some of the drawings I've made recently. —*You know, you should tell them that being cut off from all of those things isn't healthy either. That's how people end up in cults.*— Her voice trails off as she loses her train of thought. I glance up at her and see she's holding two pieces of paper in her hands. They are nearly identical to the drawing I'm doing now and she notices. —*What are these about?*— she asks. —*They're pretty.*—

—*They're of that girl . . . the one whose body they found*— I say, because the truth is I've been thinking about it a lot too. —*I'm trying to draw her a way into her own private heaven.*—

Kayliegh is used to hearing me talk about heaven. We used to pretend about it for hours when we were younger. We played heaven in my room, or her room, or even outside. I would tell her how I thought heaven was just another place like Oz or Wonderland—someplace more magical than here and that every person has their own. Dorothy had Oz, Alice had Wonderland, Peter had Neverland, and so on. I told her we could invent our own and play there for as long as we wanted. But we don't talk about it much anymore. It makes Kayliegh uncomfortable.

Her forehead wrinkles and she puts the drawings down. —*Honestly, I don't get this obsession of yours with heaven*— she says. —*You're not even religious. You've never even been to church in your life.*—

—*You know it's not about that*— I tell her. —*Not for me anyway.*—

—*Then what is it? Ever since we've been friends, even way back in third grade, you were always talking about this. Sometimes, I think you think about this more than you think about real life*— Kayliegh says. She's not upset or anything. She's just curious.

I open my mouth to tell her when I realize I don't really have an answer. —*I don't know*— I say. —*I guess, it's just . . . like I feel there's someplace else I belong. It's stupid, I know.*—

—*It's not stupid*— Kayliegh says. —*I mean, it's weird . . . but not stupid. At least you're creative with it, right? Not like Eric, whose other world is just staring at nude girls on the web.*—

We both smile and I wonder if there is any way to draw my own way into heaven.

The nurse on duty in the common room doesn't like us sitting so close together on the sofa. She keeps looking at the place where my jeans touch up against Alec's with disapproving glances. It makes me shy, but he doesn't seem to care. That's one of the things I love about him—when he's with me, nothing else exists.

When he holds the piece of paper directly into the light, the water-colors shimmer, giving them a weight much heavier than the paper they're painted on. —*I think this might be the best one you've done yet*— he says.

I've painted a picture to give him for four days in a row. He has them taped up on the wall of his room—each new one arranged in a circle that's growing around the first. Each one is a door that leads from my dreams into his. At night, I like to imagine him staring up at them, looking for a way to visit me.

The pictures are of things we've done together. The first one I gave him is of him sitting on the tire swing, shirtless in the shadows like he was the first time I met him in my dream. Whenever I paint him, I always leave the paper white where his hair should be.

There's one I did of how the sky looks when we lie in the grass and stare up at it. Another one is just shades of orange with a runny watery stripe of brown curving from the top and halfway down. He knew straightaway it was the wall in the cafeteria that I face every time he sits beside me.

This new one is special though. It's not of something we've done but of something that is yet to come. Something perfect.

—*It's me and you*— I say, blushing as I tell him.

—*I can tell*— he says, leaning his shoulder against mine and smil-ing. That makes the nurse even more uncomfortable—makes her stare a split second longer until I'm certain she will tell Dr. Richards and I will have to listen to her questions about it in our next session. But that's all right. I like hearing Alec and me mentioned in the same sentences.

—*These are our shadows and this is the sun*— I say, pointing to the purple figures surrounded by a yellow so bright it shows through the other side of the paper.

—*Yeah, I see it. It's awesome*— he says, looking at it closely. Then he leans back and lets his eyes drift far away. With his finger, he makes a large sweeping circle around the painted sun. —*This reminds me of the Ferris wheel on the pier in Santa Monica. You know it?*—

—*Sure. I've driven by it a million times with my parents*— I say. —*My dad likes to drive along the ocean whenever we go on a trip.*—

—*Ever stop there?*— he asks, and I shake my head. —*I go there a lot just to hang out by myself. It's kind of cool there. At night and on the weekends it's real touristy or whatever, but during the day it's not like that. There's always these totally spaced out people wandering around. Old beach bums and kids getting high, you know? Rejects, kind of like me. I feel like I fit in there.*—

—*Maybe that's where we're supposed to meet then*— I say.

—*What do you mean? When?*—

—*I mean, maybe that's where our perfect world begins*— I say, sliding my hand around his waist. Then I lean in closer to kiss him on the side of his face, passing all of the images of heaven from my lips onto his skin so he'll never forget.

The nurse is over in a flash, pulling at my sleeve to separate us. —*One more time, you two, and that's it. I mean it. Your schedules will be changed. I'm not about to start dealing with this every day.*—

She stands over us until we each give her a guilty nod. When she retreats, Alec whispers in my ear —*I'll wait there forever if I have to.*—

CHAPTER SIX

Some memories are presents that I'm able to unwrap over and over again. In one of my most special memories, I'm sitting in the backseat of our car and my dad is driving. My mom is next to him. Her left hand is resting on his knee while her right hand fumbles with the volume on the radio. One of our favorite songs is on—one we all sing together whenever it comes on, and already I'm humming along from behind them.

It's the middle of summer and still hot even though the sun has nearly set. The windows are rolled down because I like it that way. I hate being trapped inside of the air-conditioning when we could have wind whipping all around us instead. And since I'm only eight years old, I still get my way most of the time.

When the first verse starts, I have my hand held out the window. I make it dance up and down with the words. We are on the freeway and traffic is traveling fast, so my hand jumps pretty drastically. During the chorus, I angle my fingers to direct the breeze toward my face. My voice is choppy in its wake and my mom turns around and smiles at me.

—*How close are we to home?*— I ask after the song is over.

My dad looks at me through the rearview mirror. —*What's the matter, Breen Bean? Are you getting ants in your pants back there?*—

—No. I'm not even wearing pants— I say, giggling. It was too hot in the car to put my clothes on after we left the beach. I only have a towel wrapped around my waist that was meant to keep the seat from getting wet. I've been dry for hours though—now it's just a skirt. I don't have a top on even though I'm probably a little too old not to. I can't help feeling like I'm getting away with something. It's exciting—makes my breath as fast as the wind rushing into the car.

—We should be pulling into the driveway in about an hour— my mom says. *—Why? What do you need?—*

—Nothing— I say honestly. *—Actually, I was just hoping it would take longer, that's all.—*

I see my dad squint at me the way he does whenever he thinks I'm being silly. After checking the mirrors, he turns on the signal and switches lanes. We pass a row of slow-moving trucks and then he asks *—Why's that?—*

—I don't know. Just because— I say, fingering the postcard in my lap. It's glossy and bright and my fingerprints leave an oily streak on the photo of the dolphin leaping through the air.

—You enjoyed this trip, didn't you?— my mom says, reaching back to pet my cheek until I smile at her and nod.

—It was the best yet— I say, happy that there is still an hour left for me to savor before it ends in our driveway with the turning of a key in the ignition and the quieting of the car's overheated engine.

I sit on my bed with the Sea World postcard in my lap. The dolphin has faded quite a bit over seven years and the smudges have grown darker. My mom must have taken it off my wall and put it with the things she packed haphazardly the morning they drove me to the hospital. It was stuck inside a book that I hadn't picked up until this morning. With nothing to do, and an hour before the daily schedule began, I randomly grabbed for that book and watched the postcard fall to the floor like a dead leaf.

I had no idea at the time that our vacation to San Diego would be the last really perfect one we would take. There were others after it that were okay, but none quite like that trip. A few years later, I got to choose the destinations. Even those never lived up. I mean, I liked San Francisco. And I'd always wanted to go to the Grand Canyon. Those were fine. Better than fine even, they were great—but never magical. We just all got along like a perfect family on that trip.

In my memory, I've often returned to that trip down the coast. The postcard stayed tacked to my wall, right next to my bed where I'd stuck it the second we got home. Walking home from the bus freshman year, I would recall all the details. I'd think about the seashells I collected and the way they fit in my palm. I'd picture my parents' smiles as I raced out of the waves on the beach. Then I'd rush up to my room, take off my clothes, and stay perfectly still on top of my covers with the window open and the breeze on my bare skin, focusing all of my attention on the leaping dolphin until the rest of the world dissolved and that one perfect car ride would last forever and the song we loved to sing would never end. Sometimes I think it's one of the memories I will return to in heaven.

But something inside of me has changed.

I notice it right away when I try to drift back there—the first time I've attempted to drift anywhere in weeks. It doesn't feel the same as it used to. I can't place what's different at first. It's just a feeling pulsing through my body. I lay in the hospital bed watching clouds get torn apart as they move through the sharp branches of pine trees. They make no noise moving across the window. They don't change colors as they die, and the world stays with me just as strong as the second before.

The clatter of squeaky carts being pushed down polished hallways floats through the crack under my door. I can hear other familiar sounds, part of the hospital's routine. The opening and closing of patients' self-locking doors. The toilet flushing in the room adjacent to mine. A brief shout from outside the window like the sound of children running. It is quickly covered over by the rumble of a truck gaining speed as it leaves the parking lot.

It's strange being able to hear so clearly when I was expecting this place to fade. Concentrating used to filter out everything around me. This morning it only seems to make it clearer.

It's not just sound, either. My hands feel more real. I wrap them around my chest and press them into the space between my ribs. They are ice cold and it stings as they warm.

The smell of disinfectant in my room is suddenly overpowering.

Even the blanket around my legs is warmer. Tucked tighter. Almost suffocating me as I realize my knees are drenched in sweat.

In fact, everything is more precise except for the memory of being in the backseat as our car sped along the summer coast seven years ago. It didn't flood to the front of my mind like I hoped. If anything, it seems to slip farther away the harder I try to capture it.

When Nurse Abrams enters my room, I'm shivering. She stares at the blanket draped over the side of the bed and half on the floor.
—*Everything okay?*— she asks.

—*I don't know*— I say.

—*Why? What's the matter?*— she asks, approaching me with more haste than usual.

—*I don't know exactly*— I admit. I place the back of my hand on my forehead and tell her —*I think maybe I have a fever or something.*—

Nurse Abrams takes me gently by the wrist and lowers my hand. She's always so careful when she touches me. I guess that's because some of the patients here don't like to be touched. I've seen them. The way they freak out frightens me. Not because of how they shake or scream, but because their outbursts are so sudden and seem so unnecessary. It makes them look—crazy.

I don't mind when Nurse Abrams puts her hand against my forehead because I'm not crazy. I watch her lips counting silently to ten before she grins. —*I doubt you have a fever, but I'll take your temperature just to be certain*— she says with a wink, and I like that about her. That even if she thinks I'm wrong, she'll listen.

After checking the thermometer, she declares that I'm completely normal. Within range of normal anyway, and she can tell the news disappoints me. —*Something's clearly bothering you though. What is it?*—

—*It's . . . hard to describe*— I tell her.

—*Try me.*—

My mouth is dry and the words are hard to form. I swallow a few times trying to find them and Nurse Abrams studies me. She tilts her head so that her short blonde hair nearly touches her shoulder. Finally, I explain to her about the blankets and smells, but leave out the part about trying to drift away and how the magic feeling of my memory has dulled. —*Dr. Richards said eventually things might start to feel more . . . real. Is this what she meant?*— I ask.

—*You should ask her about it this afternoon*— Nurse Abrams says. —*But I would guess this is part of it. You've been here for quite a few weeks now and have been getting better day by day. It sounds to me like your symptoms are finally fading into the background.*

Dr. Richards will be able to tell you for sure. But I imagine you'll be able to return to your normal life soon enough. Won't that be nice?—

Normal life? My breath seizes inside of me for a split second at the very thought. The idea of going back to school and seeing the same crowds in the halls makes my brain get claustrophobic. But then I realize that the suggestion is supposed to make me happy and I smile in agreement. *—Nice. Yeah—* I say as cheerfully as I can manage.

My hands are still shaking. I stick them under my legs, trying my best to hide my fear from Nurse Abrams. I don't want her to know I'm upset. She'll tell the doctors and then I'll have to answer questions about it.

What really scares me, even more than having to go back to my old life, is the thought of having to go back there without the safety of getting lost in my daydreams.

The more I think about it, the more I believe Alec is right—that this is what they want. I wonder then, how long will it be before I'm just sleepwalking through life like everyone else?

I take the postcard off my bed and put it back inside the book, feeling more confused than ever. Alec will help me figure it all out. He understands how I feel better than anyone else. He'll be able to explain it to me, I know he will.

I hop off the bed and dress in the clothes I threw over the chair the night before. Nurse Abrams raises an eyebrow and smiles. *—I thought you weren't feeling so well?—* she asks. *—Where's this burst of energy coming from?—*

—I don't know— I mumble, thinking I've done something wrong. But when I glance up at her, I can tell she's only trying to be friendly. I speak more clearly then, talking through a smile. *—Just want to get started. You know, get something to eat.—*

The way Nurse Abrams nods is like she's hiding a secret. *—And* *maybe see your friend Alec?*— she asks in a teasing tone that reminds me of Kayliegh. But not like recent Kayliegh—more how she used to be back when we shared everything. She used to tease me too about whichever boy I liked. It wasn't to be mean. She knew I sort of liked it because just bringing it up made a crush feel more like a romance somehow.

—*Yeah, maybe*— I say shyly, tucking my hair behind my ears.

I hurry for the door. I want to see Alec as soon as possible— before all of these questions get muddled in my head. As I pull on the handle and enter the hallway, Nurse Abrams calls out —*Hold on there*— so excitedly that I freeze.

She takes three heavy steps away from the side of my bed where she'd been folding the blanket and approaches me. She's holding a small paper cup with my medicine.

I take it from her, seeing the two blue pills still sitting at the bottom.

I place them in my mouth and swallow. They slide like chalk down my throat and I'm free to go.

I enter the cafeteria with words ready to pour out of me but Alec isn't there. I want to wait by the door but I know it isn't a good idea. It attracts attention from the nurses. Attention attracts suspicious questions and I know from firsthand experience that one hesitant answer can disrupt the entire day. I did that once before and that was all it took—sent off for an entire day of tests and observation. They're so nervous and protective here. Nothing we do is ever separated from our illness. If they see me outside the cafeteria, tapping my foot while waiting impatiently for Alec, in their eyes it would be because of my schizophrenia and not simply because I'm anxious to see him.

I'm not risking a whole day without him just for the chance to wave as he turns down the hall. It's better to go inside and wait with a tray of food at a table. Acting normal is always better here.

The food is laid out on a buffet table near the back of the room. There's also a counter to the side where I could order something hot: eggs or oatmeal or pancakes. But I still feel a little feverish from earlier and not really hungry.

What I really want is coffee or tea, but we're not allowed caffeine here. Hospital policy says it's too dangerous because it might mix with our medicine the wrong way. It doesn't matter that my mom let me drink one or the other every morning for the last two years. The hospital's rules cancel out all others.

I miss spending that time with my mom. It was the one thing we always did together. I would come downstairs and she would already be in the kitchen with two mugs out on the counter. Our kitchen at home catches all the morning sun and I would have to blink at its brightness until my sleepy eyes adjusted because it floods the room with watery halos that seem to turn the wooden cabinets into gold. My mom says it's one of the reasons she wanted to buy the house. —*It's hard to start the day in the dark*— was one of her favorite sayings. She has never painted the walls in the nearly twenty years since she and my dad moved in. She says the sunbeams paint them a better color than she could ever choose.

I always liked to sit quietly at the table in the same room with her. I'd watch the sunbeams dance in my drink, making it sparkle. It didn't matter if my parents had been fighting about me the night before or if they were angry with me about something I'd done—the mornings were always calm. There was always the chance in the morning that everything would be better by the end of the day.

I think we all believed that. My dad, somewhere upstairs, invisible in the steam of a shower and running late, believed it most. Me at the kitchen table, studying the subtle shifts in light as cloud-animals paraded across the endless sky, I believed it the least but hoped. My mom was in the middle and kept herself busy to ward off doubt. In the mornings, she was a wildfire spreading throughout the kitchen. The entire house would come alive with the clanging of dishes being placed hurriedly into their cabinets after spending the night drowned in the dishwasher.

I would sip my coffee or tea, never stirring the milk I poured into both. I was always worried about the spoons spending so much time underwater. They are the only utensils with faces—faces we lend to them each time we look into their deep bend. I imagined them screaming and waving their heads around as they drowned. I stopped using spoons when I was eleven. My mother couldn't stand watching me eat cereal with a fork only to drink the milk from the bowl afterward.

The idea of not using a spoon suddenly seems so odd. I pick one up, wondering why I ever felt so strongly about such a little thing.

I take a bowl filled with diced watermelon, pears, oranges, and apple slices nicely arranged like a kaleidoscope. I don't plan on eating them. I just want the candy smell of fruit near enough to cover the sterile scent of Band-Aids that clings to the plastic tables and chairs and trays.

For over a week now, Alec and I have sat at the same table every day. Now nobody else sits there. It's saved for us. But as I take my seat, he still hasn't arrived.

He's late.

I don't take my eyes off the door—expecting any moment to see his eyes shining like green stars in a green galaxy. Then mine will grow brighter too.

Over and over, I picture him walking in, trying to rush the future forward. I close my eyes and imagine taking the journey from his room to the cafeteria. I count the seconds. I count the number of steps it would take—trying carefully to remember just how many doors he needs to pass and how many turns he needs to make to get here. I'm almost at the end when I hear him laughing. —*Do I even want to know what you're doing?*— he asks, pulling the chair next to me out from under the table.

—*Alec!*— I say a little too quickly and too loud.

—*What's wrong?*— he asks, sitting down and taking my hand. It trembles inside his and I see the concern creep across his face. —*You seem frazzled.*—

—*Nothing's wrong*— I sigh with a sense of relief. —*I was worried you weren't coming, that's all.*—

—*Why would you think that?*— he asks through a smile, gently blowing on my hand and rubbing it between his until I stop shivering. —*It's not like there's a lot of places for a mental patient to go*— he says, trying to lighten the mood. But once he sees that I'm still a little on edge, he stops. His voice gets serious again. —*Sabrina? What happened?*—

My mind drifts back to the morning in my room—to the feverish nerves and the faded postcard of a dolphin that used to shimmer with magic. I start to worry all over again. —*Nothing happened. It's just . . . I don't know. This morning, I've been feeling different.*—

—*Different how?*—

—*Well. I used to have these . . . like dreams*— I tell him. —*They call them dreams anyway, but they weren't really dreams. Not like the going-to-sleep kind or anything. It was more like being someplace else, you know? But lately, I don't know. I don't see them anymore and I'm starting to wonder if that means I'm getting better or getting worse.*—

—*Do you want to see these things?*— he asks me.

—*This morning I did.*—

—*Then how could it possibly be better for you not to?*—

—*I don't know, but that's what Dr. Richards says*— I tell him. —*She says seeing those things are part of my illness. That being the way I am causes me to be . . . delusional.*—

—*Delusional? That's what they told you?*— Alec is visibly angry now. I can feel the tension in his grip.

—*They say the things I see aren't real*— I tell him.

—*Like what?*—

I lift up my shoulder and press my chin against it nervously. —*Sometimes*— I say —*I can see the sky change colors. I just move my hand and rainbows appear. Other times, it's more than that. It's like . . . I go someplace else. Everything around me changes then.*—

When I lift my head, Alec isn't staring at me like all the other people I've ever told. His eyes light up with curiosity. There's an excitement in his voice when he speaks. —*Changes how?*—

—*Like everything, I don't know*— I say. —*It's like all of this . . . this room and these chairs and whatever . . . they all disappear. Then something more beautiful takes their place.*—

I watch his fingers gently circling over my skin—his thumb slowly petting my birthmark. It's his way of telling me that he loves all things that make me special—all the things others say make me broken. A sleeping star inside me is suddenly shining and I begin to glow.

—*You know something? You have to be the most amazing girl I've ever met*— he says, and I feel my cheeks flush.

At that moment, I wish more than anything that he and I could walk off into our own world and leave everybody else behind. We could live in the place from my dream that I haven't told him about yet. The dream where the sunlight was so bright that I never quite saw his face but knew who it was the moment I saw him in the hospital. There we'd be able to escape all that is terrible in the world.

It all seems less possible sitting in the cafeteria.

Suddenly it feels—more like a dream.

—*But what if they're right?*— I ask. —*What if I'm wrong about it? What then?*—

—*That's crap*— he says. —*If you said you saw Jesus or something, they wouldn't even think of calling you delusional. They'd put you on the evening news and morning talk shows, and some poor village in Peru would probably make a statue of you out of twigs and mud. Don't you see, all they really care about is conformity and making sure you see things exactly how they do. If you ask me, I'd say you're lucky. You get to see past all the things that are fake and ugly. The problem is that most people look at the world and see a bunch of strip malls. You actually see something worth seeing and they don't think that's fair.*—

—*Do you really think so?*— I ask.

—*Definitely.*—

—*But what am I supposed to do then? I don't see those things anymore*— I tell him. —*I feel like that part of me is going away.*—

Alec lowers his eyes and shakes his head. —*Soma*— he says quietly.

—*What's that?*— I ask.

—*It's the so-called medicine they're giving you*— he says. —*It's what they're giving all of us.*—

—*Soma? That's not what it's called*— I tell him, trying to remember the complicated names of the pills I have to take. —*It's something like chlor zine and something dol. I can't remember exactly.*—

—*It doesn't matter what the names are on the labels, it's all the same. They all have the same purpose*— he says, growing more animated. Sitting up straighter, his eyes glow brightly as he glares at the nurse across the room as if she is our enemy. *—Those pills are just to keep us from thinking. In this book I read about the future, everyone is on this pill called Soma that makes them easy to control. That's what this place is all about. They stick us in places like this so they can drug us. Then presto . . . suddenly we're robots like everybody else.—*

—But there's nothing we can do about the medicine— I say.

—Sure there is— Alec says. *—Stop taking it. Don't let them brainwash us anymore. I haven't taken anything they've given me since I got here.—*

—You haven't?— It surprises me and my voice goes higher. I'm given pills twice a day. Four pills each time. It seems dangerous to miss that much medicine. *—Doesn't it make you sick?—*

—No. It's those pills that make you sick. They turn your head into plastic. Look, there's nothing wrong with us. There's nothing to cure.—

The idea scares me and I begin to suck on my sleeve. It's not that I don't believe him—part of me has always felt the same way, but it still frightens me.

—But isn't medicine supposed to make you better?—

—Medicine? Give me a break. It's just a drug like any other— Alec says. *—They always tell us how bad drugs are, but here they try to give us tons of them? And it's not just us. Everyone I know has parents on pills. Every bathroom cabinet in America is filled with little brown bottles with long names that all mean the same thing. Soma. Mind control. I'm telling you, if we let them, they'll change us to the point where we won't ever be able to remember who we used to be.—*

—I don't want that— I tell him—my voice muffled by my sleeve.

—So you're with me then? You'll stop taking them?—

I nod—slowly at first but more decisive once he squeezes my hand. —*Okay*— I say. —*But what if they find out?*—

Alec reaches for the hand near my mouth so that both of my hands are now wrapped up in his. —*Don't worry about them*— he says. —*All that matters is you and me.*—

SEVEN

I have to be careful not to use too much glue. The magazine paper is so thin that if I use the slightest bit more than a dab, the glue bubbles up and shows through to the picture on the other side. But even being careful, holding the picture flat on the table and measuring the drop with a squinted eye as it seeps from the orange cap, I manage to get too much on the paper. I have to smear it flat with my finger in a spiral pattern until it's thin enough for me to press the picture on the collage paper without wrinkling.

—*This is so dumb*— Alec groans beside me. He's been complaining the entire twenty minutes we've been in the art room. I don't mind though because he's cute when he's grumpy and I'm pretty sure he's mostly doing it to make me laugh.

—*I don't mind. I like it actually*— I tell him for the tenth time.

—*Art collages?*— he sneers. —*What are we, in first grade?*—

—*It's supposed to help us express our feelings*— I say, doing my best imitation of Mrs. Weaver, the therapist in charge of instructing us in this activity. She says sometimes words aren't the best way to describe our emotions and that making collages might help us get in touch with our inner selves. Today, she wants us to make a piece about our relationship with our parents. For some reason, it bothers Alec more than the others we've had to do. —*Try to have some fun with it*— I tell him. Then I reach over and press my gluey finger on his nose. Before he can wipe at it, I stick a red piece of paper on him that I've cut into a circle and now he has a clown's nose.

He smiles for the first time since we started working on our projects. Looking at himself in the reflection of the windows behind us, he laughs. —*Can this be my project?*— he jokes. —*This says everything about the way I feel toward my dad.*—

—*I'm pretty sure Mrs. Weaver had something else in mind*— I tease him, pulling the paper off his face.

I've been in a good mood all day. Last night before bed, I hid the medicine under my tongue until the nurse left. As soon as the door clicked closed, I got up and spit the pills out in the toilet. This morning, I did the same thing. Nurse Abrams was more distracted than usual and I had no problem getting away with it.

Already, I'm noticing the changes.

I don't feel so on edge today. It's the same kind of feeling I get after taking a big test in school and can let go of all the memorized information stored in my brain—instantly I'm lighter once it's been emptied. This morning has been just like that. I've been floating all day.

Mrs. Weaver is strolling around the room. The tables in the art room are pushed together into a giant horseshoe. Inside the opening, she wanders from patient to patient, pausing to look at everyone's work and asking us a couple of questions apiece.

The tapping of her heeled shoes stops inches away and I know she's examining mine. —*That's very pretty, Sabrina*— she says, and I glance up at her with a smile on my face.

—*Thanks.*—

In the center of my collage is a black-and-white photograph of a mother and young daughter hugging in the snow at night. They are wearing heavy winter coats and ribbons in their hair because the picture is supposed to be of a scene in the 1800s and that was the way most girls and women wore their hair, I suppose. Around the photograph, I glued pictures of flowers I'd cut from the stacks of magazines Mrs. Weaver set out for us to use. The flowers are bright and colorful against the black-and-white snow. I painted the sky with watercolors. I used dark purples and blues and painted them really wet so that the colors ran together in interesting shapes. I used a little bit of pink paint on the girl's cheeks.

—*Can you tell me something about the images you chose?*— Mrs. Weaver asks.

—*Sure*— I say. I love talking about my pictures and I'm smiling like crazy. Even Alec can't help but grin when he sees me so happy. —*Well, obviously this is me and that's my mom.*—

—*I can see that*— Mrs. Weaver says. She allows a quick smile to flash across her mouth before it turns into a grimace and fades completely. Her features scrunch together then. With a quizzical look, she taps on the image of the girl who symbolizes me. —*But why are your cheeks pink in the picture? Are you cold? Is your mother hugging you to keep you warm?*—

I shake my head. —*No. I'm not cold at all.*—

—*Oh. Okay, then why? Did you have a reason, or did you just like the way it looked?*— she asks.

—*Not exactly. My cheeks are painted because I belong with the flowers and the sky. They are colorful and that's where I'm going.*— I tell her. Right away I wonder if I shouldn't have said that about going someplace else. It's probably the wrong answer but then again, I'm not sure I care. Alec says I shouldn't hide what I see and I trust him.

—*What about your mother?*— Mrs. Weaver asks.

—*She's trying to keep me with her. In this place . . .*— I say, drawing an imaginary circle around the black-and-white scenery with my finger. — . . . *this place with all the snow. Because that's where she belongs.—*

—*Why don't you feel you belong in the same place as her?*— she asks me, and I shrug.

—*I don't know*— I say. —*I just . . . don't.*—

—*Hmmmm*— Mrs. Weaver says, twisting up the corner of her mouth. There's a look of concern on her face that makes my stomach drop. —*What about your father? Where is he in this picture?*—

—*Somewhere nearby*— I say, thinking of him running toward us. —*He's coming to help her. They both want me to stay.*—

There's a brief moment that passes where neither of us makes a sound. She stares at my collage and I keep my eyes fixed on her. There's something about the way her eyes focus on the image that makes me wish I'd never told her. I could have just said I liked the way it looked and she would have moved on the way she always does.

—*I'm wondering if you wouldn't mind me showing this to your doctor once you're done?*— she asks.

—*I guess not*— I whisper nervously. She's never asked that before—not of me or any other patient as far as I know.

Alec hears my voice crack. He notices my hand dive into my pocket where he knows I keep at least one stone at all times. Once he sees my fingers moving like insects inside the fabric, working over the rough edges, he looks in Mrs. Weaver's direction and sighs. —*Something wrong, Alec?*— she asks, turning toward him.

—*Yeah*— he says. —*Why do you have to interrogate her?*—

—*I'm sorry if you feel I'm interrogating anyone*— she says, straining to remain calm. —*My job is to try and help you all explore feelings you may not even know you have.*—

—*What a load of crap*— Alec says under his breath—just loud enough for her to hear and quiet enough so that she can pretend to ignore it. She takes a step over to stand in front of him.

—*Mind if I look at yours?*— she asks.

—*No problem.*— Alec pushes his paper across the table so that it takes flight just above the table's surfaces and slides nearly onto the floor.

Mrs. Weaver catches it before it falls and holds it in her hand. She examines it for a few seconds before turning it around. It is a picture of a man in a suit, carrying a briefcase. Next to him is a woman in a suit, carrying a briefcase. Alec has used the red paper nose I gave him and made an identical one. He's glued both on the foreheads of the two figures with squiggly red lines running down from them.

—*In this picture . . . who do you imagine is the shooter?*— Mrs. Weaver asks. —*Is it you?*—

—*No*— Alec says. —*It's nobody . . . because it's just a stupid picture. There is no shooter because nobody got shot.*—

—*Yes, I understand that. But what would you say this means?*—

—*They're photos from a magazine!*— he shouts, pushing against the table with both hands so that the legs squeal across the floor. The violence of it startles Mrs. Weaver but not me. I know how much he doesn't like her. —*It doesn't mean anything . . . none of these mean anything, so why don't you just leave us alone!*—

Like all of the nurses and doctors, Mrs. Weaver is very good at not getting upset but I can tell she's struggling this time. —*I'm going to ask you not to speak to me in that tone.*—

—*Then why don't you stop harassing us.*—

—*I'm sorry? Harassing?*— she asks.

—*Yeah. You kept picking on Sabrina when she obviously didn't want to talk anymore. Then you accuse me of wanting to kill my parents or something*— he says.

—*It's okay, Alec*— I say because I don't want him to get in trouble. If he gets in trouble, we'll be separated. Even if it's only for a few hours, I hate when we're separated. —*It's fine.*—

—*No it's not*— he says. —*This whole thing is ridiculous.*—

—*Maybe it would be best if you left for the rest of this session?*— Mrs. Weaver suggests.

—*And maybe it would be best if you went off to teach grade-school art class*— Alec barks, but Mrs. Weaver is already walking away. She's on the other side of the room using the phone on the wall to call the nurses' station. —*I don't even belong here! They put me in this place as a favor to my dad! Some favor!*—

The rest of the kids are staring at him—at us really, because I've locked my elbow in his hoping to keep him close the same way the mother in my art collage is doing with me.

When the door opens, the nurse has two security guards with her and Alec shakes his head. Once they approach, he throws up his hands. —*This is crazy*— he says. A guard puts a hand on his shoulder and asks him nicely to come along. —*Fine! I'm going. Happy?*— he shouts at Mrs. Weaver on the way out.

I want so badly to follow him but I'm not allowed. As soon as I take one step, Mrs. Weaver stops me. —*He'll be fine, don't worry*— she says to me. She sends me back to my station where I finish my collage without much interest. She doesn't ask me any more questions. And when it's time for me to go to group, she doesn't ask for my picture. The only picture Mrs. Weaver keeps is Alec's.

I follow the other kids out of the room. All of us have group sessions next and I shuffle a few paces behind. Even in the middle of their voices, I feel lost. My hand feels empty without the familiar shape of his long skinny fingers. The sooner he's back at my side, the better I'm going to be.

They are talking about him—the two girls in front of me who I don't know. I hear them say they were scared when Alec yelled. They don't know he was only protecting me—that he would do anything to protect me.

Before we enter group, one of the girls turns around and stops me. —*You must have been relieved when they took him away, right? Did you see his eyes? I thought he was going to kill somebody.*—

Her eyes are the color of rust around the edges.

She has a habit of biting her nails until they bleed.

I shrug and avoid answering her questions.

—*You're with him a lot, aren't you?*— she asks. I feel small when she turns to stand in front of me. She's so much taller—she's a redwood and I am a sapling shrinking from her glare.

—*Uh-huh*— I mumble.

—*Thought so.*— When she nods, the longer strands of hair look like soft teeth chattering against the shaved parts of her head. —*I'd be careful if I were you.*—

The other girl stands with her hands curled into fists. She's breathing sharp and fast through her nostrils. Her behavior gives the words she says next the ferocity of a dog bite. —*Alec is bad.*—

—*I don't know what you mean*— I say as soft as a whisper.

—*She means just what she said. He's no good*— the first girl tells me, pronouncing each word clearly.

—*Why would you say that?*— I ask. —*Alec would never hurt anyone.*—

—*Don't you know why he's in here?*— she asks in a high-pitched voice as if she's just won a game of some kind. —*I bet he never told you, did he?*—

—*It doesn't matter why*— I whisper.

All that matters is that we're here and we found each other and understand each other as well as two fish forever swimming as one in a circle. That's how perfect we fit together and that's all that matters.

—*Well, he told me . . . our group anyway*— the other girl says. —*He talked all about it during our session yesterday.*—

—*You're not supposed to say what others tell in group*— I remind her.

—*Yeah? Well, you're not supposed to shoot no one either*— she says. —*You should know your new boyfriend planned on shooting up his school and half of everybody in it.*—

I shake my head violently.

—*You're wrong*— I say. —*He's here because people don't understand him, that's all.*— She shrugs and keeps walking to her group, talking loudly with the other girl again, and I'm relieved when they're gone.

I go into group and take a seat in the circle. I try to ignore what they said. I try telling myself there are a lot of reasons why Alec might have said those things in group—why he would lie. Or even if it isn't a lie, I'm sure he had a reason that those two don't understand. Nobody but me would.

I hope he's not in too much trouble. I've seen other patients yell at nurses and stuff. They're usually put back into a regular routine by the end of the day. I hope it's the same for Alec.

My fingers work over the sharpest edge of the stone in my pocket. It hurts quite a bit to keep scraping my skin against it, but already I can feel it wearing down. I'll only have to suffer a little longer. It'll all be worth it when my wish comes true.

––––––––––

Later in the afternoon, I'm out on the lawn when I see Alec coming. I'm sitting in our spot by the tree and he waves at me. I've been waiting for him and I hold my hand up quickly before putting it back in my lap. I need to see for certain that it's still him before I let myself get too excited. I've seen how they change people here. There was a girl in the common room not too long ago who didn't stop screaming because someone changed the channel on the television. When they brought her back, she was just a shell—a shadow of a ghost and nothing more. If that's happened to Alec too, I don't know what I'll do.

Part of me knows how crazy it sounds because he's walking and waving. But the other part of me can't let go of doubt. Right now, that side is stronger. Every thought I have is more magnified today— especially doubt. Maybe it's because my medicine is floating somewhere in the hospital's plumbing instead of running through my bloodstream, or maybe I'm just anxious. Whatever it is though, today is a struggle to figure out what I believe.

A panic rushes through my body as he gets closer. My heart thumps and my hands tremble terribly. I bring them up to my face where I can steady the shaking by placing the corner of my sleeve in my mouth.

I remember my breathing then. I remember to take deeper breaths the way Dr. Gysion showed us before group once. He says careful breathing is a technique to relax us whenever we get worked up.

It helps.

—*Look . . . I'm a free man*— Alec says, holding his hands up at his side and spinning around once. The sun shines directly on him and his shape is lost for a moment in the afternoon light. It takes a second for my eyes to adjust and see features within his silhouette. Once they do—I see his familiar smile and my hands stop trembling.

Alec is still Alec even if we have been apart most of the day.

I stop worrying about what those girls said to me too. They're wrong about him. I knew they were. I've always been able to tell good people from bad. Everyone's soul gives off a light. Some are bright and soothing like shadows illuminated under a full moon. Others are the color of dark corners in basement closets.

I have nothing to fear from Alec.

His glow is blinding.

He sits next to me and immediately lies down with his arms stretched out in the grass behind him. The sun begins to warm his skin and he purrs. His rib cage shows through his T-shirt. I watch it rise and fall at a sleepy pace. —*That was exhausting*— he says.

—*What did they do to you?*— I ask.

—*Bored the life out of me until I thought I'd turn into stone*— he says. He opens one eye and looks at me. This time he's the one having to squint to see through the glare of the sun. —*It took a while to convince them I wasn't going to snap and go on a killing spree.*—

—*Is that because of what you did to get sent here?*— I ask.

Alec pushes himself on his elbows and looks at me curiously. —*Yeah. I'm sure it is*— he says in a more serious tone. —*Did somebody say something to you?*—

—*Kind of*— I say.

—*Yeah? What did they say?*—

—*That you were going to shoot kids at your school*— I say.

Alec blinks and I can almost see his heartbeat increase in the movement of his eyelids. —*Who was it? It was that psycho girl, Pam? The one with the shaved head?*— I nod and he shakes his head. —*Figures. She's one of those girls who needs to stir things up, even if it means lying, you know? Everything that comes out of her is exaggerated for effect. People like her are why I did what I did in the first place.*—

—*What did you do?*— I ask.

—*Nothing really*— he says. —*One day in class, I just said that most everyone at my school might as well already be dead and that killing them would be doing the world a favor.—*

I hold my breath for a split second before exhaling. *—But you didn't say you wanted to . . . kill them?—*

—Not at all. I was just making a comment— he tells me. *—It wasn't like I had some plan to go in there with a gun and kill people. It's ridiculous how everyone reacted. It's like they never heard of freedom of expression.—*

—You told me they sent you here because you didn't fit in with the others— I remind him. I don't want to believe that Alec would lie to me, but I need to make sure. *—Why didn't you tell me about this?—*

—Because— he says, and lies back in the grass again and closes his eyes. When I don't say anything, he squints up at me. *—I didn't tell you because I didn't think it was a big deal. God! Now you're mad at me?—*

I shake my head. *—I'm not mad. I just want to know, that's all.—*

—I hate this— he sighs. *—I hate that I could be sent to a place like this for just saying something. I hate that because my parents have all this money and privilege that they could convince whoever they needed to that their son has a disorder just because I think the kids I go to school with are stupid. And I really hate that now you might look at me different because some girl told it to you all wrong.—*

—No. I won't— I say because I realize now that he didn't lie to me. He's told me this before. He told me exactly what happened, at least the way he saw it. It's the same as I've told him. *—It's okay. I believe you.—*

Alec turns to look at me, thanking me with his eyes before telling me more. *—You know what the worst part is? The angrier I get about it, the more they say it just proves that I belong here. Like today with Weaver and before with my group doctor. They keep trying to make* *something out of nothing. They say I'm showing a pattern of behavior or whatever. But that's only because they refuse to stop searching for one and it makes me lose it. You can't trust these doctors. You can't tell them anything.—*

I know how he feels. I know what it's like to be misunderstood. *—If you don't want to, we don't have to talk about it anymore—* I say.

—But that's the funny thing— he says, sitting up again. *—I actually want to tell you. If there's anyone who understands, it's you.—*

There's a moment then when neither of us says anything. It's like the moment in my dream just before our skin touches. There's something pulling us closer together. There's no way to stop us from connecting—it would be like trying to stop the waves on the ocean.

—Tell me then— I say. *—What happened?—*

—Well, I guess it wasn't only because of what I said in class— he says. *—The school searched my locker after that and found this list I wrote in one of my notebooks. It was a list of all the kids I hated. It wasn't connected to what I said at all. I wasn't going to kill them. But it didn't matter because the school and the cops made all these connections that didn't exist. It was out of control.—*

As he adds new pieces to the puzzle, I can't help but think about what my dad would say. He'd think everyone else was right about Alec and that the real story was finally coming out. It's like when I'd tell him the truth but not the whole true. He says partial truths are the same as lies. He'd want me to believe that about Alec, just like those girls after art wanted me to. But I don't. I've known the truth about him since before we met.

—They blew everything way out of proportion— he says. *—I kind of knew they would as soon as I said it. I guess that's why I said it in the first place. It's like what you and I talked about the other day . . . trying to wake people up.—*

81

—*Because they're sleepwalkers?*—

—*Yeah exactly! And they don't even realize it*— he says. —*That's all I meant by saying they'd be better off dead. I'd rather be dead than terrified of everything. It's like these people who hear about some flu outbreak on the other side of the world and start wearing surgical masks. They overreact to everything. But don't dare try pointing that out to them.*—

—*Sometimes I think it's better not to tell anyone*— I say, thinking about all the times I've sat silently facing Dr. Richards. —*They never understand.*—

—*You can say that again*— Alec says, plucking dandelions from the lawn. He twists the stems around his finger and watches his skin turn a shade of green that matches his eyes. —*First I got expelled. Then they wanted to send me to some detention center, but I was sent here instead. I didn't really care where they sent me as long I was out of that school.*—

—*Maybe it was fate*— I say with a smile. For the first time since he's joined me, I reach over and let my hand rest on his leg.

—*Yeah, fate or my dad*— he says. —*He was the one who pushed for me to get sent to the hospital even though he knows I don't belong here. He used his connections and convinced them that I just needed a little therapy. He's so full of it though. He used to be some kind of activist for the environment before he sold out with the rest of his generation.*—

A flash of faraway anger colors his eyes for a split second like an electrical storm way out over the ocean that I watch safely from the sand. It's nothing like the static though. It's something real that has always been inside of him and there's something protective about it— something that makes me feel safe.

Alec picks another dandelion from the lawn to murder beautifully in his hands. He twists the stem violently in his fingers until it snaps like frayed rope. —*Sometimes when I meet people, I tell them my parents died in a plane crash, just because it sort of feels that way. It's a more interesting story than the truth, which is that I'm invisible to my parents*— he says. —*Or at least the reality of my life is invisible. Sometimes I wonder why they can't see things that are so obvious to me.*—

—*That's the noise*— I say, and Alec tilts his head. I've never told him about the noise before and he's curious. —*Once it gets inside people, it makes it so they can't see the way things really are.*—

—*Noise?*— Alec mumbles, considering the sound of the word as he twists another stem so tightly around his finger that the tip under his nail turns white. Then he finally looks up at me and our eyes meet. —*That's a good way of putting it.*—

—*Yeah? Nobody else thinks so*— I say, looking down into my lap.

The flower end of the dandelion disappears in Alec's fist.

It bleeds yellow and turns his palm the color of his hair.

—*Doesn't it ever make you angry?*— he asks. —*Everybody always telling you that you're wrong about everything? Sometimes it makes me so mad that I just want to blow my brains out, you know?*—

I blink and see a gun flash beside his head like a lightbulb exploding.

—*No. I don't ever think that way*— I tell him, holding his hand so tight that he'll have to agree with me.

—*How can you not?*—

—*Because, I know they're wrong. I've seen what's going to happen . . . I know I'm going someplace that's worth waiting for.*—

—*Like one of your dreams, you mean?*—

—*Yep*— I say as a gust of wind blows by us. My whole body glows when it touches me. I can't quite see it the way I used to, but I sense it all around me—a world different from this world. I reach up and push aside the hair hanging in my eyes. The sky doesn't change color when I look up at it, but it wants to. —*It's close too. It's not too far away. Then it'll be perfect.*—

—*Is that really what you see when you think about the future?*— he asks.

—*Sure*— I say. —*I see it for both of us.*—

Alec lies back again and closes his eyes. He holds out his arm as an invitation for me to use it as a pillow. I lean back, lie flat on the grass, and close my eyes too. The sky is so bright on my eyelids, it's easy to imagine the world has been erased.

—*Tell me about it?*— he asks. I can feel him roll onto his side. He rests his head in his palm, brushes my hair with his other hand. —*Everything about it.*—

I lay perfectly still with my arms folded across my chest the way I used to when I was little and Kayliegh and I would lie in front of gravestones and pretend we were angels. Alec pets me like a lullaby. The wind coming over the mountains is warm. My dreams return to me then. I can see it all so clearly. —*It's beautiful.*—

—*Am I there?*—

—*Of course you're there*— I say. —*We've known each other forever there. Sometimes I think it's where we came from. Like maybe you and I got lost and now we're just trying to find our way back.*—

—*Yeah? How do we do that?*—

—*We walk through the sun*— I tell him.

—*Like wait for it to sit right on top of the ocean . . . then just walk out into waves?*— he says.

It's a good way of picturing it and I nod enthusiastically.

—*Yeah . . . just like that*— I say. —*And once we're on the other side, all of this won't be real anymore. It'll disappear and then it'll just be us. Forever. In a place that changes with however we wish it to be.*—

—*You really think so, huh?*—

—*I know so*— I say. —*As long we're together, I know it will come true.*—

—*Don't worry about that. I'm not going anywhere without you.*— He says it like a promise that will last long after the sun dips down just below the taller trees on the tallest hills. The nurses will come then and take us away, but it doesn't matter. They can take us to different wings of the hospital but they can't really separate us. Not anymore. We are connected in a dream—that can't be broken.

—*I'm glad I was sent here after all*— Alec says.

—*Why?*—

—*Because you're here*— he says.

EIGHT

—*We just want what's best for you.*— My mom keeps repeating the same phrase over and over. She's like the spinning rainbow when the computer freezes. —*We just want what's best for you, that's all.*—

I'm sitting on the bed as she goes through my closet, pulling tops off of hangers, jeans from the floor, piling all of them in the same travel bag I've used for every car trip we've taken in the past four years. Knowing that they are taking me away to a mental hospital, the pink canvas fabric seems too cheerful—the koala bear keychain that dangles from the zipper even more so.

—*You know that, don't you? You know we just want what's best for you?*— she asks, grabbing the first books she can reach from the shelf near my desk and tossing them on top of the clothes. It doesn't seem to make a difference to her that half of them I've already read and the other half are schoolbooks that I won't need where I'm going. —*We just want to help you.*—

I don't bother to tell her how I don't need any help because I've stopped trying to make them understand.

My dad's role is to pop his head in the door and tell us both —*It's time we should be leaving.*— My mom sobs on cue and he crosses my room sympathetically. I watch as he puts his arm around her and kisses

her on the forehead the way I've seen fathers do in a hundred different movies. They've rehearsed their parts so well.

As we pull out of the driveway, I can almost convince myself we are
going on one of our road trips. I am in the same seat, with the same
view of my parents. My mom's hair is pulled into the familiar brown
ponytail so that I can roll down the window and her hair won't get
tangled whipping her in the face at sixty miles per hour. I have my sleeve
in my mouth and my head tilted back to see the rainbows streaking
through the clouds as we drive.

—It's a trip. Just a trip like going to see dolphins or the Grand
Canyon— I mutter. I pet the birthmark on my left hand until my skin
gets pink and sore. It reminds me of the wimp tests that boys I know
used to play in grade school by rubbing pencil erasers over their arms
until the skin peeled away like a sunburn. The first to cry out failed.

The drive is three hours and eleven minutes from our driveway to
the Wellness Center. The radio is on but nobody sings. We stop only
once to eat. My dad orders food for me that I leave in the bag without
touching.

When we arrive at the hospital, it's early evening. The sky is light
purple and my mom's eyes are red and swollen. We drive through a
heavy gate with a guard who says he's expecting us. Our car's headlights
turn the building into a haunted house with lightning in the windows. A
seven-foot-high stone wall surrounds the hospital like a cemetery and I
wonder if this is where I'm being sent to die.

I ask my mom —Am I going to be buried here?—

—No, sweetheart— she says. —You're here to get better.—

—Hello, Sabrina.—

I blink my eyes a few times, staring at my reflection in the window. My eyelashes flutter—my eyes are blue butterflies with black wings.

The size of everything gets confused in the glass.

My face appears as large as Dr. Richards when she enters the room. When she sits down, she appears to be sitting in the dark jungle of my hair. The doll in my hands is invisible because I hold it below the level of the window.

I turn around and everything returns to its normal size.

—*How are you feeling today?*— she asks.

I feel much better. I haven't taken my medicine in two days.

—*More like myself*— I tell her.

—*That's good to hear*— she says, leaning back a little in her chair.

I know everything she is going to do before she does it. I know she is going to lean forward and place her right hand on her left knee. I know she's going to raise her eyebrows and smile at me with her eyes. We have spent forty hours and sixteen minutes in this room together since I first came here. That's plenty of time to memorize every one of her habits. And I'm just as sure she has memorized mine. She knows when something is different and I have to be careful about how I answer things.

This is the same room where my parents and I first met with her. My mom's makeup had run and given her raccoon eyes. My dad was tired from driving and kept grinding his teeth. He paced. My mom and I sat in the kind of overstuffed chairs found in the waiting rooms of every doctor's office—comfortable-looking yet nobody is ever too comfortable in them. They did all of the talking then. Dr. Richards asked them how I was feeling. —*Okay*— my mom answered uncertainly. —*The car ride was difficult. It's a long drive.*—

She placed her hand on my knee, trying to get a response or to reassure me, or both maybe. I ignored her. My mom didn't seem to notice, but Dr. Richards saw. She watched me the entire time she spoke. —*I realize we're pretty far from Burbank, but I think it's for the best that you brought her here. I truly think she'll respond in an environment like ours*— she said. I remember thinking it was some sort of trick.

It's strange. I haven't thought about any of this in weeks.

Dr. Richards opens her notebook and looks over our previous conversations. I watch her now with newly suspicious eyes. When she looks up at me, she has the smile of a reptile.

—*The other day you were telling me that you didn't like the way the prescriptions made you feel*— she says. —*Has that passed?*—

—*Sort of*— I lie.

—*Good. That's good*— she says. —*I can tell you, it's made a huge difference.*—

—*How so? I mean, how can you tell?*—

Dr. Richards closes the notebook in her lap and puts it aside. She only does this when she wants it to feel like we're chatting. The way friends would, instead of a doctor and a patient.

I put the doll back in its place with the others and sit in the chair opposite her. This always pleases her the same way people are pleased when a puppy gives them a paw and behaves.

—*Can you tell me what day it is today?*—

—*Sure*— I answer. —*It's Tuesday.*—

—*Do you think you would've been able to answer that question when you first arrived here?*— she asks.

She knows the answer so there is no need for me to say it. I just shake my head because she knows time moved differently for me outside of the Wellness Center. The world is too fast there. I couldn't keep track of things like days. My parents told her all about that.

—*You see, the lapses in time you experienced have improved*— she explains. —*Don't you feel like it has improved?*—

—I guess so— I say. *—But that doesn't prove anything. It's harder to keep track out there. It's so busy and there's so much more going on.—*

.—Maybe so— she says. *—But you're also communicating more clearly than before. You're making friends here. You're able to make yourself understood. All of this is the benefit of what we have accomplished in the time you've been here. Sometimes, the transition can be stressful. I think that's what you've been feeling lately.—*

Lately, I've been feeling like the wires in my brain have been switched around—disconnected from where they belong. It makes everything too sharp—makes my skin tingle like little shocks made of glitter. Without the medicine, they are growing back to where they belong. Already, my dreams are coming back—little by little.

—Sometimes, though, I miss the way I was— I admit.

—That's natural— Dr. Richards assures me. *—What you're going through now is something like waking up from a dream. It tries to linger but you have to fight the urge to fall back asleep.—*

—But what if the dream is a good one?— I ask.

Dr. Richards looks sad for a second—sad for me or just sad in general, I can't tell. Then it passes and she presses her lips together, nodding not only her head, but her whole body. *—The world can be a terrifying place sometimes. As your mind begins to get clearer and you realize this, the memories of the way you saw things before may feel comforting. It may seem like everything was easier then, but that's simply because you forget the confusion you felt and only focus on the positive aspects. That's why it's so important we talk about the occasions when those dreams of yours turned into nightmares. Can't you think of a time like that?—*

I turn away from her and stare out the window again.

—You still with me, Sabrina?— Dr. Richards asks after a moment. There are thin lines of concern etched in her face. Lines like rivers

dividing a map, they carve her face as she studies me with tired eyes and a polite grin. —*What are you thinking about?*— she asks.

There's a faint smell of sanitizer soap when she speaks.

—*Not much . . . just thinking*— I answer.

There's a sour scent of saliva when I speak that is like the smell of my sleeve or a pillow in the morning when I first wake up.

—*Were you remembering one of the bad times?*—

—*No.*—

I lie because I know what she's trying to do. She wants me to be scared into letting them change me. She wants to confuse me into believing the static and my dreams are the same thing.

She's a liar.

She wants to put me to sleep. I want to wake up.

Dr. Kunstler lied too. He was the first doctor my parents took me to. He said I would get better, but I got worse. He said I was suffering from simple anxiety and gave me pills to take.

When my parents finally committed me here to the hospital, Dr. Richards said that Dr. Kunstler diagnosed me wrong and that is why I didn't get better. She said it wasn't anxiety making me act the way I act but acute schizophrenia.

—*Schizophrenia? That's not our daughter. She's just . . . having a difficult time*— my mom said.

—*For Christ's sake!*— my dad said. —*She's not speaking in voices for crying out loud! She's not schizophrenic!*—

But Dr. Richards is really good at lying. I didn't know it then, but I do now. She convinced them. She raised her eyebrows to make her eyes look big and pulled her lips in to make her mouth look small as it curled into something between a smile and grinning frown. It's her way of disarming people—of making them feel unsure about what they have just said.

—I'm not talking about multiple personalities— she explained. *—That's a common mistake people make when they think of schizophrenia. Acute schizophrenia is something very different and very treatable. Sabrina is showing all the classic symptoms and it most commonly appears in teenagers. But we won't know for sure until we've spent some more time with her.—*

—But if you don't know, what are you doing in the meantime?— my mom asked. *—You told us you were prescribing two different medications. How can you do that without knowing what's wrong? And is that even safe? Giving her medication she might not need?—*

—Perfectly— Dr. Richards said.

It's all so clear to me now—the way she tricked them and why. If I'm here, she thinks she can control me. She's trying to control me right now too. I feel it. I feel her words tugging me in one direction.

—You seem upset— she says.

—No. I'm not.—

The room falls silent between us then. Neither of us speaks because I have nothing more I want to tell her and she is busy sorting out her own words. There are so many deceptions inside of her that she looks swollen with words, waiting to split the seams until they seep from her, spilling onto the floor to collect in puddles.

—I know this is hard— she sighs. *—Reliving the past is painful for most patients, but it's important. Only by doing this will you see how sometimes your mind creates what you wish would be true. The chemical imbalance in your brain causes this. But now that we've corrected it, you are able to distinguish between reality and fantasy.—*

Alec says it isn't that easy.

He says they invent what is reality and that they do a poor job of it. I can do better on my own.

—Can I go now?— I ask.

She glances at the clock, then at her notebook. —*Alright*— she says. —*I think we've taken another step today. You should be proud. I know I'm proud of you.*—

I nod. I have made progress—a breakthrough even. But if she knew the kind of progress I've really made, I don't think she'd seem as happy as she does. Because I've got a secret: Nothing bad can happen to me again as long as I ignore everything they tell me.

I run as fast as I can but my skinny eleven-year-old legs are too slow to outrace those chasing me. They are boys with sneakers and I'm wearing sandals. They run and play soccer all of the time. I play tennis and only ever need small bursts of speed over very short distances.

I scream when the closest boy reaches for me in the darkness. Trying to switch directions, I nearly slip in the grass. If it was daytime, I'd know who it was—whose hand was grabbing for me. But we don't play during the day. It's more fun at night.

—*Gotcha!*— the boy shouts. His sweaty hand clutches my shoulder and I squeal—half terrified and half giggling. —*Let's go. Off to jail.*—

It's one of Kayliegh's neighbors. I don't know him very well. He goes to private school, but I know the other two boys with him. They're in the grade above me and they're smirking at the capture of another prize. —*No fair*— I tease. —*I would've gotten away if I had real shoes on.*—

—*Whatever*— one of them says. I don't see who it is because I'm being led away with my hands behind my back in compliance with the rules of Jailbreak as it's played in Kayliegh's neighborhood. In my development, we go on the honor system. Nobody is escorted to the jail—the green electrical box in Phoebe Warner's front yard.

In Kayliegh's development the jail is better. It's the clubhouse attached to a swing set in Kyle Michlen's backyard. It's cooler because it
has an actual door. Since it's in the backyard, nobody can spy on it as
easily as the electrical box in Phoebe's front yard. They take a game of
Jailbreak way more seriously here. That's why I always come here to
play. Every Friday night, all summer long.

As I'm being marched off to prison, I wonder how many of my
teammates have been caught. I was caught pretty quickly, so I doubt
that many other inmates are waiting. We're playing with teams of twelve.
If there are even seven or eight of us free, I'm sure I'll be broken out soon
enough.

—*How many of us did you catch?*— I ask Mike, one of the two
boys I know who has been charged with taking me in. —*Are there a
lot of us out there still?*—

—*Not sure.*— He shrugs. —*I'm wondering that too. We were
after you the whole time. You're faster than you look.*—

—*I might be small, but I have superspeed*— I tease.

We're both still panting for air three houses away from where I
was nabbed. A drop of sweat runs down the side of my face and my
skin is clammy all over. It's one of those rare humid nights where the
steam gets stuck in the valley. Even though it's uncomfortable to run
around in, it's not so bad at night and I sort of like it because I can almost pretend we're playing on an island or something.

—*In you go*— Mike says. The clubhouse door swings open on
creaky hinges. It smells like mildew and cobwebs inside. —*You got
company*— he says, and I see Kayliegh's brother Eric is the only other
prisoner.

—*Hi*— I say, holding up a hand. —*Guess we stink, huh?*—

—*I nobly gave myself up*— Eric jokes. —*My sacrifice allowed four
others to get away.*—

—Mine didn't— I say, and we both laugh. *—Do you think we'll get freed?—*

—Eventually— Eric says, peering out the window for any movement in the shadows. It's against the rules to shout out from jail. But it's also against the rules for the other team to place a guard any nearer than the far edge of Kyle's backyard. *—Since we're the first ones, it might be a while before anyone makes a run at the jail. If you're going to risk a move like that, you want to make sure it's worth it.—*

—Yeah. That makes sense.— I sit down on the little bench. It's damp and dirty and I can feel it making a mark on the back of my shorts. I jump up quickly, bumping into Eric. I have to catch myself on him, grabbing his shirt. *—Sorry.—*

Eric's hands unexpectedly slide onto my narrow hips. There's a kind of weird moment where we stare at each other in the dim light coming from Kyle's back porch. There is this small flutter of romance in my heart that I don't really get because I've known Eric for four years and never thought of him as anything other than Kayliegh's dorky older brother. But something about the way his hands feel moving up my side causes me to tingle all over. There's something about being confined with him in the dark that erases the past.

My lips are quivering when he leans closer.

I close my eyes when he kisses me. I don't know why, but when his tongue touches my lips, I get the feeling like we're suddenly not in a moldy clubhouse but in a kind of glass submarine because there is the thrill of drowning inside of me. I see all of these bright colored jellyfish floating past like underwater stars. It's my first real kiss and I know now why grown-ups are saying how they remember it perfectly—because there's something magical about it.

—Jailbreak— a voice shouts, opening the door on us. The porch light shines in and I get nervous they saw us kiss, but our teammate is

already sprinting back off into the shrubs. The magic of the moment flees with him.

Eric and I emerge from the clubhouse. He doesn't specifically ask me to keep it a secret from Kayliegh but he doesn't have to. I'm not going to tell her. She thinks her brother is gross and says all he does is look at porn on his computer all day long. She'd think I was gross for kissing him. Anyway, I wasn't really kissing *him*—it was just the idea of kissing that I wanted.

We run in opposite directions.

I can still smell him on my palms. I can still taste him in my mouth. I wonder if that is something that will stay with me for long as I search out a better hiding space than my last one.

I'm pushed into the corner and Alec is leaning into me. We both ignore the cleaning products and mop handles that rattle each time we bump into them. We're not supposed to be in here—in the supply closet just off the cafeteria. But it's the only place private enough for us to be alone and do what we're doing.

My hand is up the back of his T-shirt, tracing the curve of his spine. His hand is under my sweatshirt and he can feel my heartbeat. It is a tiny bird in his palm, fluttering wildly.

We keep the light off so the nurses won't find us. A small rectangular window above our heads lets in the only light. It's enough to see his face and for him to see mine. Then our eyes meet and time stands still.

He leans his head in closer. The scent on his skin reminds me of sand and strawberry shampoo. For the first time, I really notice the small freckles under his eyes and they are beautiful. It's when I point to touch them that he kisses me deeply for the first time.

Alec isn't the first boy to kiss me.

Not counting the times in second grade when I got married every other day during recess, I've been kissed six times before. Some have been stolen kisses and some have just been clumsy. Some were okay, but none have been romantic. Only the first one was ever magical.

This is the first kiss that makes my mouth thirsty and my legs melt.

I breathe his breath and he breathes mine. There is an ocean around us and I don't let him come up for air. I hold him tight like a mermaid saving a drowning sailor to keep him for her own. I pull him closer whenever he twitches and tries to move even an inch away. Because I know if we keep sinking, we'll find a place more wonderful than Eden at the bottom.

He bites me gently before we get there and I stop.

I open my eyes and his are shining and I'm certain at that moment that he loves me. And when I smile, he wipes the corner of my mouth with his thumb.

—*They'll be looking for us soon*— he says.

—*I know.*— We were supposed to be in the cafeteria five minutes ago. Seven minutes is when they start a search here.

Alec bends his elbow and touches the door handle. —*Shall we?*— he asks, already starting to open the door. I grab his arm and squeeze down. He stops, leaving the door in place. —*What is it?*—

—*I just . . . I don't want to go in there*— I say. —*I don't think I like it here anymore.*—

—*Then let's leave*— he says as if it's the easiest thing in the world. He's grinning as he flicks his hair away from his face. I have to pinch my lips together and cross my arms so that he knows I'm being serious. —*I mean it*— he says in response. —*Let's take a field trip.*—

He pulls the door open in a gust, poking his head into the hall. He gestures for me to follow and then he's off. Gone. I push away from the wall, chasing after him.

Instead of turning into the cafeteria, Alec disappears through the door marked STAFF right beside the large double doors leading to the small sea of lunch tables. —*Come on! Hurry!*— he shouts. He's laughing and breathing as fast as he runs. I'm behind, following him through the maze of silver metal carts filled with dirty trays from lunch. The plates are piled in a delicate balancing act that requires us to sprint with gymnastic agility.

I barely hear myself laughing over the symphony of clattering silverware. The cafeteria staff moves dishes by the dozens as we cut through the kitchen. We race behind all of the workers in their pale green smocks and pale green shower caps and latex gloves that cover their hands. They look like a team of fallout rescuers in radiation suits— wrapped head to toe because even though the illnesses in this hospital aren't contagious, they still don't want to touch us.

We pass by them in a blur. Invisibly clean.

If any of them notice us, they don't let it show.

Alec keeps pushing faster ahead. I'm dizzy and laughing and staring at the reflection of the fluorescent lights bouncing off so many shiny surfaces. From one and back to the other, the beams go on forever like a world that could only exist inside a disco ball.

Something warm and electric is pulsing through my veins. It's joy. A kind of joy that has been far away for so long I thought it may have died and turned to dust.

—*Where are we going?*— I shout.

Alec hesitates a step so that I'm close enough to reach out and grab the end of his shirt. I ask him again where we're going and he answers —*Who cares?*—

Our breath turns to ice crystals as we pause in front of the open door to the freezer room where it is always winter. I can't see behind the frayed plastic curtain but I imagine the room is an ice cave that goes on and on, emptying out onto the shore of an icy world where our skin would remain as pale as ghosts.

The exit is just at the other end of the kitchen, near the storeroom. Alec takes off and bursts through the doors that open up into the heart of the sun. The blinding white light swallows him whole, but I'm not afraid to follow because somehow it feels as if we've done this before and I let the sunlight swallow me as well.

Outside in the fresh air, my arms are wings.

I spread them as I run through the parking lot.

—*This must be where they make all the deliveries*— Alec says as he huddles behind a large truck, leaning against a steel wire fence. He tucks his hands through the small diamond-shaped links and rattles it like a cage. —*See? This lot is fenced off from the rest of the hospital. Look over there. We can escape easily.*—

I see where the parking lot narrows into a short driveway before it opens onto a one-lane road. There's a guardhouse like at the main entrance but there's only one person in it instead of three. The gate is flung wide open on its hinges. Probably because it's just a simple gate that someone needs to push open and pull closed, while the main one is electronic and works at the push of a button.

The road vanishes out of sight behind tall pines.

—*Where would we go?*— I ask.

—*Into town to get some real food for starters*— he says. —*You still want to, right? We can always just come back.*—

—*Yes. I want to*— I tell him.

We both spin around when the door opens behind us. It's the same door we left from, but we're far enough away to duck behind a stack of crates piled to the side of the delivery truck. Peeking through the spaces between them, I see one of the nurses in her blue scrubs. It's the nurse from the cafeteria. She looks around like someone searching the sky for shooting stars.

—*I think we're officially missing now*— Alec says, biting his lip to keep from laughing.

The nurse glances briefly in our direction and I cover Alec's mouth with my hand. The shadows dance on my skin and I see the outline of a cat whispering for us both to be quiet because the nervous excitement is making our hearts thump louder under our rib cages.

—*She's going*— I whisper.

The door closes. The nurse's blue scrubs disappear like water down the drain. For the moment anyway, we are free.

—*Follow me.*— Alec dips and hides between cars parked so close together we barely fit through the spaces. Suddenly we are mice scurrying away from the lab—white mice in the blinding glare of a sun that looks slightly golden whenever I glance up at the sky.

As we crouch below the window of the guardhouse, I'm terrified someone is going to step outside of the building and find us. I'm not so worried about the guard. We can hear the radio playing one of the same dozen or so songs that always seem to be playing on the radio. He's not paying attention to it though because he's reading. His head is facing his lap where a book is open. In a split second of silence between notes in the song, I hear the book's pages flap in the breeze.

Alec doesn't speak.

A twitch of his head tells me it's time to go.

It's a short burst from the gate to the enormous tree trunks across the road. Maybe a hundred yards from where we are. If it's more, it's not by much. I can make it. I used to run that distance twenty times a day in tennis practice.

As I take my first step from the parking lot to the asphalt painted with white lines on either side, I make sure to listen for the noise. I know it lives in the skies outside the hospital walls. I know it's there somewhere. The static never goes extinct—it only hides.

Alec races out in front. I wait half a step longer to see if I'm torn apart by a shrieking in the sky. When nothing happens, I smile and begin to sprint away—running toward Alec with my arms held up by the rushing air created from my speed. Neither of us stops until we're hidden by the trees.

—*He didn't see us*— Alec says, poking his head around the trunk of a towering pine. —*He's still reading. I don't think he saw us.*— His voice grows in volume and pitch with each syllable. The excitement pours out of him and into me when his arms circle around my waist and we kiss—this time for slightly longer than before. Then Alec slips his arm free until only one is left resting on the small of my back.

Once we start to walk, we are careful to duck from tree to tree. At least for a little while until we're out of sight of every window. Then we cut off into the woods away from the road, where we can talk like normal people.

—*You're pretty good at that*— he says. —*You had a lot of practice making out with boys in supply closets?*—

—*Not really*— I tease. —*Actually the last boy I kissed was before summer even started.*—

Alec raises his eyebrows. —*Boyfriend?*—

I shake my head.

—*Spin the Bottle?*— he guesses.

—*Sort of*— I say. —*Truth or Dare. I guess that's the same thing.*—

Alec groans, slapping his forehead. —*Those are always the worst. Somehow I always get paired up with the most awkward person. Does that happen to you too?*—

—It did that time— I tell him.

Kayliegh and I were over Thomas's house after school in the spring. His parents didn't get home until late so we could do whatever we wanted—us, Thomas, and his friend Scott, who was a year older and kind of ugly with zits all over his face. I didn't want to be there but Kayliegh wanted to make out with Thomas and begged me to come along. It was her idea to play Truth or Dare. She said it would be fun as long as we made every question and dare something *hot*. Then she laughed the fake laugh she saved for when boys were around—the one where she touched her teeth with her tongue. She copied it from an old Marilyn Monroe movie, but she does it so naturally anymore that I wonder if she even remembers that it's practiced.

Kayliegh let me know beforehand that she wanted all of my dares to involve her and Thomas. I never said I wanted mine to be with Scott but that's what she did anyway. I would have just picked truth every time and she knew it. She made sure I picked dares by asking truth questions she knew nobody would answer—questions like what I thought about while masturbating. She wanted all of us to pick dare so we would dare her back. She was drinking from four different colored bottles in the liquor cabinet and just wanted the game to be an excuse for fooling around. *—Sabrina, I dare you to climb on Scott's lap and French him—* she dared me the first chance she got. I thought he was gross, but I did it.

—It was the worst kiss I've ever had— I tell Alec as I slip out of my sneakers to feel the grass tickle between my toes.

—What was the problem? A drooler? A vacuum kisser? What?— Alec asks, holding my hand and letting our arms swing in rhythm.

—It wasn't so much the kiss. The kiss was kind of nothing . . . just like blah. But of course, he bragged about it at school the next day. I'm not sure why, he had nothing to brag about. All he did was stick his

tongue in there until I thought I was going to gag.— I stop walking and look up at Alec. I'm not sure why. I guess I just want to remind myself how much better he is than any other boy I've met. *—It wasn't at all like it was with you.—*

Alec's cheeks turn pink. *—Yeah? How was I?—*

The second time we kissed, I had my eyes closed while it happened but I opened them just before we stopped and I saw the sky change colors. The outline of his hair was sprinkled with shining sparks. *—You were . . . kind of perfect—* I say.

—Kind of?— Alec throws his hands out to his sides, pretending to be offended. *—Can I try again? I'd hate for my reputation to be spoiled by a "kind of."—*

The first houses and stores from town are in sight as we stop on the last hill looking down. Alec holds me and I hold him. Our bodies press together until we are Siamese twins. The warmth from his body against mine makes the tiny pebbles in my pocket glow brighter than bright so that I don't have to see it to know it's happening.

—I like you— Alec says. *—A lot. I think you're so incredible, but I'm sure you already knew that. I wanted to tell you anyway.—* When I don't say anything, Alec looks nervous. *—You got quiet. I hope you're just speechless because you like me too and this is just one of those perfect kind of movie moments. Because it's either that or you're thinking "oh my god, how do I get away from this lunatic?" and that would just be plain wrong.—*

I watch the color in his eyes dance as he talks.

There's a halo around him that tells me he knows the answer, but still I'm not saying anything and I know he's getting more nervous. But then I answer him by touching his bottom lip to my upper one and kiss him until my cheeks turn a darker shade of pink and I feel the rest of the universe is revolving around us and only us.

The town is split down the center—half on one side of the street and half on the other. The perfect symmetry of cars and shops is amazing. The shape and size of the buildings remind me of towns I used to build from Legos, only not as colorful.

There aren't many people around. But the ones who are there, shuffling into and out of stores, all glance at me and Alec; just long enough to make me feel as if we don't belong. I squeeze Alec's hand a little tighter under their glare. I tuck my shoulder under his and walk in step with his pace.

In the hospital, people are one way or the other. We are either slightly dazed patients or sterile nurses and doctors with mannequin skin. There is nothing in between. Here is different. We stand out here. *—They keep looking at us—* I say.

Alec swivels from side to side, absorbing all of the strangers' dirty looks. *—Yeah. Screw 'em—* he says, and his words become a spell that protects me.

I notice everything as if being in the world is a new experience. Every little detail seems meaningful and I try to keep track of them. A discarded coffee cup fumbles around in the breeze. The plastic lid, still half on, rattles over the cement. A stirring straw sticks out. It makes a sound like the clicking of insect antennae. I try to memorize it exactly— even how the shadows fall on the stenciled logo as the cup rolls slowly back and forth.

Dr. Richards tells me my obsession with details is an unhealthy symptom of a wider problem. She doesn't understand that clues can be hidden in even the smallest places. It's the same as stones giving off a dim halo—I have to search every last inch to find flaws in the scenery. They'll lead me to the place I know is heaven if I follow them.

I have to pay attention because I don't want to miss our chance when it comes.

I catalog the cars parked along the road. They are parked in a pattern of colors. Red, silver, blue, black, red, white, and silver—ranging in size and shape but lined up neatly like a child's toys practicing a traffic jam. The parking meters tick away silently and digitally. The time left varies for each car. Seven minutes. Eleven. Three. One hundred and six.

The buildings are uneven. Slanted roofs touch up against shorter flat ones. Other buildings are set apart with driveways or skinny alleys between them. All of the ones with stores are wrong. It's obvious the buildings were meant to be homes. The shops are intruding into living rooms and kitchens.

I try to keep track of the people I see. I watch who goes in which door or which car, but it's hard. Things here happen without planning. There's no routine. Outside the Wellness Center, not everyone moves on the same schedule. It makes me nervous to view the chaos that comes with people acting independently. Coming face-to-face with the world, I feel anxious—like being shut in a dark closet with a hidden ghoul breathing on my neck. But Alec is a light in the dark. Being scared doesn't scare me in the same way when I'm with him.

I grip his arm and he holds me.

—*Looks like there's a place up there*— he says over the humming of car engines. He points to a pale blue building on the other side of the street. Above the wraparound porch is a sign that reads THE QUIET MAN in large loud letters and SANDWICHES, SOUP, & SNACKS in smaller ones. With the sun at his back, Alec looks skinny and frail. But frail like flames that dart away from a fire because there's something fierce about him too—something warm when pressed close to me, but it will burn others if they get too near. —*Want to check it out? I'm starving.*—

—*Okay*— I say even though I'm not hungry at all.

We lock elbows, cross the street, and walk into the store. The chime of jingle bells on the door greets us. —*I hope they have burgers*— Alec whispers. His mouth hangs open and he pretends to drool.—*Big, greasy, disgusting burgers that soak through the bun and drip cheese all over my hands.*—

There's a familiar smell of cinnamon and firewood inside. It is the same kind of quaint general store found in all of the out-of-the-way towns my parents like to stop in whenever we'd load up the car for a road trip. These stores are all the same everyplace in America and I'm always afraid of moving too fast in them. I worry that any quick move will send up a cloud of dust the size of a sandstorm in the desert.

I walk slow and quiet between the heavy wooden shelves. Shifting my feet in a delicate ballet through the aisles, I pass rows of jam and syrup and cookies from brands that don't exist in the electric wonderland of supermarkets placed every two or three miles in my town. I whisper the brand names in my head and commit them to memory as we make our way to the back of the store where there's a deli case and a chalkboard menu.

—*It doesn't look like a burger joint*— Alec mumbles, reading the sandwich descriptions scribbled out in pink chalk.

We're the only ones in the store besides the lady at the cash register by the door and the man in the apron behind the sandwich counter. They're both old. The woman's hair is mostly gray but there are a few black strands here and there. Her skin is gray too, the way old people's skin always seems to turn gray. Or maybe it just looks gray because of the shadows. Or maybe her lipstick absorbs all of the light. It's such a bright crayon red, painted on larger than her lips really are. I've often wondered why old women do that. Why they try to cover where their lips have gone thin. It's the same as bald men wearing hairpieces—it exaggerates what they are trying to hide.

The man at the deli counter must be the woman's husband because they look alike. That's another thing about old people. Once they've been married long enough, they grow to look the same. They also learn to communicate without words. When the woman clears her throat, the man stops what he's doing and turns. As Alec and I approach the back, the couple follows us with their eyes. One from the front and one from the back as if we only exist in their line of sight and if either of them blinks, we'll vanish.

A shiver runs through me and I pull Alec closer.

I used to have a recurring nightmare when I was little. I would be lost somewhere, either in the mall or an airport or some other place like that and this couple would find me. Always the same couple no matter where I'd been. They always promised to bring me home to my parents, but they never did. Their real plan was to eat me and I fell for it each time. I trusted them. And every time, the dream would end with their hands turning into claws—their mouths growing sharper teeth to tear me apart.

The old couple in the store, with their dry expressions, gray skin, and gray eyes—they remind me of the couple from my dream. I can almost see their faces waiting to change. Dr. Richards would say I was projecting. She would tell me that my fear of the world is finding a way of expressing itself in an old nightmare tucked away in the attic of my mind. *Irrational* is a word she might use to describe it. But her words don't make it any less real. She doesn't understand that my dreams are like instincts. Right now, they are telling me this place isn't good.

I squeeze Alec's hand, slightly pulling him away. *—We should go.—*

—Without eating?— Alec asks with eyebrows arched to the ceiling and his stomach rumbling and growling.

The old couple's eyes remain locked on us. Intense and serious and humming with static so strong that I know it's there even if I can't see it.

My stomach does somersaults inside me. —*It's just . . . this place gives me the creeps.*— Alec turns his head and snuggles his face against my neck where his breath is warm on my skin. I let out a long, slow breath and let my heart fall into the same steady rhythm as his.

—*Let's see what they have first*— he says. —*Okay?*—

I bite my lip and nod, never taking my eyes off the old man who now has both hands on the counter. They are in the shape of fists and are as square as cinder blocks.

Alec has a way of tilting his body as he stands that makes people uncomfortable. I've seen him do it with the nurses and they react by stepping away and sounding suddenly irritated when they speak. He does the same thing here in the store and I see the man's cheeks flush with a color halfway between annoyance and hatred. —*What can I get you?*— he asks in a voice too big for the narrow space between the deli counter and the wall behind him.

—*Ladies first*— Alec says. —*What do you want?*—

I feel confused and dizzy inside and simply shrug. I try to read the words on the chalkboard but the letters don't seem to make sense. I mean, I can read words like *ham* and *turkey* and *pesto* but I can't put them together into thoughts because all I can focus on is the old man's eyes which spin in slow-motion like gasoline rainbows rising off the blacktop in summertime—his knuckles *tap-tapping* faster than seconds ticking off a clock.

Alec stares at him. —*Easy, man! She's thinking*— he snaps. —*Can't we even get a minute to decide?*—

The sound that comes from the man's throat is the sound of a rhinoceros—the sound of horned rage deciding whether or not to charge. —*Take as long as you need . . . just as long as you kids really are planning to order something. Otherwise you're just wasting my time.*—

Alec makes a show of looking around. —*I'm sorry. I didn't notice*

*the huge crowd! We must be keeping you from all these other cus-
tomers.—*

—*Look here . . .* — the man growls threateningly.

Alec is about to start in on him again but I pull at his sleeve so that his ear is pressed against my mouth. —*I don't want anything*— I whisper. —*I just want to go.*—

—*Yeah, okay.*— Alec nods in agreement, taking a step away. —*I don't think I want anything either. Not anymore.*—

The old man's face swells with blood. His cheeks puff with angry breaths of steam. I'm waiting for his mouth to explode with razor teeth and his fingers to become knives.

My hand darts toward my mouth and I begin sucking on my sleeve. The old man's eyes grow steady. He stares at the piece of plastic wrapped around my wrist. It catches in the dim light at just the right angle to attract his attention. —*You kids from the hospital up the road?*—

Now Alec is the one who wants to leave.

He leads me back through the aisle as the man hollers for us to stay.

—*Linda? Call them up at the hospital. Tell them we got two of their kids down here in town. They're probably searching for them*— he shouts over our heads to the lady in the front who already has the phone pressed to her ear.

On the way out, I take a last glance over my shoulder. The man is still hollering something to his wife but as soon as the sun touches my skin, his words sound like nothing more than noise.

TEN

Alec and I run from the store. I sprint across the porch, leaping over the three creaky steps. The soles of my sneakers clap loudly on the sidewalk. My arms swing wildly. The sleeve of my sweatshirt slips off my shoulder, the hood falls halfway down my back, and the teeth from the zipper scratch my neck, but I still push faster. I don't ever want to stop. I want to keep running all the way to heaven.

—*Sabrina, that way!*— Alec is waving for me to cut through the space between two buildings. The bottoms of my shoes are worn flat and my feet skid when I change directions. My right leg twists and I slip, scraping my knee and hands when I brace myself. A rash of blood dirties my skin, but I keep running. Alec grabs me—his arm hooks my waist even though my legs keep moving. —*You okay? That was a nasty spill.*—

—*I'm fine. Let's just keep going*— I say, panting breathlessly.

—*We're cool for now*— he says. —*We don't have to kill ourselves running a marathon.*— He is bent over with his hands on his thighs trying to catch his breath. He wants to slow down. I don't, but I trust him. I'll go at his pace.

—*Okay, no running*— I tell him. —*But can we just . . . keep going?*—

—Sure. Where?—

—Away from here . . . from those people.—

The old couple, they were static people. They are the first I've seen since going to the hospital. The first to show it outwardly anyway, because I still have my suspicions about Dr. Richards and some of the nurses and the girl who wanted me to stay away from Alec. Out here they don't hide. Out here they are stronger and will attack like vampires.

I'm remembering how dangerous it is outside the walls of the hospital and I'm frightened. My hands are shaking. Sweat runs down my face, but I'm shivering. Alec puts his arm around me. His hand rests on my collarbone where my heart flutters rapidly.

—Hey, relax— he says in a soothing voice. *—You'll give yourself a heart attack. It's fine. We're not going to get in trouble. Even if they find us, we didn't really do anything. We'll just go back with them and that's it.—*

I'm not sure I want to go back, but I'm not sure I want to be here either. I want to be someplace else—someplace where there is only us. If we keep walking, we'll find it. The sky is already starting to change. The blue is drying up and disappearing.

—Whoa! You see that?— Alec leaves my side and takes off in the direction of a parking lot behind a drugstore. His eyes are as large as moons and he is practically skipping, taking little leaps as he surges ahead. *—A shopping cart! Not fenced in and free to go?—* His hands grasp onto the handle of the rusty cart and he immediately spins it around in a squeaky circle. *—This really is our day. Come on. Hop in. I'll push you first.—*

He smiles at me like in a dream. The sun bleaches away his hair—bleaches away his clothes—and I see him like I did on the tire swing in my backyard. He invites me to get into the cart with the same playful voice as he invited me to join him on the swing. Only it's happening for real—in the present instead of the future. And I feel like the end of the world must be getting closer. It's all coming true just the way I imagined.

I'm chewing on my sleeve but still Alec can see I'm smiling.

—*Come on . . . you're not chicken, are you?*— he teases, spinning the cart in rapid circles that leave rainbow trails in their wake. It has one broken wheel that keeps it going round and round like some strange piece of playground equipment.

I climb inside with Alec's help. The back of my sweatshirt rides up my spine as I fix myself into the wire cage. The skinny metal bars feel good against my skin. I clutch my fingers through the tiny spaces and hold on as Alec pushes—slow at first but picking up speed as the ground slopes.

I watch the trees race by, trying to predict which of them will fall first when this world is wiped away. Alec is grunting and laughing, pushing as fast as he can. The parking lot reaches a dead end out in front of us. Beyond that is a field of grass tall enough to tickle the back of my knees and I'm speeding toward it. Eventually the cart is speeding too fast for Alec to keep up and his hands slip from the red bar and I hear him tumble to the blacktop.

The wind rushes against my face, reminding me of the first drop on a roller coaster. My father and I have ridden every one in Southern California. We always wait extra long in line to be in the front. My mom thought we were crazy to ride them at all, let alone the first car. I loved the feeling of being safely out of control. But I always kept my eyes closed. My dad kept his open, teasing that I missed half the fun. He didn't realize all he missed though.

I close my eyes as the cart rolls swiftly downhill, wobbling and unsteady. The sky catches on fire. It burns hot and white. The metal wheels strike a crack in the pavement and there is a moment where I am flying, screaming happily. I open my eyes and see the clouds crashing toward me. It feels as though I will climb higher forever . . . until I start to fall.

I land with a thud on the soft ground. The dry grass sways above my head like the million arms of golden jellyfish. The ink on my hand is still drawn in the shape of a cat. —*Want to do that again?*— I ask Fred and he responds with a permanent smile.

Alec charges through the field. I see his shoes before anything else. I hear his breath rushing out of him quick and concerned before he speaks. —*Jesus! Are you alright? I'm sorry . . . it slipped out of my hands.*— He bends down, sees me laughing, and is relieved I'm alive.

—*That was close*— I say. —*We should try again. We almost made it that time.*—

—*We almost got you killed is what we did*— he says, collapsing in a heap beside me. The shopping cart rests on its side—one wheel still spinning in the air. Alec puts his arm across my chest and buries his face in my neck. His breath is a hot wind coming in gusts.

I have a clear view of the sky. There are no trees or buildings or power lines in my sight. One color fades as another glows brighter. They take turns like blinking Christmas lights. I can see shapes scribbled over the surface like the messy crayon figures children draw. I've missed them. When they're absent, it is too easy to forget the comfort they bring me.

—*Isn't this perfect?*— Alec says.

—*Perfect*— I say.

His fingers crawl through my hair and mine press into his arm. —*Being in this field, this is freedom. I get so sick of being scrutinized, you know? It's like you can't get away from it*— Alec says. —*At my school, there are cameras in every hall. They're inside those black*

114

spheres. *You know, like the kind they use in malls to catch shoplifters. Then they also have hall monitors and armed guards at the door. It's all the same as prison. So is the hospital. Sometimes I wonder if you can ever get away.—*

    —It gets to me— I say.

    —Yet, we're the crazy ones.— Alec shakes his head at the thought.
—Sometimes I just want to get away from it all.—

    —I want to all of the time— I tell him.

    —Yeah . . . I guess I do too.—

Alec begins kissing the skin behind my ears. His hand moves under my shirt like water. He doesn't hear the screaming in the air. He misses the flashes of the storm coloring the sky blue and red. It grows louder and thicker like a weapon and I cover my ears.

    Alec looks up. He can see them. *—It's okay—* he says. *—Just act normal.—*

A wave of panic comes over me as I stare at the police car parked at the edge of the field. Its sirens are flashing, taking pictures from the sky. I'm only able to stay calm because Alec is next to me, squeezing my hand. Nothing bad can happen to us when we are together.

    The town stretches out in front of us. It sits against the horizon like the backdrop on a stage. It is thin and almost see-through but becoming more solid every second we stand here.

    —Are we going back to the hospital?— I ask Alec.

    He shrugs. *—Do you want to?—*

    I see a stone by my feet. It glows brighter than any I've seen since leaving home. I bend down and pick it up. The world seems so different than I remember and it scares me. *—I'm not sure . . . maybe we should.—*

115

The flashing police lights create halos above Alec. —*Something tells me we're not going to have a choice*— he says.

The headlights are watching us. Even in the afternoon sunlight, they are on full blast—taking image after image to steal us bit by bit. It's how they do it. If we won't go along, they'll just absorb us one picture at a time until we become ghosts inside their machines.

The driver's-side door opens and a police officer steps out. He is dressed all in brown so that he fades into the dusty air spiraling up from the ground behind him. The sun shines directly down on his pink forehead. His black boots melt into the asphalt and he becomes an approaching storm. When he waves his hand to get our attention, the sky changes color. It's not like when I do it though. There are no rainbow trails lingering in the air. No, when he waves his hand, the sky turns dark with violent clouds.

—*You kids hold up there a second*— he hollers. —*I want to talk to you.*—

My heart is a bird at the edge of a cliff wanting to leap—full of thoughts of flight. I have wings in my feet, ready to carry me into the sky, but Alec continues to hold me. His fingers slide under my sweatshirt, petting the small of my back.

—*Why? What did we do?*— Alec calls out. He is ready to defend me.

The police officer never takes his eyes off of us. He reaches for the small radio clipped to his shoulder. He mumbles something I can't hear and is answered with a burst of static that startles me. —*I'm going to need you two to come with me*— he says to us. With a flick of his head, he motions toward the car.

The muscles in Alec's body grow tense beneath my fingers. I can feel his bones—smooth like the rocks I collect.

The policeman's footsteps are crashes of thunder, rising up from

116

the ground instead of raining down from above. His face is twisted into the kind of strained grimace sewn into puppets—resembling something between friendly and suffering from a stomachache. His body is swollen like a worm too full with blood. His uniform tugs at every angle. He is expanding. There is enough static inside of him to fill me and Alec both if we aren't careful.

He holds his hand up like a crossing guard. His hand shakes like the smallest earthquake ever noticed. —*Take it easy*— he says to us, shuffling forward with the clumsy steps of a diseased werewolf—terrifying and unpredictable while Alec and I stand entwined like pale angels.

A burst of sunlight shatters the sky and for a split second, I see through everything. I can see through the veil that covers the truth of the world. I see the horror that eats away at the beauty of the grass and trees and strips the color from rainbows until there is a sickness in everything that surrounds us.

I turn and hide my face in Alec's shoulder. —*Make him stop*— I say. —*He's not real . . . he's only pretending. Please make him stop.*—

Alec pets me softly. —*It's okay. I'll take care of it*— he says. Then he raises his voice, shouting out over my head. —*We don't have to go anywhere with you. I know my rights.*—

—*Son, I think you know perfectly well what's going on here*— the man in the uniform says with the same authority as a teacher telling someone in class to keep quiet. —*Let's just get you kids back to the hospital. If there's a problem there, we can work that out. Okay?*—

—*Like you'd even care?*— Alec yells. —*Besides, aren't there any crimes or anything you should be taking care of? Any old ladies need help crossing a street or anything like that? You think because we're kids you can just bother us?*—

I press my mouth to Alec's ear and whisper —*I want to go. I want*

to go back now. It's not safe here. I want to go back. Not forever. Just
for now.—

Alec turns to face me. He puts his hand under my chin and makes
me look him in the eyes. —*Sure. Whatever you want*— he promises,
kissing me on the forehead. His arms relax and my grip loosens. I bite
down on my sleeve and keep close to him. My heart is a rabbit in my
chest, kicking and thumping as we take a step forward.

I count my breaths and the storm starts to retreat.

Everything will be okay once we're back—we'll be hidden again.

—*Why don't the two of you take a seat in the back of the car*—
the officer says with his hand on the top of the door, ready to seal
us inside. He clicks the button on his clip-on radio a second time, feed-
ing the sky with more noise that seems both in front and in back of
me. —*They're sending somebody down to pick you up. It'll only be a
minute or so.*—

I shiver with the sudden spark of a fever when the cop touches
the top of my head, helping me to climb into the car. His fingerprints
tingle with static and I'm glad to be set free so quickly. Glad to be in the
squad car, separated from the world.

—*What? No handcuffs?*— Alec says, getting in beside me.

The cop exhales deeply and closes us up inside.

—*Don't say anything to anyone when we get back, okay? They'll
just twist everything you tell them into something else*— Alec says as I
stare at the sky through the window like a fish looking out of an
aquarium.

There is a smell in the plastic seats like the bleach smell at the hospital. A smell that has comforted me during the weeks I've stayed there.
My thoughts grow clearer as I inhale. —*What do you think they're
going to do to us when we get back?*— I ask.

—*Probably keep us from seeing each other*— he says, tapping his forehead again and again against the window. He hits the door lightly with his fists too. There is an explosion inside of him and I have to keep reminding myself that he's doing it for me. —*They're not going to let us be together. For a little while anyway.*—

His words frighten me worse than anything.

—*They can't though!*— My eyes are wider than oceans as I think about us being apart. Without Alec, this me, the special me who he loves, will fade into nothing. —*We can't let them!*—

—*Hey . . . don't worry*— Alec says, holding my hand tighter. His touch tingles. His eyes radiate a soft glow. —*It'll be a day, maybe two at most. They'll never stop me from seeing you longer than that, I promise.*—

—*Will you still visit me . . . in my dreams, I mean?*— I ask.

—*You couldn't keep me out if you tried.*—

I see the lights of the hospital's security car approaching. Their flare on the car window reminds me of the crystal figurines in our cabinet at home—fairy figurines that my mom collects. And when I close my eyes and let Alec's mouth become one with mine, I can almost feel my own wings—sparkling and invisible to anyone without the right kind of eyes.

ELEVEN

—How long do I have to be in here?— I ask the security guard. I want to go back to my room so badly that my voice comes out high-pitched and fast. The guard mistakes my nervousness for anger at first. Then he sees my hands wound tightly together and knows that I'm only afraid.

His face turns kind after that. Even though his skin is dark like the center of my eyes, there is a glow to him. *—I don't think it will be long—* he explains, reaching for the door handle on his way out of the room. *—A doctor should be by . . . soon, I guess.—*

I'm alone then, sitting in a tiny room at a tiny table.

A mirror takes up most of the wall facing me. There's a reflection in the silver glass, but it's not me. It's nearly a perfect clone but something about the eyes is darker and different as they stare back at me. Her eyes don't glow like mine. They are blue like the sky, but mine shine like electricity underwater.

It's hard to breathe for a second and I have the impression that this other me has stolen the air from my lungs as she watches from the other side of the mirror in disguise.

The imposter me is small and only takes up a fraction of the space in the mirror. I keep watching—waiting for her to make a mistake and make a move that I don't. Even if she only blinks, I will have proof.

I've seen this girl pretending to be me before. I've seen her in the bathroom mirrors at my school. Only glimpses though. I've seen her longer inside the computer. I remember her from there. It's where she was born. That's where she lives, but she wants out—wants to switch places with me for good.

She is one of the secret people. There's a secret person for every one of us.

My chest tightens when I see her here and so stable. What if she has already done it—has gotten out? It's possible. Everything is brighter in the reflection. It's cramped in the room. The gray walls connect to form a metal box—a silver piece of glass like a computer screen in front of me. But which of us is on the outside and which one is looking in?

———————

—*Okay, I'm almost done*— Kayliegh says. She thinks I'm mad at her for spending more time with Thomas than me this summer. She's been spending the whole week before school starts up again trying to make it up to me. She says it's bad luck to start sophomore year separated from your best friend. I've told her at least a hundred times that I'm not upset, but I guess I haven't been too convincing. This is Kayliegh's newest attempt to make up before then. My birthday is coming up soon and she's giving me my present early—setting up a profile for me online without my parents knowing. —*You're going to love this*— she says, clapping her hands in anticipation as she laughs.

There is gravity in Kayliegh's laugh that pulls everyone around her into orbit. Her gravity is strongest with me—I am the planet revolving closest to her star. —*Okay, okay. Show me already.*—

We are sitting on my bed with the door closed and locked so my mom won't walk in. She'd freak if she knew what we were doing. My parents don't think these kinds of web sites are safe. They don't let me use them, which is actually fine with me. Sure, I used to bug them about it back when my friends were first getting their profiles. But lately, it all seems like more noise—just another way for the static to watch me.

—*Ta-da!*— Kayliegh says, spinning her laptop around so that it faces me. —*Welcome out of the stone age.*—

A picture of me stares back from the upper left hand corner of the screen. In the photo, my lips are pushed up in a fake kind of kiss like a picture in a celebrity magazine. It was taken up in Kayliegh's room last spring. I'm wearing one of her really old tank tops that's much too small for me. It says SWEET on the front because it's meant for little girls but we thought it was funny because it means something different at our age. In the picture I'm leaning forward and it makes my breasts look bigger. She snapped it when we were playing around—just a second of acting silly that was never meant for sharing. It's the kind of picture my dad would never want to see of me. Really, though, it's nothing like me at all. But inside the computer everyone will think that is what I'm like. They will all believe I'm posing only at them.

—*You like it?*— Kayliegh asks. There's a glow around her, so bright she's practically bursting. I rub my hand over my mouth and shrug one shoulder. She can read my mind. —*Level with me . . . what's wrong with it?*—

—*Nothing, I guess*— I mumble. —*It's just . . . why did you use that picture?*—

—*Because it's fun . . . and you look hot*— Kayliegh says. It was her idea to take the pictures. I took the same kind of her and she kept laughing and asking me if I thought Thomas would like them. I told her that of course he would because Thomas is all hormones. I would never tell her to her face, but he kind of gets on my nerves. He is always saying lewd things to me on the walk home. I really don't know why she likes him so much. —*Trust me, you look great in the picture so just lighten up. Anyway, it's just a picture, it's no big deal. Your parents got you all messed up about this stuff. That's why I set up a profile for you, so you could see. Besides, you don't want to become a social outcast.—*

—But won't a lot of people see this?—

Kayliegh falls back on my bed laughing. *—That's the entire point, Sabrina!—* Something about her tone is like a parent scolding a child and when I don't smile, she frowns. *—Look. You already have five friend requests. This is going to be great.—*

When she smiles, the lavender walls in my room turn to gold. Sparks fly up around her. I want to feel them on my skin. Part of me wants to reach across the bed and trace her smile with my fingers but I know better than to act on every whim the way I used to when we were younger.

I want to describe it all to her—to draw her a picture, the way I'm so used to doing. But then I remember she doesn't want me doing that any longer. Not after the last time, just before spring break when I drew her with flower petals for hair and me beside her, smiling at the scent. *—It's cute—* she said when I showed her, but the smile she wore as I was drawing it faded as soon as she peeked. *—It seems kind of . . . weird though. Other people might get the wrong idea—* and I haven't drawn a picture for Kayliegh since. Without them, sometimes I have no way of telling her how I feel.

At that moment, I feel like I want nothing more than to delete myself from her computer entirely. But it's impossible for me to argue with Kayliegh when she's this excited. At times like this, she is a whirlwind in the center of a thunderstorm. There are only two choices—go along with her or get left in the ruins.

I'm not ready to be left behind. Besides, maybe she's right. It might not be such a big deal.

I take a closer look at the screen. I scroll through the page and it reads like an advertisement—my photo next to a list with my age and sex and interests so people can choose me or not. Like everyone else in my grade, it says I'm older than I am going to be. —*Oh don't worry about that*— Kayliegh tells me. —*You have to be sixteen to join the site, so everybody just says they are, even if they aren't.*—

There are five faces asking me to approve them. They are all boys from places around the country that I've never been to. —*Why do these guys want to be my friend? They don't know anything about me.*—

—*They probably think you're cute and want to flirt or whatever*— Kayliegh says. —*That's what people do. It's just for fun, it doesn't have to mean anything.*—

—*So what do I do?*—

Kayliegh shrugs, putting her hands up in the air. —*You pick.*—

I wonder how she knows if these people are even real.

They don't feel real to me.

I try my best to act like I'm enjoying it. I type a few messages and send a few requests to kids at school. I don't know why, but something about it feels wrong—feels like the computer is trying to read my mind. I start to wonder if the more information I feed into it, the more real the fake me becomes. If I keep giving away pieces of me, it will take my place. It disturbs me to even think about it.

—*Are you hungry? Want to go downstairs and get something to snack on?*— I ask. I think Kayliegh suspects I'm only making an excuse so we can turn off the computer. But she says okay anyway and I close the screen. I won't look at that page again for another two months when my vice principal has it open on his computer at school.

———————

The image in the mirror is smiling. I keep looking at the door hoping somebody will come rescue me, but they don't. There is no sound of sneakers through the hall, no trays of medicine being wheeled, and in their silence there is only the noise that is never supposed to be inside the walls of the Wellness Center.

The girl in the mirror enjoys it.

She is smiling and her eyes are evil.

—*You're her, aren't you? The secret person*— I whisper, and she mimics me. —*You're what will replace me once they are done.*—

She answers without moving her lips. Her reply echoes through the walls—buried inside the noise like thunder in a hurricane. —*I already have*—is what she tells me.

—*No*— I mumble.

It can't be true.

I can't be stuck here—not when Alec and I were so close.

Alec.

I want to see him.

I want to see him right away, so I jump out of my chair and grab the door. It's locked. I jiggle the handle and pound on it with my fist. The girl is laughing at me. I can feel her laughter in my bones and I scream.

—*I want out! Let me out!*—

My hand hurts, but I bang harder. My throat is raw, but I yell louder.

When the door opens from the other side, I rush out into the hall-way, gasping for air like someone half-drowned being pulled out of the water. The nurse catches me before I get too far. I try to escape and another one tackles me.

There is a tiny prick on my arm like a bee sting—then everything dissolves.

—Hello, Sabrina. How are you feeling?— Dr. Richards asks as she enters my room.

There is a sick feeling in my stomach as I notice that it is nighttime.

—Was I asleep?— I ask.

—We gave you something to calm you down— Dr. Richards says. *—You were sleeping for a few hours.—*

My hand wraps around the stone in my pocket. It's the stone from outside of the hospital—the one I took as the police car was watching. I know its shape by the way it cradles in my palm. It's more powerful than the ones I find here and the heat from my body causes it to sputter and spark. I check to make sure the light doesn't shine through my sweatshirt and am relieved to see that it doesn't. My hand must be absorbing all of the colors it sends out.

—You realize that you gave us all a bit of a scare?— Dr. Richards tells me.

I nod shyly. *—I guess. I never really thought about it.—*

Dr. Richards drags the chair from under the desk in front of the window and pulls it next to my bed. The sound of the chair's legs scraping across the floor is horrifyingly loud and I flinch. *—What was it that upset you in the waiting room? Can you remember?—*

—Mmmm, hmmmm.— I remember.

—Will you tell me?—

I look around the room and see my stuff scattered around. The pink bag with the koala keychain sits in the corner. The books on the desk are the ones I brought with me. The photos taped to the wall are ones my mom sent and the drawings are ones I've made. *—It was nothing . . . just that room I was in. I was getting claustrophobic, that's all.—*

—The nurses said you were talking to someone in there. Who

were you talking to?— she asks me. I just shake my head because I don't want to say. When she asks a second time, I answer by touching my tongue to the sleeve of my sweatshirt. —*Okay, we won't talk about that then*— she says, encouraging me to bring my hand back into my lap. —*Instead, can you tell me what made you want to leave?*—

—*I don't know*— I say.

—*Then why did you?*—

—*It wasn't really like leaving*— I say. —*Or it wasn't about leaving, I mean. It was more about . . . like wanting to fly or something. Flying just to fly, you know?*—

I watch as Dr. Richards scratches down every word I've said, turning the sound of my voice into blue ink in her notebook. —*You went to the town. How did it feel being out there after spending the last several weeks here?*—

I think about Alec walking with his arm around my waist and how the sky changed colors with each step. I picture the sun sitting low in the sky, calling for us to walk into its center and out of the world completely and how wonderfully amazing it felt to be free. But then I remember the old couple with sharp teeth and hungry static in their eyes. I remember the headlights of the police car and the idea of every move I made being followed. I notice the hum of the fluorescent light above my head then. It hurts my eyes and makes everything shiny like the shoes I used to wear with white dresses on Easter. I twist a strand of hair around my finger and examine it. It looks wet and blacker than its normal dark brown.

I'm being watched still.

I bite my bottom lip and hold it between my teeth.

It's all true. They are working together—the hospital and the static working to make us into sleepwalking mannequins that behave exactly like they want us to.

The thought tightens the skin over my ribs.

127

But every thought I have is fleeting. Each one is like the piece of a puzzle and no matter how many times I try, I can't make them fit together. It's as if they know the precise moment when I'm about to figure out their plan and that's when they flood the air with a stronger storm to confuse me.

—*Sabrina? Did something happen in town?*—

I try to concentrate, but the lights blink too fast for me to think straight. They scramble my thoughts.

Alec is right. To be safe I shouldn't tell them anything.

—*For me to help, you have to talk to me.*—

When I refuse to answer, Dr. Richards folds her arms in front of her, leaving the notebook open in her lap. She arches her eyebrows and her hand scratches out a few words in the notebook.

—*I had to contact your parents*— she says. —*They needed to know about this incident. Also, to be honest with you, Sabrina, I'm concerned about how things have been going with your treatment lately.*—

I try to follow what she's saying but it's not easy.

The lights continue to flicker and her voice keeps fading.

She sighs and leans back. —*Perhaps we should talk again in the morning. You're probably still drowsy from the medication.*—

Medication.

She said they gave me a shot and it dawns on me now. That is why I can't concentrate—why my thoughts are all swimming around in circles. We never should have come back here.

—*Where's Alec?*— I ask forcefully.

—*In his room*— she says. —*We'll discuss it in the morning after you've slept some more.*—

Dr. Richards waits with me until a nurse comes. She crosses the room to meet her and whispers something to the nurse before she leaves. The nurse hands me a cup with six pills and watches me so closely that I have to sit on the edge of my bed for five minutes and forty-two seconds with the medicine under my tongue until my entire mouth burns with the chalky taste of acid. After she's gone, I finally spit out what's left into the palm of my hand and wash it away in the bathroom sink.

Whatever it is they are trying to do to me here, I'm not going to let them.

TWELVE

In my dream, I'm standing in my yard in Burbank. The house at my back is like mine only different, the way it always is in my dreams. It's turned at the wrong angle so the sun shines on it differently. Also our driveway is grown over with grass as tall as my knees that has dried to a golden brown in the forever drought. The roads in my neighborhood have suffered the same fate. There are fields between the houses and the houses are marked by trees taller than normal instead of street numbers painted on a curb that no longer exists.

Somewhere, a few lawns behind me, a fence rattles in the breeze. The sky above me is bleach bright, but I know the horizon at my back is purplish black with rolling waves of storm clouds screaming their thunder into the landscape. I refuse to look over my shoulder. I know there is only horror there.

In front of me is the familiar creaking of a tree branch as the tire swing sways back and forth. I run ahead, rushing around the side of the house where I know the boy is waiting for me—the boy who never had a name before but now is Alec and always has been. Yellow dandelions sprout through the grass and their flower tops snap off as I tear through the yard. They rise up around me and flutter like yellow starfish before becoming part of the sunbeams that dance warmly on my bare skin.

I see him as I round the house. He is exactly where he is supposed to be. He is naked just as we always are when we meet here —*There you are*— he says. —*I've been waiting for you. Are you ready?*—

I stand with my legs crossed and my toes digging into the soft dirt. My entire body blushes as I nod. —*Yes*— I say, pressing a finger up to my mouth to straighten out the crooked smile on my lips.

His eyes are glowing, following me as I approach the swing with careful steps. His eyes are beautiful and I don't mind being watched through them. My legs rub against his as I slide onto the swing opposite him. Our knees touch. Our hands clutch the same spots on the rope and we start to swing—moving only inches at first but quickly climbing higher.

I lean back as far as I can so that my neck is draped toward the ground. The grass seems to fall farther and farther out of reach—the sky sinking closer and closer to greet us.

We pump our legs faster as the storm chases across the ground, turning houses into dust. My house will be next but that doesn't make me sad. It's not like the house I grew up in—this is only a shell, empty inside of anything I've ever cared about. We swing one last time and then let go of the rope. We fly away as the house is destroyed. We become thin birds sailing toward the sun—our arms spread like featherless wings.

We are holding hands, speeding toward the horizon. The city blankets the world below us. Its streets are tentacles expanding its reach. Buildings sprout up like weeds and quickly grow taller to turn into rockets ready to shoot us down. Before they launch, before they can ever catch us, the sky peels back like a curtain made of paper.

I see figures appearing on the other side. They pop up like fireworks exploding into the world—a million colorfully scribbled faces, the kind Picasso or maybe a toddler would draw. —*They are angels*

131

saying hello— I tell Alec and he says he knows. They wave their hands and the storm dies below us as the world is coming to an end.

Alec guides us to a mountaintop perch where we watch the valley fill with seawater until it is a swimming pool the size of an entire state. We are the last two people alive and the rocks beneath our feet crumble and dissolve into sand and we are staring out into a new ocean—the sun's reflection burning a hole in the center of the water.

—*We have to swim out there?*— Alec asks.

—*Then we'll fall through the center*— I explain.

—*Won't we drown?*—

—*We can breathe underwater until we arrive.*—

—*Where will it take us?*— he asks.

I smile because we've been through this all before and he always forgets. —*Heaven, remember? We're angels now. We're safe.*—

I race for the water and Alec trails behind. But as soon as my feet touch the warm waves, the dream fades and my eyes shoot open. The ocean is instantly swallowed by the darkness of my hospital room— the sun replaced by the glare of a security light outside my one window, locked and sealed for my own safety.

I wrap my arms around my chest and hold the memory of him close to me for as long as I can. Even though I miss him now, I'm happy he came to visit me. And I know he is in his room thinking the same thing because I visited him. Our dreams are connected. They have always been that way, even when we were little kids. We just didn't know it then.

I try to remember every detail of my dream because in this one we came closer than in any other one I've had. It showed me what we have to do. I was confused before and thought we needed to learn how to fly. I was wrong. We have to be on the beach, not in the sky.

We have to be on the sand, waiting for the sun to open up a place for us to sink through.

I close my eyes, but don't even try to fall asleep. I pull the blanket over my head to make a cocoon. My breath fills the space around me, warming my skin. Like a baby waiting to be born, I lay restlessly counting the minutes in my head. I want morning to come and my door to be unlocked so that I can find Alec and see if he saw it too. It is the one wish I make on the stone pressed against my stomach.

I haven't been able to leave my room all day. My breakfast was brought in on a tray and my lunch also. The walls inch in on me, hour by hour. I've been in here for twenty hours, four minutes, and twelve seconds exactly. That's not terribly long, but time stretches out when I'm confined and kept apart from Alec.

The sun has moved away from my window to the other side of the hospital and I want nothing more than to travel with it. I want to be outside. I want to see Alec. They know that. It's the reason I think they are keeping me in here.

—*It's afternoon*— I say. —*Aren't I even allowed to go outside?*—

—*It's just a precaution*— Nurse Abrams says, clearing away the untouched fruit salad and preparing my dessert—six pills measured into paper cups. —*Tomorrow, perhaps.*—

—*What about group? Aren't I supposed to go to group? Dr. Gysion will wonder where I am*— I say.

—*You're not going today. Dr. Gysion knows all about it, don't worry.*— Her voice is a gentle lullaby in the shade. I can tell she wants to let me leave. But there are rules that she has to follow even though there are others she is allowed to make up. Keeping me in my room is someone else's rule. That much is obvious to me. —*You have to be cleared by Dr. Richards before resuming your normal routine. Maybe that will happen after today's visit*— she explains. —*I know your visit with her is scheduled for a bit longer than usual. It's nothing to worry about. Just some simple tests, I promise. Nothing too bad. Then maybe it's back to normal.—*

—*Is that why you're here early?*— I ask, looking up at the clock. It's only five minutes to three o'clock. Normally I wouldn't see Nurse Abrams for another two hours when she'd come to fetch me from the lawn where Alec and I would be talking about things we would never share with our doctors.

—*Yes*— she answers. —*We're going to head down there in a minute.*—

—*Are they going to give me more needles?*— I ask, wrinkling my nose at the thought. They've given me two injections since I came back—long needles that appear to be filled with rusty water. I hate the needles. I can never tell if they are taking stuff out or putting stuff in.

—*No needles. Cross my heart*— Nurse Abrams says, and there's something strange about the way she's talking to me today. Not detached and mechanical like the past weeks, but softly as if I were so fragile her words might break me. —*Ready?*—

—*I guess so*— I say, and we walk out together.

I keep looking over my shoulder as we make our way toward the examination room. I've spent so much time here that I could wander around blindfolded and never bump into any of the furniture inside. It's two long hallways from my room and I'm hoping to see Alec along the way. I look all around and poke my head into every room, hoping for a glimpse around a corner or even just a flash through an open door, but he is nowhere.

—*Everything okay?*—

—*Fine*— I say.

I'm not fine though. My hands are trembling inside my pockets. My feet are cold even as sweat tickles behind my ears. I know what's going on just by the way she's acting. I know I'm in trouble. It's just as it was in school when my teacher sent me to the office. She wouldn't say what it was I'd done. She didn't want me to be prepared. It's easier to lie when you're expecting the questions. Everyone knows that.

As we walk through the hall, there is something else bothering me. I wouldn't ever dare to tell her. It's my secret for now. I know about the noise inside the hospital. I can't tell anyone here that it followed us back or they will keep injecting me twice a day. Anyway, the noise is still small like the sound of a television whispering in the next room, but it's growing louder. Soon it will echo through the hollow halls and ring inside my ears.

My heart races, fast and frightened, as I follow Nurse Abrams with tiny steps. The static is here. Watching me inside the walls of the hospital. Spying through the invisible cracks in the scenery. Listening and recording everything I say. I'll have to be more careful than ever.

Nurse Abrams opens the door and steps aside to let me pass. —*Go on in and take a seat wherever you like*— Nurse Abrams says. —*Dr. Richards should be by any minute.*—

I move into the center of the room and stand there. The door clicks closed behind me, shutting out the noise. I'm thankful for the momentary silence.

The school receptionist glances up at me as soon as I enter the main office. —*Just take a seat over there, Sabrina. Mr. Harris will be with you shortly.*— She points to a little waiting room off to the side and I wonder how she knows who I am since I've never been in here or spoken to her before in my life.

Through the frosted glass window on the office door, I see two students pass by. Their faces are distorted and they move like creatures underwater. I want to follow them, but I have to stay here. Mrs. Green, my first-period teacher, said the office sent a note requesting me to go down. She didn't tell me why. I'm sure it said why on the note, but she kept it from me.

—*Now, please*— the receptionist says when she notices I haven't gone into the smaller room as she requested. I guess I didn't move fast enough and her tone is sharp and short-tempered the way school officials' voices always are with bad kids even though I've never been in trouble.

I walk through the open door marked VICE PRINCIPAL. I'm not expecting to see Skylar waiting there too and I freeze up. She is sitting in a chair obscured by the door—a tiger hiding and ready to pounce when I step in. Her eyes narrow at me and her mouth curls into a snarl. —*If you say anything, I swear you'll regret it.*—

I bite down on my lip and take a seat in the chair farthest away from the one she is sitting on. I shove my hands under my thighs—my hidden fingers firmly crossed.

Skylar huffs and swears under her breath. She is annoyed to be here and more annoyed that I'm here too. I'm not annoyed, only nervous. My stomach is a net of butterflies—my belly full with them like when I imagine the ocean inside my womb, but it's making me sickish instead of happy. I stare at the blue and green checkered pattern on the rug under my feet, feeling like I might throw up.

—*Did you rat me out or something?*— Skylar growls. I shake my head but she doesn't believe me. She knows why we are here. She knew as soon as she saw me, but I still have no idea. —*I can't believe you would tell. God, can't you take a little joke? Besides, you were the one who got yourself into this mess. Just remember that. You can't blame me for it.*—

I don't know what she's talking about, so I say nothing.

When Mr. Harris comes to the door, he calls my name first. Skylar flashes me a warning look. I see the skeleton of a snake under her skin and shiver. I'm as small as a mouse in her stare. If I get too close, her jaws will unhinge.

—*Come with me*— Mr. Harris says. He is shaped like a pear or a deflated beach ball that is wide only in the center. He takes up most of the space in the doorway and has to step away before I can follow him into his office. He closes the door behind us. Then he gestures for me to sit down in one of the small chairs opposite him.

Mr. Harris turns his computer screen at an angle so that we both can see it. I recognize the photo of me in the corner—the one where I'm blowing a kiss at the camera. This is the profile page Kayliegh set up in the summer, but it looks different than it did. Even though I haven't touched it, or even looked at it, there are now more than three thousand people who are my friends. Many of these friends have left comments like the ones Kayliegh and I found on the pornography sites in her brother's computer. They describe in detail all of the sexual acts they want the girl inside the computer to do with them and how much they are willing to pay me for each.

—*Is there anything you want to tell me about this?*— Mr. Harris asks. His words sound thick and slimy as if his mouth is full of paste. It makes his cheeks puffy and his skin red and the rolls on his neck fill with sweat.

—*I don't know*— I say because I don't know what else to say.

Mr. Harris stares at me with insect eyes that want nothing more than to spin a cocoon around me and swallow me inch by inch in the thick saliva caught behind his teeth. —*It would be in your best interest to talk to me*— he says, and I can hear his stomach growl when he wipes his chin with sticky fingers.

His eyes are hungry.

They chew away at me until I'm soft and easy to devour.

The entire office is like the inside of a stomach. The scent of digestion is woven into the wallpaper's pattern. The air is thick and made of grease as thick as jelly. The lights fight through it and cook me from the outside in until the meat will slide slowly from my bones.

—Look, Sabrina— he says. —You're a good student. You've never been in trouble before. Somehow I don't think you're the only one involved in all of this. I've talked with some of your teachers and they tell me some of the students have been giving you a hard time lately. I'm prone to believe they are involved. But if I'm going to help you, I need you to cooperate with me.—

—That's not me— I say, pointing at the screen. —I don't know anything.—

Mr. Harris gives me a hard stare, takes a deep breath, and lets it out. Then he moves his mouse around on the screen and double clicks. The screen changes and a video pops up. He refuses to look as the video plays silently on a loop.

I watch out of the corner of my eye. I see an image of myself spinning like a ballerina in the grass with the school behind me. Dressed in only blurry sunshine from the waist up, I turn slowly with my eyes closed. But it's not me, I can tell. The girl inside the computer is pretending to be me, but she's different. She sees only white spots where the sun shines through her eyelids. It's not the same for her as it was for me when I was where she is. The warmth has evaporated and the colors have turned dull and cloudy.

—Are you trying to tell me that isn't you in the video?— Mr. Harris asks.

—It's not me . . . not really— I say, wringing my hands together and bending my fingers back until they sting in pain. —It was brighter that day than it shows. The colors were brighter. It's all wrong in that video.—

138

Mr. Harris stares at me as if I'd just entered the room. —*So you admit you were there . . . then it is you. Now what I need to know is if you made this video and posted it by yourself or if other students at this school were involved.*—

—*I've never seen that video before*— I tell him honestly.

—*But this is your profile?*—

—*Yes . . . but none of that is me. I never wrote any of those things.*—

—*Who did?*—

He clicks back to the profile page and I point to the girl in the photo. —*Her*— I say, and Mr. Harris looks at me the same as the kids in my classes and in the halls. —*It's true.*—

—*Okay, we'll assume for now that this isn't your page. But that's you in the video. Who made it?*—

—*But it's not. It was different*— I say. Then I start talking faster and faster, trying to make him understand. —*The grass was a darker kind of green. And the afternoon sky too . . . it shimmered like the gold breath of a dragon.*

I want so badly to make him see it all, to make it crystal clear for him, but the noise swirls so heavily around him that I know he'll never understand. It looks nothing like that in the video. It's not at all how I saw it and I bet it doesn't feel the same either. Each blade of grass was a tongue tickling my bare feet. And when I spun around . . . it rained glitter like flashing sparks from power lines.

—*Sabrina, did you let somebody take this video?*— Mr. Harris asks again.

I shake my head.

—*No*— I whisper —*I don't like to have my picture taken.*—

Mr. Harris's mouth wrinkles into a frown. He doesn't believe me. I can tell because his expression is the same one my dad makes whenever I try to tell him about good and bad halos hanging over strangers.

But it's true, and it's true about having my picture taken too. I hate seeing pictures of myself more than anything.

My mom took a picture of me on the first day of seventh grade. I'm wearing a flower barrette. Even though I'd worn one a thousand times before, this time the kids at my bus stop harassed me about it. This kid from down the street ripped it off my head and played catch with another boy, keeping it away from me until they finally tossed it out of the bus window. Every time I see the photo, I feel stupid all over again.

My mom never took the picture down even though I asked her a hundred times. She says I look pretty in it. But I think I just look dumb and I have to see it every time I get something out of the fridge. My mom doesn't even get the cruel irony that it's stuck up there with a magnet shaped like a dog that we got in the mail from the ASPCA. Now it's there forever, mocking me with my own smile. That second of my life is stolen away because that's what pictures do. They rob from us and keep every moment exactly how they want it to be remembered.

—*I never want time to be so dead. I want it to be slow . . . like swimming underwater. But I don't ever want it to be frozen. It's like the Native American thing . . . like how they say photographs steal part of your soul. That's how it is for me too.*— I explain this to Mr. Harris because if he can understand about the photographs, then maybe he'll see what I mean about the girl pretending to be me inside the computer.

Mr. Harris rubs his chin. —*Listen, all I want to know is who took this video on school grounds. Don't try to protect them. You should be worrying about yourself. A video like this is a serious issue for whoever took it or uploaded it. So . . . are you going to tell me or not?*—

—*You're not listening to me!*— I say louder, trying to be heard over the storm inside his office. —*It doesn't matter because it's not*

me. Don't you understand? That part of me was stolen. It doesn't be-
long to me anymore.—

He gives up trying to understand then. He clears his throat and frowns. —*I'm going to have to call your parents*— he says, already holding the phone to his ear and dialing from a number printed in my school records. —*Please wait in the other room again.*—

As I walk out, Skylar stands up to go in. Mr. Harris holds up his large hand, signaling for her to stay put and for me to close the door. When I sit down, Skylar looks at me with her mouth hanging open.

—*You didn't tell him I put that video online, did you?*— she asks.

I don't say anything.

I sit perfectly still, waiting for my parents to come and take me home.

The windows in the examination room are bigger and face the opposite direction than the ones in my room. They are almost too big—too bright. The sunbeams are spotlights with all their attention focused on me. The room gives me the feeling of being the only actress on a stage—an actress without lines or cues.

Dr. Richards still isn't here and I stand alone in the middle of the room. Somewhere out of sight, there are a million pairs of eyes studying me. I can feel their glare like tiny pin pricks on my skin.

Shadows divide the room, leaving one corner in darkness, and I walk over there to escape the spying lights. I crouch down in front of a bookcase that comes up to my chest—completely hidden then.

The top shelf is lined with dolls. Each of them stares up at me with empty eyes. They fascinate me and scare me at the same time because their bodies are waiting lifelessly for a child to tell them what to say and what to do. They appear almost real, or like they once were real but have had their souls removed. I can't help but wonder if that's how I'm going to end up—an empty doll without thoughts of my own.

I run my hand over their small faces until I find one that interests me more than the others. I pause to stare at her. Her brown hair and blue eyes are so much like mine. I pick her up in my hands and trace her mouth with my finger. Then I hold her up close so that I can whisper in her ear. —*Are you where they're going to put the parts of me they don't want anymore? Is that what they do here? Do they make a doll for every patient? I bet they do. I bet they store what's left of us inside of you and send a sleepwalker with pretend thoughts out in our place.*—

Turning the doll over and around, I wonder how much of me will fit inside. I wonder what the world will look like through plastic eyes or how things will feel touching them with plastic fingers. Perhaps I'll even be adopted by some little child. I guess it wouldn't be so bad to be loved that way. Part of me wonders if it wouldn't be better than being a real person in such a messed-up world.

I close my eyes and imagine slipping inside a life of hollow eyes and blank expressions. Colors sprout and swirl on my eyelids like stepping into a dream. I can sense my clothes fading away—my feet sinking into sand. It feels nice to drift farther and farther away from this room that tries hard to feel like a home, but where no one ever wants to live.

When the door opens, my eyes snap open at the intrusion. Spinning around on my heels, I drop the doll. My hands return back into skin. I'm alert and nervous all over again.

Dr. Richards strides into the room. Her white coat is buttoned professionally. Her glasses sit high on her nose and there is no trace of a smile on her lips. Everything about her is serious in a way that is different from any other session we've had. —*Hello, Sabrina. Feeling any better today?*—

I turn a shoulder to her, turning my attention back to the book-shelf. —*I feel trapped*— I answer.

—*Trapped? That's a curious answer*— she says. I don't have to see her to know her eyebrows are raised, or that her head is tilted to the side. Her reactions are always the same. She is mechanical and with machines there are no surprises.

—*Not really*— I mumble. —*Not when I can't leave my room to do things I like and everything.*—

—*What is it that you would like to do?*—

I shrug as my hand reaches for the doll again. Turning her tiny wrist in my palm, I search her plastic skin for a cat-shaped birthmark. —*I don't know. I don't really feel like talking about it.*—

Dr. Richards leans back, making the chair squeal under her. —*Is seeing Alec one of the things you're looking forward to?*— she asks.

My head turns toward her instinctively when she mentions his name.

My eyes flash with sparks of electricity.

—*Is he in trouble?*— I ask.

—*Should he be?*— she asks in return.

I shake my head, placing my hand near my mouth. I stop before putting my mouth on my sleeve. I know she waits for me to show habits like that. She uses little things like that as proof to show I'm not well. But I'm fine. Or I'll be fine as soon as they let me go.

—*I want to talk to you about your friendship with Alec*— she says. —*Specifically, I want to know what happened the other day. Was it like the incident with the boy who lives down the street from you?*— She pauses a moment, flipping through the pages of her notebook before finding the name she's searching for. —*Was it similar to what occurred with Thomas Merker?*—

—*No*— I say so forcefully I'm nearly shouting. —*Alec is nothing like Thomas. Alec is like me.*—

—Are you sure?—

She's trying to confuse me again—to change my thoughts into hers. I have to stay focused. I have to keep my fingers tightly wound around the stone in my pocket. *—I'm positive.—*

Dr. Richards folds her notebook closed, but keeps her finger in the middle to mark the page. *—Did Alec make you run away? Did he say anything to you that made you feel as though you had to leave?—*

—I already told you, we didn't run away— I say.

—Okay— she says in a voice meant to calm me. *—Let's talk about Thomas then and what happened when he made that video of you at school.—*

I narrow my eyes into the shape of a sliver moon.

—Who told you about that?— I demand.

Dr. Richards raises one eye until there are small wrinkles of confusion covering her forehead. She opens her notebook to the page she has saved and shows it to me. *—You did—* she says. *—Twenty-two days ago. Don't you remember?—*

———————————

Thomas keeps touching my hair and I keep jerking my head away. It's the same dance brothers and sisters do during a long car ride, trying to annoy each other. Only he's doing it for different reasons. His hands don't tug or yank, they slide slowly, making sure his fingers brush the skin on my neck with every stroke.

—No way, man. That band's awful— he says to Scott as his other arm crawls in the grass behind my back. *—What's up with all the garbage that guy's always singing about anyway?—*

His fingers are large insects walking down my spine. I try to wriggle away by arching forward. Thomas's eyes flash from Scott to my chest and he smiles like a game show host with porcelain teeth. His eyes are recording me as they stare.

I'm aware of the changes that have taken place inside of him. The boy I grew up with and rode bikes with and helped to build forts out of old wood and mud is disappearing. Even as he gets taller, his shoulders broader, Thomas is shrinking and becoming so small under his bones. It is something else that makes him move and makes his tongue speak. The boy I used to know as Thomas Merker has been erased—replaced with a personality programmed by television and commercials to act a certain way. Like most every other kid in school, Thomas is nothing more than a mannequin with breathing flesh.

—*Come on, man! You're being a bit too harsh, don't you think? They're not that bad of a band*— Scott argues. He doesn't know that Thomas is only pretending to have a conversation and isn't really interested in the discussion. Thomas is only interested in me—in the way his palm presses against the bare skin between the bottom of my shirt and the top of my jeans.

—*Yeah, you're right*— Thomas says. —*They're so much worse.*— He turns his head to the left so he can watch my cheeks turn pink as his hand goes lower and then lower still. His fingertips sink below my belt and my ears hum with a children's tune inside my head that goes *itsy bitsy spider, down Sabrina's back.* His palm is a flame pressed against my skin as one of his fingers worms its way into the space where my spine ends and my body folds together.

I want so much to tell him to stop but my mouth doesn't work. My tongue ties into knots and is too clumsy. I haven't been able to speak at all since we came out here onto the lawn behind the gym where the afternoon is brightest. I'm not even sure I've been able to breathe either, but I guess I must have; otherwise, I'd be dead.

It started during last period. Sitting at my desk, the teacher's words changed into a humming noise that mixed too easily with the fragments of conversations passing from desk to desk. It all came together to form a ringing sound in my ears that I can't shake off. This happens more and more, it seems—happens closer together, day after day. It used to feel like forever between episodes. Now it feels constant—like the storm is getting nearer and I need to get away.

I should have gone straight home. I would have but Kayliegh begged me to stay after. She said she wants us to be close again—that she's sorry for not sticking up for me against the rumors Skylar has been spreading. Really I think she only wants me here to distract Scott. Whatever her reasons are, it's okay because I want Kayliegh back. I'm tired of being alone. Everything will go away then, I'm sure of it.

—Hey, 'Brina? When did Kay say she was coming anyway?— Thomas asks. He has a habit of shortening every name that Kayliegh is crazy about. She says it makes him dangerous because it means he's always pushing ahead.

He pushes his face nearer my neck.

His breath is the beginning of a hot wind approaching from some- where far off beyond the parking lot where cars are twinkling like metallic stars—coming from farther than that even, from out past where the lawn turns into soccer fields and football fields and baseball diamonds that fade away into thousands of houses, all looking identi- cal in the hazy distance. The wind begins there. Thomas is merely bor- rowing tiny bursts of it from a reservoir of static that blows in from the deserts that swallow up the landscape behind the mountains on the horizon. The cell towers rising above the trees pull it forward like mag- nets. A tornado is on the way and I make my hands into fists to be ready for it.

Kayliegh is supposed to be here with me.

She is supposed to meet us here after she's done talking to her geometry teacher about getting extra credit. Then the four of us are going to walk the two miles back from school to her house, stopping at the pizza place on the way to rest. Thomas keeps looking over his shoulder in the direction of the school so that he'll know when she comes. I know he won't stop touching me until she does.

The longer she takes, the closer the wind gets. It's already so close that I feel it in the soft center of my bones—feel it warming the inside of my soul in a rush of heat that floods over me. If Kayliegh were here, it would settle down.

—*She can take her time for all I care*— Thomas whispers as I watch a parade of kids hurrying off toward the traffic of buses parked in front of the school. Some of them glance down at us in the grass and watch Thomas's hand fumbling with the top button of my shirt. I stare anxiously at the sea of faces—all of them are like the living dead.

I look toward Scott as he tries to stare in the other direction. His head is turned, but his eyes don't go along for the ride. They stay focused on each inch of my bare skin being revealed, button by button.

The longer strands of Thomas's hair tickle the nape of my neck— wayward bangs that hang below his cheek like streaks made from a black marker. It's one of the things about him that makes Kayliegh write his name on her hand with a heart drawn around it.

—*You're cuter than Kay, you know that?*— he whispers to me. —*I know you think she's prettier, but she isn't.*— His left hand moves up the back of my shirt as his right hand moves down the front where the two sides are no longer connected. My ribs soak up the sunlight and the few freckles on my stomach stand out against my pale skin. I'm staring down at my belly button when I feel his lips touch the place

147

under my jawbone. His tongue escapes like a wandering snake between rocks. When it presses against my skin, I feel as though I've been stabbed. —*You taste better too*— he says and I feel his words hissing in my ear more than I hear them.

It's not that I'm letting him. I just can't seem to bring myself to do anything to make him stop. I keep telling my arms to shove him away but they won't listen. I'm paralyzed until the wind reaches me.

His fingers dig under the strap of my bra and slide it over my shoulder so that there is space between me and the fabric—a space just large enough for his hand to creep in like a burglar through a basement window.

His palm covers my breast, pressing me flat.

My mom says the women in our family develop late. She tells me this as if she's apologizing—as if there is something wrong with the shape I am. The way Thomas smothers me makes me think he doesn't care so much. Whatever I am right now, right at this second is enough for him—at least until Kayliegh joins us.

He must be reading my thoughts because his hand goes limp as he glances at me. —*We don't have to tell her anything about this, right?*—

With all of my strength, I force myself to swallow in order to speak. —*Don't*— is the only word I manage to get out and even I know it sounds like I really mean for him to keep going.

—*I know you like me, Sabrina*— he says. He undoes my bra and it falls across my body like the strap of a backpack. His fingertips barely touch my skin, moving in small circles over the pinkest part of me. —*You've liked me since fifth grade, just admit it. I've always thought you were kind of cute too, in that shy girl sort of way. But that's just an act, isn't it? You're not as shy as you pretend to be.*—

He takes his hand away and reaches into his pocket. He pulls out his phone and smiles at Scott. Scott has been watching jealously until then. Now he's jealous but he's also excited as the blinking red light tells him Thomas is filming me.

Static hovers over me like a vulture.

The sky fills with screams that only I seem to hear.

I close my eyes and look up at the sun. It becomes a white spot dancing on my eyelids. The wind comes and moves my hair. It passes over and finally I can move again because it pushes the static away and holds it back.

I don't say anything as I slide out from under Thomas's arm. I simply stand up and start to walk away. My shirt hangs open behind me like fabric wings, leaving part of me naked to the sun. He keeps the camera phone pointed at me but it doesn't matter. It can't see into my dreams—the static can't record that.

The scenery begins to fade into something resembling a blurry shadow as I head toward the area near the tennis courts where the grass is thin and the pebbles in the dirt dance like fireflies on the ground. The colors change with every step I take. With my head tilted to the sky, I spin in circles watching the blue change to gold—spinning so that I can see rainbows form perfect circles around my eyes. It feels good to be in control of the universe in this way.

Through the windows of the examination room, I see the bleached outlines move against the golden afternoon sky. They are just shapes and shadows. Ghosts more than people. None are Alec, that much I know.

I'm not sure how long I've been sitting and staring at them without talking. It could be hours or it could be minutes. The way

Dr. Richards studies me as I turn my head away from the glare suggests it's been longer than what she considers healthy.

I rub my eyes. They are dry and sore.

It feels like forever since I blinked last and it frightens me a little.

—Sabrina? How are you feeling?— she asks. *—You were mumbling and seemed agitated.—*

—No I wasn't.—

Dr. Richards looks concerned. *—Can you tell me why you wanted that doll?—* she asks. I look down and discover the doll in my lap—the one that resembles me.

I let go of it—let it fall as if it were on fire.

—I didn't. I have no idea where it came from— I tell her.

—You got up to get it— Dr. Richards says, but I don't believe her. *—Wait here one second.—* She gets up and leaves the room. When she returns, she's carrying a laptop. A few seconds later, a video appears of me in the examination room dressed as I'm dressed now. It shows me standing up and walking over to the bookshelf with the sleeve of my sweatshirt tucked into my mouth. I grab the doll and bring it back with me. Then I sit down and stare out of the window as Dr. Richards watches.

—What is that?— I ask in a panic. *—Where did that come from?—*

—I'm not sure what you mean?—

—Liar!— I scream, lashing out and knocking the computer onto the floor. *—You're a liar!—*

—Sabrina? Calm down and tell me what's got you so upset— Dr. Richards says in a steady, slow voice.

I stand up and ball my hands into fists. I keep them by my side and roar at her like a lion—my face burning red with anger. *—You recorded me! This whole time!—*

150

—*We record every session here*— she says. —*I'm sorry if you didn't realize, but . . .*—

—*Liar!*— I start to rock back and forth on the heels of my feet. A headache swells behind my eyes and I feel as though my brain will explode. —*You tricked me! You all did!*—

Two nurses rush into the room then. I swing my arms out at them, but they are able to grab hold of me. I feel weak—almost invisible—thinking about all of the hours and all of the pieces of me that have been stolen. I wonder how much of me is even left.

The needle glides through my skin without much effort.

There is a rush of pressure in my arm before the lull. I tingle all over for just a second before my senses dull. Then I'm easy for them to maneuver back into the chair—as easy as posing a doll.

Dr. Richards takes a medical pad from her coat pocket. —*Sabrina, I'm going to prescribe another medicine for you*— she says. Then she hands the script over to the nurses and instructs them to take me back to my room.

—*I don't want any medicine.*— I try my best to yell, but the words come out deflated.

—*It's just something a little different than what we've been using*— she explains, scribbling away on the pad. —*Given your behavior over the last few days, I'm worried the current prescription is losing its effectiveness.*—

—*I'm fine. I don't want any more medicine*— I repeat.

Dr. Richards pauses and looks at me. I can see the beginning flurries of static in her eyes. —*Can you tell me what day it is?*—

The question hangs in the air like a sickness.

I rub the back of my hand over my mouth and try to look everywhere but at her. I know it was Friday at some point but I can't remember if that was today or the day before yesterday.

—*What does that matter?*— I say.

Dr. Richards presses her lips together tightly. —*Hopefully this new drug should make things a little clearer for you again.*—

My hand starts to tremble as my mouth searches for the comfort of my sleeve. Before I can reach it, the nurses gather me up and place me in a wheelchair. I am asleep before we ever get back to my room.

THIRTEEN

They finally let me resume my schedule two days after Alec and I were brought back. When I leave my room, the sun is on the right side of the building and hasn't passed over to the left side yet. At this time of day we are always in the common room and I have to count one second between my steps to keep from running all the way there. If they see me run, they will put me back in my room. They will give me another needle.

When I walk into the room the sunlight through the windows is blinding. For an instant before my eyes adjust, everything evaporates in the excessive color. Then shapes start to form and I identify the outline of the sofas and tables and the many silhouettes moving around. I focus on them.

A panic builds and I'm not as good as I should be at slowing it because Alec should be here. If they've let me back into my routine, they should've let him back too. He would come here too. He'd want to see me just as badly.

I search everywhere with my eyes, turning my head like a lost child in a store. One of the nurses sees me. From across the room, she is watching me sway like the last leaf on a tree, clinging to its branch and trying not to fall.

—Is something wrong?— she asks, suddenly standing next to me. Without waiting for an answer, she places her hands on my shoulders and leads me away from the door.

The nurse guides me to a chair. Pulling it away from the table, she expects me to sit down but I shake my head. *—I'm okay—* I say, and I have the feeling I'm telling myself more than her.

I don't want them to send me away for an examination or back to my room. I remember my breathing and about taking deeper breaths.

It helps.

—I was just . . . I was looking for somebody, that's all— I explain. *—You don't happen to know where Alec is? He's usually in here at this time.—*

The corners of her mouth turn down as she gives a small shake of her head. *—I'm afraid I can't really give out information on another patient.—*

—But he's always here! Don't you need to know if something is wrong?— I can tell she's about to repeat the same answer. That she's going to say it's the policy of the hospital. So I put my hands together and say *—Please—* before she can. *—You don't have to tell me anything, I just want to know if he's okay.—*

She sighs and hesitates before going over to her station to look at the patient log. *—He's fine—* she says once she returns. *—But he's going to be with the doctors most of the day.—* Then the soles of her sneakers squeak as she leaves to take her place at the other end of the room where she was when I first walked in.

I see some of the girls from my group session on the other side of the room. They are talking and smiling and I don't want anything to do with them because everyone here is changing. They're not real anymore. They are becoming just like the kids at school. I know they'll eventually turn on me too.

I stay by myself at the table and start to draw. I need to figure out our way into heaven before I see Alec again. I need to illustrate the path we're supposed to take.

There isn't much blank paper in the bin and I run out quickly. I start to use the backs of paper where other kids have been keeping score for card games. I use the little white subscription cards from magazines and any other scrap I find that has enough clear space to fit an image because I'm trying to draw everything I've ever seen in my dreams. I think if I can only put them all together in the right order, I will know what I need to do.

—*What are you doing?*—

I look up and see Amanda looking down at me. —*I'm just working on something*— I say. That's all I'm going to tell her. She might be spying on me. —*It's very important that I finish*— I mumble. There is a race going on between me and the static. If I don't win, I'll disappear.

Amanda leans over the papers spread over the table like islands in the sea. She picks up a handful of drawings that I've laid on the corner. I'm nervous she will put them out of order and flash her a look. She's flipping through the pictures though and doesn't notice.

—*Did you do all of these just now?*— she asks me.

—*Most of them.*—

—*Wow. This is a lot of work*— Amanda says.

My head spins with images of turning cartwheels on Kayliegh's front lawn. I can even smell the summer grass stains on my palms. I remember how we always said that we would explore heaven together, leaping from cloud to cloud, hand in hand. It seems connected somehow and I rush to find a fresh piece of paper to draw it.

Amanda sits down and watches me. She has several checker pieces in her palm and keeps stacking them. It's a quiet noise but those are the most distracting.

155

I lose focus and look up at her. We both stare at the strange pattern of colored marker, pencil, and crayon that stains my skin. Below it all, though, I still see the two eyes of the grinning cat promising to protect me.

—*We all wondered where you were the last couple of days*— Amanda says. —*They told us you needed a twenty-four-hour treatment. Is Alec getting that treatment too?*—

I remain silently staring and Amanda moves her hands into her lap. She's a stranger to me. I don't know anything about her except for our walks back from group session. It makes me suspicious, like maybe she's a spy for the static.

When the common room door opens, Amanda stands up, returning back to the sofa where she had been before. The way she retreats makes me hopeful that Alec has entered and I look over at the entrance. It's not him though. It's Nurse Abrams. She's talking to the other nurse and I can hear them. —*She was asking about him*— the nurse on duty says, and I see their eyes dart over to where I am. I pretend to draw.

—*Poor girl*— I hear Nurse Abrams say. —*I'm sick of kids like him being admitted. We're supposed to be helping kids with real problems, not babysitting the delinquent offspring of rich people. Look what he did to her, she was almost better.*—

I won't look at her when she's done talking and calls my name.

I start to draw again—scratching the pen's tip so fast and violent that it is ripping through the paper. She comes toward me then. Nurse Abrams reaches for me, but I yank my arm away like a cornered animal.

—*Sabrina, I need you to come with me*— she says softly.

—*It's not time*— I say.

—*I know it's not, but you have a phone call.*—

All phone calls are taken in special rooms set up for us in the north wing of the hospital by the main entrance. They are private rooms but they are watched. Everything is watched by the cameras, I know that now. Nurse Abrams offers to walk with me, but I want to go alone. I heard what she said and I know she's not on my side. She's on their side. Besides, I want to go the long way around so I can walk by Alec's room.

I press my face against the glass in the door.

He's not in there but I mouth the words *I love you* anyway because I know the words will wait for him. Then I hurry away to the visitors' desk where a nurse leads me into a little room with a phone and closes the door.

Kayliegh calls exactly at the time they told her to.

—Hello?— Her voice sounds anxious. —*Sabrina? I can't believe I'm actually getting to talk to you! This is the first time they've let me call. I've tried calling you the past two days but they said I had to wait. So? How are you?*—

—*I'm fine.*—

—*Really? That's good. I've been worried about you. Everyone has*— she tells me.

—*Who's everyone?*— I ask.

—*You know . . . our friends. Thomas even told me to give you a message*— she says, laughing. —*But I'm not going to say it. You know how he is.*—

—*Yeah, I know.*— I want to ask why she doesn't seem to know how poisonous he is, but I don't. I don't want to talk about him.

—*Sabrina, I need to tell you how sorry I am*— Kayliegh says.

—*Sorry for what?*—

I hear her breath on the other end. I hear the words in her mouth trying to fight their way out. —*I think all of this might be my fault*— she says. —*I think I know how all of those things ended up on your profile. A couple of weeks ago . . . I was hanging out with Thomas and we were just fooling around online. When he found out I had your password, he wanted to send Scott a message pretending to be you. Just as a joke, you know? And, well, I was kind of mad that you never even gave it a try, so I went along with it. But I swear I didn't know he was going to tell other people your password. And once things started getting really out of hand, I went to change it . . . but somebody already had.—*

I have nothing to say because none of that matters anymore.

All that matters is getting to the place behind the sky.

She's trying to make me forget that—trying to convince me that she is real. The medicine flowing through my body makes it hard to keep things straight—makes my brain feel like soggy cereal.

—*Are you mad?*—

I shake my head and somehow it's as if she can see me.

—*Everyone at school is like so behind you*— Kayliegh says. —*They all want you to come back. Even Skylar feels so rotten about what she did. She even confessed to Mr. Harris about the video. They took the suspension off your record. That was pretty cool of her to do that.*—

—*You talk to her?*—

—*Yeah, she's not so bad. I mean, what she did was terrible. But she didn't know that you were having problems. None of us really knew.*— There is a pause on both ends of the phone. Then Kayliegh clears her throat and says —*I'm sorry I wasn't a better friend. If I'd known there was something this serious wrong with you . . .* —

—*There's nothing wrong with me*— I say. —*Why does everyone think there's something wrong?*—

—Because there is . . . isn't there?—

—No. I just see things differently . . . that's all. You used to like that about me— I say, wishing maybe I never agreed to take the phone call.

—I didn't mean it that way— Kayliegh says. *—Don't be mad at me, please. I just want to help you. You're my best friend.—*

—I don't need any help— I say. *—I needed you to believe me instead of Thomas and Skylar and anybody else like them!—*

Before she can say anything else, I hang up the phone. I don't care what she has to say to me anymore. I don't need her. I have Alec now. He'll never betray me—not like she did.

There is a nurse waiting for me outside the door.

—How did it go?— she asks.

—Fine— I lie. *—I want to go back to my room now. Is that okay?—*

—Sure— she says, but she makes me wait for another nurse to walk with me because they were listening and something I said has made them worry about me all over again.

FOURTEEN

It's dark when the door to my hospital room opens. A thin band of light invades through the crack, illuminating the shadowy corners. My eyes become alert as footsteps cause an eclipse.

The outline of a person appears in the doorway—backlit like an angel. The figure's head turns to the side and searches the hallways like a child looking both ways before crossing the street.

I hold my breath.

Nurses visit me constantly. They come as often as circus clowns emerging from a tiny car. Bringing medicine after medicine, they fill me with an entire diet of pills in small white cups. I haven't been able to avoid taking them. Now there's so much medicine inside of me that I'm melting away like ice on a summer street.

I dread the nurses' visits. But this is not a nurse slipping into my room and letting the latch lock behind them. Nurses never lock themselves in with me. Nurses enter with marching steps and the flick of electricity to fill the room. Their noise is as loud as an alarm—not the soft padded sound approaching me.

My eyes are adjusting to the dim haze from the security light in the parking lot outside. I watch the strange figure moving toward my bed. My breathing is fast and shallow, seeing a shadow hand press to its shadow face. —*Shhhh.*—

Just by that simple sound, I know it's Alec.

The springs on the bed squeak as he crawls over my legs to rest on top of me. With his face near mine, I can see him clearly. I trace the small slope of his nose that gets wider at the bottom, connect the freckles under his eyes with imaginary lines, and run my finger over the shape of his lips. Even with only the little bit of light, his feline eyes glow.

—*I was so scared . . . I mean, I didn't know if . . .* — I start to tell him how worried I was and how I've missed him to the point of suffocating, but before I get the words to come out right, he covers my mouth with his because he knows. It's only been two days since we've been together but it feels like lifetimes. It feels the same for him too. I can tell by the way he breathes into me all of the things he's held inside since they brought us back.

Every last inch of me begs for him. I reach under his body and help to pull his shirt over his head. He helps me do the same.

Our clothes make sparks of static electricity in the dark as they fall to the floor.

The feel of his skin pressed against mine makes me feel alive. Blood rushes through my body. I feel real again as I dig my fingernails into his back—gripping him so tightly he flinches because I don't want him to leave me alone ever again.

As we kiss, Alec keeps pausing to glance over at the door. —*I'm worried someone will come*— he says. —*I don't think anybody saw me, but you never know.*—

His hair is sweaty and sticking to his forehead. I wipe it away from his eyes and make him look at me. —*They won't*— I say because it doesn't matter that they have cameras everywhere—cameras can't see us where we're going. —*We're safe here.*—

—*How can you be sure?*—

—*Because . . . when you got on the bed, we went someplace*

else. Didn't you feel how we floated away? Like being on a boat and drifting into the ocean but that the ocean was made of stars instead of water?—

I place both of his hands over my heart. It's the only way I know how to explain. Our hearts begin to beat in the same rhythm and he smiles.

—Yeah, I guess I did feel something like that.—

—Of course you did— I say, *—because we're connected.—*

He kisses me again. This time he doesn't look anywhere but at me. The blankets drop to the floor next to our clothes as we both bend and stretch, pressing against each other until we are out of breath. Then Alec collapses in my arms and we lie like branches of a tree that have grown around each other. I run my hand through his hair and see little sparks like fireflies dance around him. For the first time since we've been locked apart, I'm calm.

In the quiet that follows, Alec nestles his face into my neck. *—I really wish I saw things the way you do—* he says. *—You're lucky. I hate almost everything I see, but you can see the beautiful part of everything.—*

I turn my head toward him.

The light rests on his body like water.

—You're the only one who thinks so— I tell him.

—Yeah, well it's clear to me that it's everyone else who's mental— he says with a deep exhale. *—I tried telling that to the doctors here today and you should've seen the look on their faces. I swear I'll really go crazy if I stay in this place.—*

Sitting up, I pull my knees under me and place my hands on his chest. I begin to trace a picture on his skin with my fingers. I make a circle for the sun and so many rays shining from it.

—Once we pass through the sun, all of this will go away. The

grass will take over. It will turn all the roads to fields and all the houses into nothing. It'll just be you and me then. Just like heaven and we'll be free like deer running through a forest.— Alec has his eyes closed as I describe it to him. Every time he breathes, I'm sure the picture is clearer in his mind. My fingers dance on his skin, showing him how we'll leap and run and swim under a sky that changes colors with however we feel at the time. *—Nobody believes me, but you know that it's real, don't you?—*

—Of course— he says, and then his eyes open. *—I see it every time I look at you. It's just that it seems so impossible.—*

—It's not.— I pull out the last drawing I made from my desk. It's the last one in the sequence I've been working on all day. It is of me and Alec on the beach—the place where we leave the world behind.

—That looks like the beach in Santa Monica— Alec says.

—That's where it is— I say. *—Remember the Ferris wheel? You told me about it and we said that's where our private world would begin?—*

—Yeah, I remember— he says. *—God, I'd give anything for you and me to be laying in the sand there right now instead of here.—*

—Me too— I say. *—If we could just get there . . . I know every-thing would be okay. But I'm scared we won't.—*

Alec pets me, kissing my shoulder. *—Why are you afraid?—*

—Because . . . I think they're changing me— I say. *—Sometimes, it's like I don't even remember who I was before and I think they want me to forget all about it. Also . . . I'm scared maybe they will take you away.—*

Alec wipes the red corners of my eyes, brings his fingers along my cheek before bringing his palm to rest on my naked leg. *—They're not taking me away. Don't worry about that—* he promises. *—I'll always find a way to get back to you. I'll do whatever . . . I don't care. I'd kill* *them if they tried to keep us apart.*— A fierceness flares up in his eyes and I know he's telling the truth. I know nothing will ever be able to stop him from being with me. And I think about what that girl said about Alec being bad and I realize she didn't understand there's a difference when a person does things that are bad for a good reason.

I lie down next to him, curling my body against the shape of his. I feel safe being so close to him. And when we close our eyes, I can tell we're going to make it—we'll survive when the rest of the world ends. Even if it's a long way to wherever we belong, we're going to get there soon. I already feel the future moving toward us like a nuclear wind, blowing closer with each passing heartbeat.

The door opens and a nurse enters my room. As soon as our eyes meet, she retreats. She is going to take him away.

Alec is asleep but wakes when I stir. —*They're coming*— I whisper.

Time stands still while we're together. Outside the window, leaves hang suspended above the ground. Trees bent by the wind stay bent. For those short minutes, we are immortal—out of the reach of time. But time has a way of speeding forward. It rushes at us like a car running a red light to collide with our bodies at rest.

We both hear the guards charging toward my room and Alec holds my hand. —*It's okay*— he says when I start to shiver in his arms. —*Whatever happens, just remember it's only temporary. Think about us on the beach and know that it's going to happen. Okay?*—

—*Okay.*—

Nobody gives us a chance to explain why he's in my room and how we need each other. Not the guards who take Alec by the arms and drag him from my bed. Not the nurse who gently holds me back.

The world spins so fast in those minutes.

I'm paralyzed by its force.

Nurse Abrams enters with two other women in blue scrubs. She drapes a blanket over my naked body and asks me questions. I can't understand what she's asking though because there is a rush of noise inside my head blurring her words together.

—*Better call Dr. Richards*— Nurse Abrams tells one of the other nurses. —*She's going to want to contact Sabrina's parents right away.*—

FIFTEEN

After we meet with Mr. Harris, I want to go straight to my room but my parents say we need to talk. They make me sit at the kitchen table with them. They want to go over everything Mr. Harris has told them. —*I don't think you understand how serious this is*— my dad says, staring at his computer on the table between us. Every time he catches a glimpse of me on the screen, he shakes his head.

—*Did somebody put you up to this?*— my mom asks.

—*Was it some boy?*— My dad's fists rest on the table like hammers. Having someone to blame matters more than anything to him— even if it ends up being me.

—*Nobody made me do anything*— I say softly.

—*Why then? Why would you do this?*— My mom's face is strained and exhausted. I want to tell her she should make some coffee but it doesn't seem appropriate. —*I don't understand. This isn't like you.*—

—*I didn't*— I say. I point at the girl twirling around. —*I didn't do that. That's not really what happened. It was . . . different.*—

My dad breathes out through his nose like an angry animal. —*I don't care, we're deleting this . . . now.*— He wants me to log in and make it all go away, but I can't. The password doesn't work and the email address for the account has been changed. My dad is furious all over again.

—*I told you . . . it wasn't me*— I say.

My dad is already on the phone with the customer service number listed at the bottom of the site—pacing through the kitchen and muttering under his breath. —*I'm going to make them take it down one way or the other.*—

My mom is scrolling through the comments. After each one she reads, she makes a sound like she's been stabbed. —*I can't believe some of these things . . . who would do this? Does this have anything to do with what your principal told us . . . about the kids at school giving you a hard time?*—

I shrug.

—*Sabrina . . . why didn't you tell us?*— my mom says. —*You didn't say anything about having trouble at school. Is that why your grades have been slipping too?*—

—*No*— is all I'll say because I can't tell them any more than that. I can't tell them about the invisible vultures I see or the noises that I hear moving through the walls. If I do, they will make me see more doctors. I don't need doctors. Doctors make it worse.

—*That still doesn't explain the video or what you were doing walking around topless at school*— my dad hollers. —*I mean, what the hell were you thinking? Do you have any idea how many creeps are out there watching this?*—

—*Honey, I don't think losing your temper is going to help*— my mom says. —*It's pretty obvious Sabrina didn't upload it here . . . she can't even log into the page.*—

—*Exactly*— my dad argues. Then he turns to me. He's still on hold and waves the phone at me. —*This is exactly why we didn't want you going on these sites in the first place. Things like this can happen and the next thing you know, it's you who gets suspended from school. Don't you get it? A suspension like this is severe. This goes on your college transcript. I have no idea how we'll even begin to explain this.*—

167

They gave me a seven-day suspension for violating the school's decency policy. My parents tried to convince Mr. Harris that I'm sick but he told them that he had no choice since I refused to help find the culprits. As a compromise, he agreed not to contact the police about the video even though he claimed he should since I am underage.

—*It doesn't matter*— I mumble, and my dad's temper gauge dials up another notch.

—*What did you say?*—

—*I said it doesn't matter!*— I raise my voice even though they never listen to me no matter how loud I talk. —*None of that is going to happen. The storm will be here before then. It's going to make everything go away!*—

My dad puts his face into his hands and wipes away his rage as best he can. He and my mother pass looks back and forth to each other and when he speaks next, his voice is calmer. —*Sabrina . . . what storm?*— I can tell he's afraid of my answer by the way he chokes on the words as if they were smoke.

—*The one that's everywhere*— I tell them. —*In the sky, in the air, the ocean . . . everywhere.*—

My dad hangs up the phone and my mom tells me I can go upstairs if I want. —*Your father and I need to talk about something*— she says. —*It's okay. We're not mad anymore.*—

I run away from the kitchen and up to my room. I fall onto my bed and fold my arms over my stomach. I stay perfectly still waiting for a dream to come—waiting for release and wondering why I'm the only person who sees the world closing its eyes and drifting off into a nightmare.

But it's no use. The static has found a way into my room.

I press my palms to the walls and the wood breathes with the effort of something trying to get in. I tear at the pictures wallpapering my room—pages taken from magazines or paintings I've made. Under all of them, the static is hiding.

I know what to do by instinct. I take the markers from my desk drawer. My hands work fast and feverish to cover every inch of wall that I've cleared of posters now spread out in tatters over my floor. I draw with both hands trying to match the scribbles I've seen on the sky—making larger and darker circles that spiral out from the center.

When the bedroom door opens, I'm on the floor in the corner of my room. My mom stands in the doorway staring at the walls. —*Sabrina? What in God's name is going on in here?*—

I stay curled in the corner, shivering in my underwear and holding my knees with ink-stained hands. She doesn't see me right away— only what I've done. —*It was trying to get in*— I mumble. —*I was only protecting myself.*—

Her eyes stop roaming my room and settle on me. It's like she's seeing me for the first time—as if I were a stranger to her. Her anger about the mess soon dissolves and I see the confusion in her eyes when she bends down close to me. An hour later, she is on the phone with a psychiatrist.

———————

In the Wellness Center examination room, my dad can't stay still and paces endlessly. The dolls follow his movements without moving their eyes. My mom's eyes shift as she watches him and I watch her. Dr. Richards watches only me. So do the cameras hidden through the room. But now that I know about them, I refuse to give them anything they can use.

—*Doesn't anyone pay attention to what goes on in this place?*— my dad asks. —*For God's sake, it's a children's clinic. How could you let this happen?*— His voice makes the walls shake. Invisible thought balloons float above his head filling with swear words he would never say in public.

Dr. Richards frowns apologetically at my mother. Her face has been frozen in the same guilty expression the entire time my parents have been here. —*I know this is upsetting for you both.*— The wrinkles around her eyes become more permanent and I think about the game Kayliegh and I used to play—trying to slap the other's back to cause a silly face to get stuck there.

—*You have no idea how upset I am!*— My dad speaks through clenched teeth like a ventriloquist throwing his voice across the room. —*Maybe after I talk with my lawyer you'll know how upsetting this is for us.*—

—*Kevin! Please try to calm down*— my mom pleads, grabbing his arm to get my dad to stand still for even one second.

He shakes her off.

His fury sweeps him back to the other side of the room where he pauses in front of the windows. From this new perspective, he glares at my mom. It's one of his talents that he can change his anger as easily as changing channels on the television. My mom is his new target. He takes aim and fires words like a machine gun. —*I don't understand why you're not just as angry as I am. How can you just sit there after they've told us our daughter was found sleeping with some boy? The same boy who practically kidnapped her just a few days ago! We trusted that Sabrina was going to be safe here. They were supposed to be taking care of her, not putting her in harm's way. The board should take their license . . . that's what needs to happen.*—

I wish I could tell him how being with Alec is the only time I'm really safe. I can't though. It has to be our secret. They wouldn't understand anyway. They don't believe in dreams. Alec says it's because they've all been brainwashed. He says they could never see things the way I do.

They don't have the right kind of eyes to be able to see the sky breaking apart and being put back together again.

Nobody asks me for an explanation. My parents can barely look at me even though I haven't seen them in weeks. They hardly spoke more than a greeting when I came in. It's like they're afraid of me or don't want me again until I'm completely changed. Maybe that was the deal when I was admitted—that they would only take back the new and improved me. Or maybe . . . maybe they're just tired from spending all morning driving the three hours and eleven minutes up here.

It was barely dawn when Alec was discovered in bed with me. It was early enough that my parents would have been asleep when they were called. They must have left the house almost right away to get here so fast. My dad didn't even shave—a shadow of a beard haunts his face. When I was younger, I used to sit in his lap and rub the scratchy stubble with the back of my hand and tell him —*You're like a lion.*— Then he'd roar and I'd turn my head away giggling until he stuck his face against my neck.

I take my hand away from my mouth and reach out for him. I want to touch his face again and see if it will make time go backward.

His eyes catch my hand stretching in his direction. He stares at me as if I were a stranger and I stop my hand in midair. I doubt it would work anyway.

—*What is this other kid's name?*— my dad asks, his frustration rising to the top again. —*I want to talk to his parents.*—

—*I can't give out that information*— Dr. Richards answers. —*Besides, I don't mean to be dismissive about what happened, but I think it's best if we focus on your daughter right now.*—

—*That's exactly what I'm trying to do*— he tells her. —*I want the boy's name. I want to press charges.*—

I listen helplessly.

They gave me one pill to make me quiet.

Another pill to make me behave.

—*There's nothing to suggest anything criminal took place*— Dr. Richards assures my dad.

—*Oh, is that so? Well, maybe I'll just have to go after the hospital then.*—

—*If you want to pursue action against the hospital, that is up to you*— Dr. Richards says. —*I'm not here to talk you out of that. I'm here to tell you that I'm concerned about Sabrina. I really think we need to discuss new treatment options.*—

—*Wait. What new options? Why?*— my mom says, speaking to Dr. Richards for the first time since I've entered the room. —*I thought she was improving. That was the impression we were given.*—

—*I'm afraid her condition has become more severe*— Dr. Richards says.

Outside the window, the sky is changing. The clouds are lower than usual and they get caught in the tree branches. They are quickly torn apart. I feel the same way—stretched between what is going to happen and what has already been.

—*But she's always had her good days and bad days*— my mom says.

—*That may be, but the fact remains she's no longer responding to the treatment. We've tried changing her meds and increasing her therapy sessions, but it doesn't seem to have made a difference*— Dr. Richards confesses. —*She's become as withdrawn as when she arrived. It also seems as if her delusions are reasserting themselves. Her grasp on reality is deteriorating.*—

My hands get fast and nervous in my lap. I fidget inside my pockets until my palm wraps around the smooth surface of the stone I've hidden there. My mom reaches across her chair and rests her hand on my elbow. Her voice cracks when she speaks again. —*We were hoping she could come home soon.*—

—*I know this is difficult. But there are some things we haven't tried yet that may help*— Dr. Richards explains. —*I'm very hopeful that after a month or so . . .*

My dad doesn't let her finish.

—*You actually think we're leaving her here?*—

Dr. Richards raises one eyebrow. She tries to stay even and calm but I can read her better than she knows. I can tell she's surprised. She hadn't expected my dad to say that. Neither did I, honestly. —*I would hope for Sabrina's sake that you'll give this new treatment a chance.*—

—*She's been here almost three months! Now you want to try something? What have you been doing this whole time?*— His words come quick and breathless and he points accusingly as he shakes his head. —*No. I'm not leaving my daughter here to be some guinea pig. You people obviously don't know what you're doing. We're going to take her to see someone who does.*—

My mom rubs my arm with her hand. —*Honey, this is the best clinic in the state*— she says. —*We need to think about this. Just because Sabrina met a boy, we can't rush a decision like this. She's fifteen. It's normal. I mean, isn't that why we're doing all of this? So that she can have a normal life?*—

Alec says a normal life is worse than dying.

He says we're better off crazy and I believe him.

—*I assure you, if this is about the incidents involving the other patient, it won't happen again*— Dr. Richards says. —*The boy has been discharged and, as of this morning, is no longer a patient here at this hospital. Arrangements have been made for him to be treated at home, so I would hope you'll keep Sabrina here.*—

As I sit up, my breath makes the sharp rush a knife makes slashing through the air. It's the first sound I've made and everyone in the room responds by staring at me. —*That's not true. It can't be*— I say softly like a whisper into my sleeve. —*Alec wouldn't leave me.*—

My dad looks at me and back to Dr. Richards with suspicion.

—*I'm sorry, Sabrina. I would've liked to break this to you in a different way. I know you and he are close*— Dr. Richards says with static swirling just behind the center of her eyes.

She's lying.

She's planned it like this all along. She never wanted Alec close to me. She's never liked him telling me the truth.

—*Regardless, it doesn't change anything*— my dad says.

He's wrong—it changes everything.

Ignoring them both, my mom turns to face me. —*What do you want? Do you want to stay here?*— she asks.

I shake my head violently.

Only bad things will happen if I stay.

—*I want to go home*— I say.

I feel desperate to leave.

The noise is suddenly so close and getting closer. It's everywhere inside the walls and I need to go.

—*Please*— I beg. —*Can we go today?*—

SIXTEEN

The twigs are still green on the inside. It makes them easy to twist and bend into shape. I've already done most of them. The pile in my lap is getting smaller. I probably won't even need them all to finish the roof.

—*How's it going down there?*—

—*Fine, Daddy*— I say, looking over my shoulder. My dad is standing at the edge of our lawn, where the grass turns into a small patch of woods separating our house from the houses in the next development. He's waiting for me to smile at him or give any little sign that it's okay for him to come closer. He knows I don't like him to see the fairy coves before I'm done.

This one is just about finished. I'm binding the last curved pieces with twine and it will become the rounded ceiling. The walls have been done since yesterday. I made those from dry sticks that I glued together, and I've already decorated too. I put three candles around the entrance. They're in glass jars I covered with pink and purple crepe paper that my mom bought as streamers for my eleventh birthday party next month. The seashells I collected on our last trip to the beach are laid out like a stone path in front of the cove. Then I used some of the new blossoms from my mom's garden and stuck them in twigs to look like windows—not too many though because she'll get mad.

My dad's footsteps crunch through what's left of last fall's leaves. He bends down and whistles as he looks over my shoulder. —*That's a fancy one. Quite extravagant. I didn't realize we lived in 90210 of Fairyland*— he says, half-teasing. Even so I can tell he's impressed.

I punch him playfully on his arm. —*I just wanted to make one that was special*— I say, tying the last pieces together. Then I carefully place them on top and the dome takes its final shape. —*Do you really like it?*—

—*It's perfect*— he says. —*I couldn't have done a better job myself.*—

—*Thanks*— I say even if it isn't true. My dad used to help me build fairy coves when I was littler and I know he could do better. But now I like to do them myself. My dad's the only one who gets to see them. I catch my mom taking a peek every now and then when she's gardening, but that's okay. I just don't tell anybody else. I don't want any of my friends to say it's silly or anything. I'm afraid if they did, it would ruin it for me.

My dad kisses the back of my head and puts his arm around my shoulder. —*Come on, kiddo, your mom will come screaming down the yard if I don't bring you back for dinner.*—

I stand up and shake out my skirt. I notice the bottoms of my feet are brown with dirt and know my mom will flip if I don't wash them before I come in the house. We start back up the yard when I remember the note in my pocket. —*Hold on! I forgot.*— I spin around and dash back to the fairy cove. The note is a welcome card for any fairies that might move in and I leave it just inside the door.

—*All set?*— my dad asks, and I nod.

As we walk, I keep fingering my star-shaped charm necklace. It's smooth and feels like good luck between my thumb and forefinger. —*Dad? Do you think they'll come this time?*— I ask, and he shrugs. —*I mean, I know it's kind of childish for me to hope for it and everything. But they must exist somewhere. Or they might. And if they really do, then who's to say they won't come here, right?—*

My dad smiles and pulls me so close my shoulder bumps into his ribs and I have to cross my legs to catch my balance. *—You know, Sabrina, sometimes I wish you could stay a kid forever—* he says. *—Promise something? Even when you do get older and grow up, stay this perfect for me.—*

My eyes light up and I smile.

—Sure thing, Dad— I tell him. *—I promise.—*

My bag rattles in the seat next to me. It's stuffed with all of the same things that were in it when we took this drive last time, only then we were traveling in the other direction. My mom did the packing again. I watched from the chair in my hospital room. The only things she left behind were the stones that flew from the pockets of a pair of jeans she pulled from the closet. She knew what they were as soon as they scattered over the floor. She knew they were wishes that had yet to come true but still she left them there.

She doesn't believe in making wishes.

My dad used to, but I think he believes I'm too old for them anymore.

I believe Alec and I can make dreams happen and that's what I keep wishing on the stones I still have with me.

We're a little more than halfway home when my mom wants to stop. My dad drove the way up, so she's driving back. She doesn't ask or take a vote or anything like that. She simply puts the blinker on and says *—I'm pulling in there.—*

From the back window, I watch the headlights gleam off the other cars in the diner's parking lot. Their metal surfaces sparkle like

Christmas lights. Red and silver, brown and green—the cars twinkle in the hazy glow of a streetlamp high above. The white lines of every parking space appear to be painted with snow. The urge to let myself get lost in the colors is overpowering.

—*Should we go in? Or just get something to take out?*— my dad asks when the car comes to a stop.

My eyes are taken over by the warm electric glow coming from the diner's many windows. They are as large as movie screens. Some show nothing but blank booths and bottles of ketchup. Others are filled with people whose mouths never rest because they are either eating or talking, but never making any sounds that can be heard from here. My dad doesn't trust me with those strangers and that's why he asks about going in or not. What he really means is whether I should remain in the backseat like a dog while he runs errands.

—*We've been driving a long time*— my mom says, pushing her hair back so that she looks as if she's just woken up. —*I think we could all use a rest.*—

With his safety belt still buckled, my dad half-turns and pokes his head uncomfortably into the backseat. —*What do you say, Breen Bean? Feel like eating?*—

He's been doing that since we left the hospital—calling me the old nickname he hasn't used since I was ten or so. I know why he's doing it. I heard my parents talking with Nurse Abrams as they were filling out the paperwork to get me discharged. She reminded them that they needed to *engage* me. Using nicknames is my dad's way of trying.

I wonder if he even realizes how fake it feels for me. He says it like an actor who hasn't yet rehearsed his lines. In fact, everything about both of them seems that way. They don't behave at all like I remember. I haven't been alone with them in weeks and weeks and they've changed more than I could have imagined. I wonder if they are even themselves anymore or if they have been taken over by static, erased completely.

—*You want to go in?*— my mom asks.

—*Yeah, okay*— I mumble, and open the door.

Outside, the world is so different from what I've grown used to at the Wellness Center. The air is warmer and tingles with the hum of electricity competing for space with the buzzing bugs. On the road that runs alongside the parking lot, the rush of cars never stops. The rumble of their tires on the asphalt swells and I can almost hear their echo weighing on me. Already there is a smell of salt water in the breeze, even though the ocean is miles and miles away. It is all familiar and hor-rifyingly strange at the same time. I walk up the stairs and into the diner quickly, hoping to escape it all.

It's not really any better inside. If anything, I feel more out of place in the diner's neon confinement as we stand by the counter. My dad looks around. There is a sign that says we will be seated, but my dad says we should just take a booth by a window.

Walking past all of the people sitting on the red vinyl benches re-minds me of wading through waves in the ocean. Each set of eyes is wider. Each stare lasts longer. I tuck my hair behind my ears and lower my head, sucking at my sleeve as I watch my feet stepping carefully across the checkered tiles.

My mom reaches over the table when I slide into the booth across from my parents. She pulls my arm down softly. There is a wet stain where my mouth was. —*Not here, please*— she says. She looks so run-down and exhausted that I nod, putting my hands in my lap where they can hide under the table.

Every sound startles me.

Every noise is magnified.

A burst of laughter from the table behind ours explodes in my ears. The clinking of the ice cubes as the waitress pours us water echoes like shattering glass. A symphony of clattering dishes rains from the kitchen like a swarm of gunfire. Each sudden sound rises above the steady whisper of static and makes me flinch—each outburst is a warning that the storm is growing closer.

The cool feeling of the stone against my palm is the only thing keeping me from putting my hands over my ears and screaming. I'm glad my mom didn't find this one—the stone I keep in my sweatshirt's pocket, near my heart. I wouldn't survive without it.

My parents pretend everything is normal. They talk about the things they'll need to reschedule at work—the meetings they missed by coming to get me, the ones they will miss tomorrow and the tomorrow after that until they can find someplace new to put me. They discuss the problems they are going to have with our insurance. My dad says it's going to cost a fortune because his mind calculates all things in dollars and cents. He knows the exact price he will pay the gas company for boiling water for tea or taking five extra minutes in the shower.

My mom talks about taking me shopping for new clothes. She says the ones I'm wearing look to be getting a little tight under my arms. She asks if maybe I want to go with her tomorrow to the mall and my dad asks her whether or not that is a good idea.

The one thing they don't talk about is where they'll put me next—but it's there, just under the surface of their conversation.

I use the small tin of crayons to distract myself. There are only four colors—orange, purple, black, and green. They are scarred from being handled by the tiny fingers they were meant for. Three of them are broken in half, held together only by a ripped label.

The orange bleeds beautifully on the paper place mat as I press down violently, making lines heavy enough to cover the ads for lawn care and patio furniture printed around the border. My wrists move in big circles that grow smaller toward the center. Around and around. Over and over. This time it's my dad reaching across the table to hold on to my arm. He wants me to stop, but my mom grabs him. —*Let her be*— she whispers.

The paper radiates heat from the center where the orange is brightest. That's when I take the purple crayon and place its point in the middle and begin to trace tight spirals that loop into one another.

—*Sabrina? Honey, why don't you tell us about this boy you met?*— my mom asks. When I glance up, she's smiling but it's the way people smile around sick people. A smile that she doesn't really feel— asking questions she doesn't really care to know the answers to because it's her turn at attempting to be my friend. —*What's he like?*—

—*I'm drawing a picture*— I say. —*It's of him.*—

My mom arches her body up and leans over the table. Her eyes are focused on the purple shadows I've made against a crayon sun. She doesn't see it though. Her eyes are too broken.

When the waitress comes back to take our orders, she looks to me first. —*What can I get you? Something to drink?*— she asks, but I don't say anything. I press harder until the last crayon snaps in my hand. —*That's a very pretty picture*— she says, changing her voice to sound like someone talking to a toddler. Then she looks at my parents and tells them —*My son's autistic too. Where is she on the scale?*—

I glance over at my dad. Staring at him from the top of my eyes, I can see he wants to correct her but decides against it. His disapprovement of me comes through even louder in his silence.

—*She'll have a grilled cheese*— my mom says before ordering for herself. The waitress clears her throat apologetically, realizing she guessed wrong about me. My mom sighs, letting her know it's okay and that she shouldn't be embarrassed.

Once we're alone, my parents exchange looks. I can read their minds. They are wondering if this is how it will always be. It won't though. I'll be gone soon—sooner than they know. They won't need to put up with me for much longer.

I slide out and stand in the aisle.

I take only half a step before my dad stops me.

—*Where're you going?*—

I hold up my hands. The skin on the round part of my palms is stained with crayon wax. —*I need to wash them, if that's okay with you*— and I do my best to sound snotty and aggravated like teenagers on television. —*I'm still allowed to go to the bathroom by myself, aren't I?*—

—*I don't know . . . you tell me*— my dad says—hours of driving showing through in his tone.

—*Just . . . let her go*— my mom says with a quick motion of her hand, chopping at the space between my dad and me. —*Sabrina, go on. It's fine.*—

I feel bad about treating them that way. Or I will feel bad if they truly are my real parents and not copies of them—not brainwashed versions of the two people who used to take care of me. That's why I left the drawing. Just in case it really is them, they'll know where I went.

I walk toward the back of the diner.

Instead of heading to the right where the restrooms are, I turn left into the kitchen. Just like at the hospital, the people in there are too busy to notice as I wander past like a shadow they maybe only think they saw.

I see the door in the back. It's already propped open to let a breeze in and to let the cooking heat out. I pass through as easily as a ghost.

It's dark outside but not pitch-black. The sky is the same strange illuminated shade of purple it always is this close to Los Angeles. I stare up at it for a second. The storm is gathering. I can sense it wrestling above the smog.

I cross the parking lot and start to run. I leave the diner in the past— leaving behind the highway and the cars and the grilled cheese that is being made for me. I reach into my pocket and pull out the stones I've been keeping there. I'm not at all surprised that one wish has already come true—the stone I stole from my dad's pocket has magically turned into his wallet.

I was lying on my bed.

My bedroom was bright.

I closed my eyes and felt the pull of a world different than this.

The wind approached like it always did—coming to set me free. All of the pictures tacked to my wall fluttered at the corners before they were blown away one by one like a swarm of ladybugs parachuting on polka-dotted wings. The walls became thin as bedsheets. They were blown into the distance too.

The wind touched me—my clothes evaporated.

I opened my eyes and the sky was perfect. I breathed in and the blue faded out. I exhaled swirling colors that scribbled across the clouds like rainbows on soapy water. The sun burned a hole through the center of it all and I followed it.

Dr. Richards always asked me why I left my room that day before I was brought to the hospital. —*I wasn't in my room*— I told her each time she asked. —*I was in another place.*— She wanted me to describe the other place to her, but she never understood—the other place is nothing like California. The colors are all different like in old photographs where the oranges and browns are bright and the blues look purple. The houses aren't the same either. Their paint is always peeling and the boards show through. If I stare hard enough, I can see the paint falling like snow because the houses are older there—nearer to the end of the world.

That day, the third day of my suspension from school, I really thought I'd make it to heaven. It was all around me—close enough to touch. I felt the ground shift under my feet as I walked. The concrete sidewalks turned to sand—the houses to dust.

There was a face in the sky like a smiling cat leading the way. There was the shadow of a face in front of the sun. I couldn't make out his features but I knew I'd seen the boy before. I knew I trusted him. The stones on the ground glowed like shooting stars leading the way to him.

With one hand pressed to my mouth, I watched the colors change—flashes of red and pink and blue like electric fireflies. With my other hand, I reached upward. The sunlight touched my skin like golden water rinsing over me. I wanted so badly to slip through the warm center.

Behind me were footsteps falling on the ground like gunshots.

I concentrated on the bleached haze of heaven in front of me, ignoring the screams of thunder that called my name in a voice like my dad's. I ran faster from it—ran until my heart felt as though it would explode inside of me. But I didn't make it. The storm caught up with me. A cold hand came to rest so suddenly on my shoulder and all of the air rushed out of me in a gasp.

A brilliant blue color returned to the sky.

The stones lost their halos—dissolved into blacktop under my feet.

My dad was taking his shirt off and covering me with it as strangers stood and watched with dizzy eyes. They were all dressed. I was the only one naked in the sun. We were standing in the middle of my street, somewhere between my house and Lillian's.

Twenty-four hours later, my parents left me at the Wellness Center. Forty-eight hours later, Dr. Richards was asking me if I had been trying to run away. The answer was no. But if she ever gets to ask me about this time—my answer would be different.

I am running away this time.

I'm running from hospitals and doctors trying to control my thoughts. I'm running from the storm. I'm running from sleepwalkers pretending to be people I know.

I run through parking lots and private lawns. I run across streets at places where there are no traffic lights. I stay to the side of buildings where the lights are dimmest to keep from being recorded and tracked. But I cannot run all the way to Alec in Los Angeles, so I scan the sky for a sign.

In the distance there are wings in the sky, waving like flowers in a field. I think at first that maybe they are fairies. When I get closer, I see they are only the blinking lights of buses parked in a bus station.

SEVENTEEN

—*Where to?*—

Heaven isn't an answer that can be printed on a bus ticket. Maybe there used to be, but there are no buses that run there anymore.

—*I can't sell you a ticket if you don't tell me where you want to go. It's as simple as that.*— From the other side of the Plexiglas, I watch the woman's lips move. Her fingers tap impatiently at the keyboard and there is a rumbling of anxious coughs behind me. I don't know how many times she's asked me for a destination but I can tell she's not going to ask again before moving on to the next customer standing in the growing line behind me.

I pull myself together.

I stop shaking long enough to focus on the sound of the words coming from her mouth and make myself understand what they mean. Then I force myself to answer. —*Santa Monica, please.*—

The woman uses the top of a pen to scratch her head. Her hair is pulled into a tight ponytail, streaked with gray. —*We don't go there direct*— she says without taking her eyes off the monitor on the counter in front of her. —*You'll have to transfer in L.A.*—

—*That's okay*— I say.

She immediately starts to type information into the computer.

—*Name?*—

—*Mae*— I answer, using my middle name. I left the diner a few hours ago—long enough for them to be searching. Every computer in the world is connected to the static. I have to keep my name out of them.

—*Last name?*—

—*Parker*— I say, and the woman doesn't even flinch. She has no idea that I'm lying to her.

—*Cash or credit?*— she asks.

There are six credit cards in my dad's wallet. They all have his name on them. They are useless.

—*Cash*— I say, and count out the bills. I hand over three twenties and the woman hands back a boarding pass that will bring me to Alec. My grip on it is so strong, I'm afraid of tearing it.

As I turn around, the woman stops me. —*If you want to wash up, there's a bathroom just over there*— she says, pointing to her own chin so that I'll instinctively wipe at mine. My hand comes away with a trace of sick that I thought I'd cleaned off already.

—*Thanks*— I say with a sense of panic in my voice.

A few miles away from the diner, I made myself throw up next to a large green Dumpster in an empty parking lot. I had to get the medicine out of my body—they gave me so much of it the last day or so. Whatever was still inside of me, I left it a few miles back in a clear puddle that splashed against my shoes. Outside in the dark, I didn't notice there were traces dried on my face and dribbled down the front of my sweatshirt. It has to be washed away as soon as possible.

The bathroom in the bus station has white tiles that are yellowing. The trash is spilling onto the floor and the walls are smeared with grime that seems to breathe under the flickering florescent light. There are rust stains in the sink basin but there doesn't seem to be any static flowing through the faucets when I turn them on.

I splash cold water on my mouth. I swallow a sip and then wipe my chin. The smell makes me sick enough to want to throw up a second time, but I hold it back. I can't stand throwing up. I hate the feeling of not being able to breathe. It's the worst feeling in the world—worse even than burning.

I click soap from the dispenser until there is a small pink lake in my palm. I scrub my hands with boiling hot water until the skin is red and raw. The smell of puke is replaced with the smell of chemicals and then I am clean.

I tear a piece of paper from the roll to dry my face and hands. I remember to tuck another few pieces in my pocket in case I need them on the bus. When I step back into the main terminal, I feel momentarily confused as if all the people and objects have been switched around while I was in the bathroom. And even though the bus station isn't very big, I'm suddenly lost.

—*Concentrate*— I mutter.

Inside the pocket of my jeans, I pinch my thigh between my fingernails. The pain calms me. The bruising of my skin quickens my breath and helps me to think.

I take in one thing at a time.

There's the booth with its glass that rises up to the ceiling. The woman who sold me my ticket is where she was before. A new customer stands in front of her but the ticket lady hasn't changed—the same ponytail stretches her skin tight like plastic wrap. Moving my eyes to the left, there are a few vending machines off to the side. They sell snacks and soft drinks in bright colors.

There's an old arcade game in the corner, spitting out electronic noises. It's one my dad used to play when he was my age and I wonder if anyone even knows how to play it any longer.

There aren't many other people waiting around for a bus. Maybe that's because it's getting late or maybe this place just never gets crowded. I've never heard of this town and I can't imagine anyone comes to visit. That makes me feel safe. I bet nobody even knows there is a bus station here—tucked away behind a highway motel and invisible to passing cars.

—*It's okay. I'm okay*— I remind myself.

I'll be fine here until the bus comes.

I wait outside by the number four painted on the ground. This is where the bus to L.A. will stop. I can't remember how long the woman said until it arrives though. I wish I did so that I could count away the seconds and know when the waiting would end.

—*You heading home . . . or leaving it?*—

I turn my head to see a man leaning against the wall just out of the glare of the overhead lights.

I study him carefully, looking for any kind of glow about him. I'm very aware of spies. The static is thick with them the closer I get to the city. I have to stay guarded.

He has one leg bent so his shoe is pressed flat against the beige bricks. His other foot is stretched far out in front of him for balance and taps a nervous rhythm. It isn't until he brings his hand up to his mouth and breathes in from a cigarette that I see he is only a few years older than me.

—*Home*— I say so he won't grow suspicious.

—*Same here*— he says. —*Can't wait to get out of this hole in the ground. I don't know how anyone can live in a place like this. Give me the city any day, know what I mean?*—

I push my hair behind my ears so that they stick out wide and awkward and then I nod. —*Yeah, I guess.*—

His cigarette falls from his fingers in slow motion. He stamps it out and steps away from the wall. He takes five steps closer to me—stopping directly under the glare of the lights. —*So? You're from L.A. then?*—

I know not to say too much. I shrug one shoulder and look away, hoping to see the lights from a bus turn into the parking lot.

—*How old are you anyway?*— he asks. —*You look like you're still a kid.*—

—*Old enough, I guess*— saying it as I face the opposite direction from where he stands.

He takes another two steps closer so that he's standing right beside me. Even though it's still warm this late at night, I start to shiver being so close to him. He stinks like ashes. His eyes are swimming with static. I'm reminded of all the times after we kissed when Kayliegh's brother would come into her room whenever she was in the shower and I was alone. He never tried anything—he was just creepy like this guy.

If Alec were here with me, Alec would hurt him.

—*Traveling by yourself?*—

If I'm rude, I know he'll linger. It's the same as it was with Skylar and her friends. It's better to be polite and uninteresting.

—*What time did the lady say the bus was supposed to get here?*— I ask because asking questions is a good way to make somebody uncomfortable. That's something I learned from Dr. Richards. She did it to me so many times that I can do it to perfection.

When he answers, it's like a reflex. —*Should be here in three minutes.*—

—*Thanks.*—

I keep my eyes straight ahead, staring out at the lights of a town that doesn't have a name. I count in my head by one Mississippi, two Mississippi—all the way up to sixty and then start over. My lips are moving as I do and it scares him. He doesn't try to talk to me anymore after that.

The bus is twenty-eight seconds late, but it finally turns off the road and pulls into the parking space marked four. Above the driver's window, it reads LOS ANGELES in white letters on a black background. It looks like a name tag worn on a silver insect made of metal. The headlights are its eyes.

The door hisses as it opens.

An extra step folds out like an inviting tongue.

Even though I'm first in line, I don't get on—my knees shake too much to move. If I were with Dr. Richards, she would ask me what I was so afraid of. She'd want me to describe how I'm terrified to step onto the bus and I would tell her it was because it feels like stepping into the mouth of a beast waiting to swallow me. She would call it delusional and suggest I board. She would push me toward being eaten.

A small group of people begins to gather around me. The driver is collecting their tickets as they go inside the bus. I watch them disappear one by one into the blackness.

—*It's going to be okay*— I mumble, sucking on the sleeve of my shirt. It's just the static trying to trick me—trying to keep me from getting to Alec. I have to be brave.

The cigarette boy moves in front of me. We are the only two left. He bends a little at the waist and leans toward me until his face is only inches from mine. —*You getting on?*— he asks, and I feel myself shrinking. —*Hey? Are you okay?*—

—*Fine*— I'm almost shouting when I say it and he throws up his hands to tell me he was just trying to be nice, but his niceness is a disguise I see past. I wait for him to board first so that when I get on, I can be sure to sit far away.

—*You coming?*— the driver says, and there's something friendly about his voice that calms me—something that reminds me of a grandfather in some movie who is always helping everybody. He tips

191

up the brim of his cap and winks. —*I promise, I'm the best driver on this route. You're in good hands.*—

There is no trace of static anywhere near him and I trust him.

As I hand him the ticket, I can see that it's crumbled and twisted the way my father wrinkles up newspaper to start a fire whenever we go away someplace cold. —*Sorry*— I whisper, but the driver tells me not to mention it.

Once I'm on the bus, it's nothing like I feared. The dark corners and shadows that hang over every seat aren't terrifying at all. There's actually something comforting about them—something protective. I move deliberately toward the back. I make sure not to glance at the cigarette boy as I pass. Out of the corner of my eye, I see that he's staring at me. I keep walking until he is forgotten, fifteen seats away from where I sit down alone with my head resting against the window.

The bus comes to life—the engine purring as we drive off. I take a pen from my pocket and hold my hands steady. The lights from passing cars on the road are all I need to trace the lines. In less than a minute, I am no longer lonely. With all of the stops along the way, it is three hours by bus to L.A. and now I have a familiar friend to keep me company. —*Don't worry, Fred. We'll be there soon.*—

I let the rumble of the tires take over after that. The headlights on the highway hypnotize me. Soon my eyes are too heavy to keep open and I fall asleep.

————————

Alec is waiting for me in my dream.

—*Hurry*— he calls out.

The ocean is behind him—a whirlpool in the center swallows the sun.

He's far ahead of me.

My feet move so fast, they barely touch the ground.

Just before I reach him, he disappears. The scenery shatters and I see the bus driver leaning across the seat, shaking me. —*Last stop*— he says.

It won't be long now before there's no escape.

If we don't hurry, heaven won't wait.

EIGHTEEN

It would terrify my dad to find me in a place like the bus terminal in Hollywood. It's empty in the predawn hours of the morning. Long shadows darken the corners and corridors to save energy. The people here are people with nowhere to go. My dad would see stranger danger all around. Not me—I feel better in places like this.

—*Sabrina, at your age, everyone thinks they are invincible, but you're not*— he said to me the week before I started high school. He was just as nervous as I was about starting a bigger school. I think he's always been worried about me. I feel it every time he looks at me. There's a spark in his eyes. I know it's love that makes them glow like that, but under it there is the fear of losing love. —*You have to promise me you'll be smart, okay? I know you think we're strict, but your mother and I make rules to protect you. We can't be with you all of the time though. There are going to be times in the next four years where you'll find yourself in certain situations where you'll have to make a choice. All I ask is that you think before you act . . . don't put yourself in danger if you can help it.*—

—*Okay, Dad*— I said.

—*I mean it, Sabrina . . . promise?*—

—*I know. I mean it too.*—

He wouldn't understand about me being in the bus station. He would think I was breaking my promise, but I'm not. My dad believes that bad disguises itself—that danger hides. I think it's the opposite. The truly horrible things about the world are always reaching out for you.

The man standing by the steel gate drawn over the closed coffee hut has dirty fingernails. He smiles at me with the grin of a crocodile. His legs are reptile and mobile. There is a shadow over him darker than midnight. He is to be avoided and I walk past.

The woman sitting in a row of chairs attached to the wall is good. She has two bags bunched under her enormous legs. She takes up two seats with her size and the halo around her spreads another two seats on either side.

—*Excuse me*— I say, and she opens her eyes, stirred from a nap that was just beginning. —*I'm trying to get to Santa Monica . . . do you know which way I need to go?*—

The woman looks around for an information booth. The nearest one is unoccupied. —*It figures*— she says. —*They ain't never there. I'm pretty sure you want gate sixteen for that bus, but you might want to double-check.*—

—*I don't want to take the bus*— I say. —*I meant, how do I get there if I leave?*—

—*Oh, that's a different story altogether*— she says, laughing. —*I'll tell you what you want to do . . . go out the main exit there*— she says. Then she rattles off street names like a grocery list that I will never be able to memorize in their correct sequence. —*If you get lost, just remember to keep the morning sun behind you until you hit the ocean.*—

—*Then . . . Santa Monica is south of there, right?*—

—*Sure is, but you're not going to walk there, are you? Child, that's far!*— the lady warns me. When I say that I am planning to walk, she puts her hands on her hips—one corner of her mouth twisting into a frown. —*Sure you don't want to wait for the bus? The next one will be here in two hours. Besides, it ain't exactly a good time for sightseeing.*—

I shake my head. There is a rabbit instinct inside of me pushing me to find Alec. Every second we're apart is time the static has to get closer to me. I'll go crazy if I sit for two hours. —*Thanks. I'll be okay. I can't wait that long for a bus.*—

She shakes from side to side like an earthquake and laughs the same way. —*Youth . . . always in a rush.*—

The sun is still underground when I get outside. The sky is washed with electric light. I watch the headlights of stray cars speeding through green lights. There is a building across the street with lights on in the second floor—muffled voices in a shouting match drift from the open window. I think about what my dad made me promise—about thinking before I act. I think the best action for me to take is to keep moving and take off in the direction the lady said would lead me to the ocean.

I try to follow the directions she gave, but I keep forgetting to look at the street signs. I keep losing track of the number of intersections I pass and blocks I go down. Instead I focus on the palm trees and neon signs. —*Keep it together . . . just a little longer*— I tell myself because my brain is starting to feel unhinged like it used to in school. The past and present no longer mean as much since I left the hospital—it all seems to run together.

By the time I reach the overpass bridge that crosses the freeway, I have no idea where I am. The noise is all around me—throbbing just behind my eyes.

There is a chain-link fence along the overpass and I lean against it. The rattling metal is relaxing. I lock my fingers through its holes and breathe. I count my breaths as I watch the river of headlights far below. They are all searching for me with mechanical eyes but they can't look up—only straight ahead.

I wrap my fingers around my wishing stone and take it from my pocket. As soon as I feel its warm surface in my palm, I see the first rays of sunlight in the sky.

I take a deep breath and start to walk again—one step after the other with the sun behind me. I'm heading in the right direction again. I don't know how far I've gone or how far I have left to go, but I'll get there.

Across the bridge, the neighborhoods change.

Office space and stores transform themselves into houses. The houses grow in size—into mansions as I keep moving. But they quickly shrink again and stretch themselves into strip mall plazas.

There is static everywhere in the air. I feel it all over my body like a rash of insect bites. It spreads from building to building through power lines. It's beamed down from satellites like disease. It's woven into the skyline and feeds off the traffic rushing by. It buzzes inside every fragmented conversation taking place all over the globe. It infects people through cell phones. It copies them inside of its computers. People are thin like paper and the static is fire—devouring its way through the population and getting hungrier.

I've tried to point it out. To Kayliegh, my mom, my dad, but nobody ever sees it. Like passengers lost on a merry-go-round, they all miss it—too distracted by the motion and the blinking colored bulbs. They go around and around, spinning so fast it creates the illusion that everything is normal. I see past it though—I see what's on the other side. I feel sorry for everyone else. They don't even know the world is going to end at sunset, the second I jump off the ride with Alec. It's all so clear to me now. Clearer than it's ever been.

—Don't you think so?—

I turn my head to the side, surprised that Alec isn't with me. He felt so close for a second that it confuses me. But then I remember where I am and what I'm doing.

I need to hurry.

Time is running out.

As I move swiftly through intersections newly clogged with strangers, I feel as though I'm coming out of a dream that has lasted my entire life. Once I'm with Alec—once his hand is touching mine—I will be wide-awake and waiting for heaven to welcome me.

———————

—Do you even know where you're going?— Kayliegh shouts. She keeps saying we're lost, but she's laughing about it. We're not really *that* lost. We just took a wrong turn or something. But we can't call our parents or anything. We told them we were going to a pool party. They have no idea we came to the city to go to the beach. Her parents would ground her for life—mine for twice that long.

I turn my head. We're both smiling nervously. *—We'll find it—* I promise her. *—The palm trees will guide us there.—* I point to the row of trees lining the sidewalk like open umbrellas. Their leaves are so shiny—they pull me along the sun-soaked streets. *—I trust them to take us the right way.—*

—Oh . . . great. I feel sooo much better now— Kayliegh says, rolling her eyes. But she trusts me and I can tell she's not as anxious.

She watches as I stop suddenly in the middle of the sidewalk. I spin around in a circle with my eyes closed and my arms out to my side. When I open my eyes again, the scenery changes. The streets evaporate and the city becomes weightless without its roads. Even the tallest buildings appear feathery. A strong wind could probably blow the entire city away. Some lucky person up in the hills would get to see it all—Los Angeles scattered to the wind like sparkling dust.

—*Sabrina?*— Kayliegh says. —*You're lost, aren't you?*—

There's a palm tree behind her and from my angle, it springs from her hair like a flower. The leaves are long and drape to the side. A purple haze surrounds them and it hurts my eyes. When I squint, it's like I can almost hear words hidden in the brightness. They are telling me to follow.

—*We're supposed to go that way*— I say, aiming my eyes at the tree that is now waving in the breeze. Without waiting for Kayliegh, I dart through a parking lot and run toward it.

Kayliegh's laughter gets tangled with her words as she shouts —*You're completely nuts! Wait for me.*—

She's falling farther behind. I reach out with my hand—stretching until my fingers slip into hers. I won't let her rest or slow us down. We have to keep going until our feet touch the wet sand where the waves end.

—*Hurry. Let's hurry*— I yell. My legs struggle to keep pace with my butterfly heartbeat. Ignoring traffic lights and horns and people moving in the other direction, I move right along—the one- and two-story buildings with their shop windows blur past. This is how it feels to fly. This is how it feels to leave the world behind when the hand I'm holding suddenly becomes an anchor—yanking me backward.

The muscles in my shoulder twist uncomfortably. The city grows heavy again in an instant—tugging at us with so much gravity, our wings get clipped.

I rub at the soreness in my arm as I turn around. —*Why did you stop?*— I ask, but Kayliegh is not there anymore.

A guy stands at arm's length from me. He has long brown hair and wears torn jeans, and I can still see the shape of my hand where

I held his. —*This girl's crazy, man!*— he grunts to his friend who is an exact copy of him with the same saltwater hair hanging loose on his shoulders. Same torn jeans. Their spines are curved the way apes' are when they try to stand taller. —*She just grabbed my hand and started mumbling. Smiling and whatever.*—

I look at my hand and look at his and sense that they were once connected. My eyes are huge in my head as I listen to them talk about me as if I'm not there.

—*Leave her, man. She's probably tabbed up, most likely.*—

—*Or a Jesus freak or something.*—

—*Nah, look at her . . . she's drugged.*—

They are transparent, yet I can't see through them as they walk away. Then they fade before my eyes. The sound of their voices scatters, getting lost in the crowded sidewalk. I tuck my hair behind my ears. It feels wet and smooth, but warm where the sun has touched it. Bringing my hand down to my mouth, I rub my lips. —*Kayliegh was never here*— I whisper in my birthmark's ear—moving my mouth but not making any sound.

I spy a girl staring at me. People move past her in both directions. She stands still—waiting. She's not really anybody—just my ghost reflected in a store window. A secret person sucking at her sleeve, which means I am too. She has black circles under her eyes dark as ink stains, pink skin around the edges and pale everywhere in between.

I touch my cheek to see if it's really me.

I feel her fingerprints on my skin and I'm not sure which is me and which is the imposter. I don't know where I am—trapped or free or somewhere in between.

Shadow cars zip past my reflection in the background. Clouds move in front of the sun like camera flashes. They all tangle together in my confusion and I have to concentrate to keep from being lost forever.

—The beach— I whisper. *—You're going to the beach to see Alec.—*

The blue pen markings around my birthmark change shape in response—an invisible smile from an invisible cat, letting me know I've figured out something important.

Kayliegh and I were going to the beach too. I just got mixed up. But all of that happened before and can't happen again. A thing only happens once and it won't happen any more. Dr. Richards says I can't control my episodes but she's wrong. I just have to pay more attention.

I break into a sprint—swinging my arms wildly. I don't care when I bump into people who stop to shout threats at me because it's all starting to look familiar. I've been past these shops before—the ice-cream stand with the large vanilla and chocolate swirl sculpture rising from its roof. Kayliegh and I went there. The guys behind the counter looked at our bathing suits wishing they had X-ray eyes and gave us cones for free.

I know where I am.

I don't stop there this time—I run right by. It's how I will keep the past from absorbing the present.

I can hear the waves over the noise in the air. The coastal highway is right in front of me—four lanes separating the city from sand. There's a swarm of people standing on the corner waiting for the light to change. I brush past them—rushing headlong into the screeching of brakes.

Faces stare at me through the windshields with identical expressions. Their mouths move rapidly, flashing angry teeth but I smile back. I push aside the sweaty strands of hair sticking to my forehead and walk between the cars like an angel as I step onto the beach.

There is a hot wind coming off the water, blowing in from a place much farther away than the other side of the horizon. The sky is brighter too. My feet sink into the sand and my steps become slower. Throwing my arms out like wings, I raise my head to the changing colors of the sky. When I turn around to face the city towering in the background, the glass windows sparkle and glow like so many wishing stones piled on top of one another.

—*I knew it was real. It's happening just as I knew it would*— I say, watching the world dissolve before my eyes.

NINETEEN

The sun has moved out over the waves. It sits behind the Ferris wheel like a spotlight too bright to stare at directly. The amusement park ride fades into flakes of white paint and metal rods that crisscross and divide the sunbeams into fractions. The colored cages blend together as they go round, making a rainbow ring around the sun.

I sit in its shadow, facing the ocean.

The boardwalk is covered in the scent of cotton candy billowing from the small snack stand a few feet away from me. The smell is so strong I can nearly see vapor trails of dissolved sugar spreading gently out over the pier. Here and there, pink clouds of candy sprout from the thin crowd of people like markers counting down the end of time.

Off to my right, there is a row of houses built right on the beach. If I squint, I can see future explosions hidden inside each of them— their tall windows holding back an intense orange light like transparent teeth trying to hold fire in a dragon's mouth.

The palm trees along the highway sway in the breeze that blows inland. Sand scatters in the wind's grasp as it grows stronger. The sand will soon become sudden tornadoes rising from the ground—the windows will burst and the trees will shed their leaves.

It's already starting. The future is rushing toward me. The shadows of another world are visible under the surface—moving around like fish under frozen water. Now that all of the medicine has left my body, there's nothing to blind me to it. Soon I will blink and all of this will be gone.

One little girl walks by me with a red balloon tied around her wrist. She's maybe six years old and the outline of her body against the sun's glare is heavy—drawn with a thick marker like my own. The two adults with her appear to be made of light pencil markings.

The girl smiles at me and waves her hand. She must see what's happening too and it doesn't frighten her. As she approaches, the balloon sags in the haze that has settled around us. She stares at my hand. —*I like your cat*— she says, pointing with a small finger that comes close enough to touch me by accident.

The sky bursts open—changes from a watery blue to a golden fog.

—*Annabelle! Leave that girl alone*— one of the ghosts shouts, and the little girl is yanked away. I hear a mumbled apology in the same thin voice but it is easily lost in the wave of sounds gathering like a flock of gulls.

—*It's okay, it won't be long. You'll see*— I whisper to the girl. The faces of those she is with flicker and flash. For a split second, I see the distorted skeletons of snakes under their skin. I'm thankful the girl will never grow up with their slithering lies. —*Don't worry*— I call out. —*I'll look for you after.*—

As they disappear, the sun grows larger than before, racing toward the horizon. In just a little while, it will fill the sky. That is when Alec will come.

I close my eyes and wait.

I imagine my skin has turned red and caught on fire. If I open my eyes too soon, the wind will turn my bones to dust, scattering them to the ground like burnt snow. I must stay perfectly still.

The muscles in my legs and arms ache. They twitch and beg me to move—sending searing pins and needles through my nerves. I shut out their cries and concentrate even harder until the pain is almost like breathing.

Shapes begin to form on the inside of my eyelids—coming clearer into focus as my pupils adjust each passing second. Out on the horizon, the ocean retreats. Tall grass grows up from the waves, long enough to swallow me if I were to walk barefoot into it. Houses emerge like sand castles from the ground. They are painted the same colors as the houses on the street where my parents live. One of them is supposed to be ours but it's turned at the wrong angle so that the front door faces the setting sun.

I can't see it from where I am, but I know there is a tire swing swaying from the tall oak tree in the backyard. I hear the unmistakable creaking as the rope twists. It's not the sound of someone swinging but of someone having swung, and I hold my breath.

His steps are deliberate as he approaches me, his hair lost in the sun. Every part of me wants to rush and meet him but I know if I move before he touches me, he will disappear. It's torture to be so still when I want to be so close.

—*Sabrina?*— he says each time his feet strike the ground but I don't answer. His voice rings inside my ears —*Sabrina, Sabrina*— louder each time until it dictates the drumming of my heartbeat.

His hand hesitates before touching mine. Time stops and I stop. After that, everything accelerates.

Alec is standing there when I open my eyes. The blazing sun burns the sky orange behind him. The Ferris wheel rotates like a slow propeller attached to his back. —*You came*— I say, smiling brightly.

He half-bends to meet me as I rise halfway and our bodies tangle together into one. There's a shuffling of shoes over the boardwalk as the crowd moves one way or the other—leaving us alone in the center.

———————

—*What are you doing here?*— Alec asks. My arms are draped around his neck and his fingers crawl through my hair, but his back is arched into the shape of a question mark and his confusion surprises me.

—*Waiting for you*— I say, pulling him closer and covering his mouth with mine. —*Just where we always said we'd meet.*—

He kisses me long and slow before pulling away.

—*How did you even get here?*—

—*How doesn't matter*— I say. —*It would be like telling you that I had a dream about you, and then only telling the parts you weren't in.*—

Alec wipes his forehead and blows a rush of air from his lungs. —*This is so weird*— he says. There is an excitement in his legs that makes him hop. —*I mean, that you're here! I was just thinking about you and then . . . man, this is so weird. It's like it's not even real.*—

—*It's real. I'm real.*— The sun on our skin is real. The ocean is real. The pier we're standing on isn't. The people aren't. But we are. —*We're together now.*—

—*Yeah . . . but what happened? Did something happen at the hospital?*— he asks.

—*I couldn't stay*— I tell him. —*I would have disappeared in there alone. I told my parents I wanted to go home, but it was a lie. I knew I was never going home.*— I'm talking very fast, tripping over my words in a way I haven't done in so long. It used to happen to me all of the time. Kayliegh's mom used to say I had a motor for a mouth. She said I talked so fast sometimes she couldn't understand me. It was only after things started to confuse me that I slowed down. That I'm speeding up again, I think is a good sign. Like maybe I'm finally getting better now. Everything finally makes sense to me.

Alec slides his hands down, resting them on my hipbones. His fingertips are cold and nervous in a cute way. He bends back, creating space between us as he stares at me with wild eyes. —*Why didn't you call? I don't get why you came here without telling me.*

—*Because this is how it's supposed to happen. All of the stuff we talked about . . . it all happens right here and I knew you'd come.*— My voice rushes out of me. My hands are quick too. I can't stop fidgeting with the collar of Alec's shirt. My fingers dig under the fabric and crawl over his shoulder blades like spiders. Here isn't like the hospital. I don't have to be careful or cautious. I can act on every impulse.

I start to pull his shirt up and push my chest against his. We are pressed so tightly together that I have to take smaller breaths when I kiss him. First on his cheek and then under his chin once before sealing my lips over his and pushing my words into his mouth with my tongue because it's easier than talking—passing pictures from my eyes to his like telepathy.

Images of us naked in the grass flash across his eyes and I reach down to unbutton his jeans. —*Hey . . . wait a minute. Hold on, not here*— he says with a smile stolen directly from the sunlight. His hands cover mine and they are now warm and excited.

—*I missed you*— I whisper with my mouth faintly touching the smooth skin above his upper lip.

—*Obviously*— he says with a slight laugh. —*I missed you too. It's hard to believe it was only yesterday we woke up together.*—

—*Yesterday?*— The word hangs above me like the shock of thunder.

—*Feels like a lot longer, right?*— Alec says, and I nod in agreement. One hand falls to his side and the other stays clasped onto mine as he leads me away to the edge of the pier where we can look over the railing and see the waves crashing on the sand. Even as they roar and crest, I can see they are drying up. I can feel the city dissolving. And when I turn my head to peek, the tallest trees atop the hills are like a thousand paintbrushes driven by the wind to make colorful streaks across the sky.

I open my mouth to tell Alec about all of it, but I can already see it reflected in his eyes. I know he sees what I see so I stay quiet. I let him speak, listening to the clear sound of his voice floating over the noise. —*You know that they wouldn't let me talk to you? They kept saying it wasn't good for you to see me. Like just talking to me would harm you or something. As if they even know anything about you—* he says, staring out over the ocean where the sun pulses with the beating of my heart. —*I freaked out so bad on them about that. They tried to get me resentenced to a security ward, but my dad took care of it. He got all self-righteous like always, ranting and raving about how he was going to get their funding cut. He's such an egomaniac, but whatever. It's better we're out of there. That place sucks.—*

—*They recorded everything I said. I didn't know it but they did.—* I start rubbing my hand over my mouth until Alec steadies me. He says it isn't right that they didn't tell me but that it's okay now. —*If I stayed another day, I don't think I'd know who I was anymore.—*

—*I know what you mean. That place can really mess with your head.—*

—*They replace us . . . with copies of ourselves—* I say.

Alec stares at me when I say this. It's the same look my dad sometimes gives when I try to tell him about shadows under the surface of the sky. It makes me nervous to see that expression on Alec, like maybe he doesn't understand. Or worse, maybe he's been replaced already. But my worry melts away the second he smiles, moving his thumb back and forth to pet the ink stain on my skin.

—I still can't believe you're here! How great is this?— He is excited all over again and lifts me up with his skinny arms encircling my ribs, spinning me around once before setting me down. *—But they're looking for you. You know that, right?—*

—They won't find us.—

—They did call my house though— he warns me. *—They gave me the interrogation from hell, asking all about where you were or where I thought you might go. I didn't tell them anything, of course. I said I had no idea where you'd go. I mean, I was sort of hoping that you'd come here to see me, but I didn't know. I doubt they believed me. Someone's going to come by and check sooner or later. We can count on that.—*

—It's okay— I say. *—They'll never get here in time. We'll already be gone.—*

TWENTY

—*Is this really what you guys do all day?*— Kayliegh asks an hour after we get to Robbie's house. She and I have spent the entire time sitting on the sofa watching Robbie and Thomas play a video game. It hasn't exactly been entertaining and for sure not what Kayliegh had in mind when we hiked over here from her house.

—*Most of the time, yeah*— Robbie says as his thumbs make a million spastic movements on the controller.

—*By 'most of the time,' Rob means when he's not jerking off*— Thomas says, elbowing Robbie in the side. Robbie pushes him away, but Thomas laughs it off. —*What? You know you're the champ at it. At least, I hope you're better at it than you are at this game.*—

—*Shut up*— Robbie grunts, and I feel bad for him. I've put up with enough of Thomas's gross remarks on the bus over the years that I know exactly how he feels. I wish he would look at me so I could smile or roll my eyes at Thomas—do anything to let him know not to be embarrassed.

Thomas is the one who looks at me though. Robbie keeps his eyes glued to the screen as his character walks through a field of tall grass and decaying houses. —*Brina? Did you know you're Rob's first choice of wanking material?*— Thomas asks, making an obscene gesture with his hand.

—Eww. Stop being so immature— Kayliegh says.

—Make me.—

Kayliegh makes like she's going to punch him and Thomas grabs her wrist. He pulls her down from the sofa, onto the floor, and rolls over on top of her. They are both laughing now and wrestling like little kids before they sneak out into the other room. Honestly, I have no idea what she sees in him. Aside from being a pin-up kind of cute, he's one of the most obnoxious boys I know.

I slide over the cushions, closer to Robbie. *—Want to see something cool?—* he asks.

—Yeah, okay.—

I watch as the game character runs through a world that seems as large as our own. There are lakes, hills, and the remains of what were once roads and buildings. He has to run through them all at the same speed we would if it were real. The light in the sky changes as day turns to night, the longer he goes. It reminds me of the little worlds I make up for myself after school. Maybe we have more in common than I thought.

In the game, Robbie's character is being chased—hunted by mutant creatures who he never sees until they are right on top of him. He uses any number of weapons to slaughter them one at a time. I watch their heads being blown apart in gory detail. It makes my stomach sick. Perhaps we are as different as I always suspected.

—I don't want to see any more of this— I say.

—Sorry for all the gut splattering— he says. *—But, I got to kill these guys to get to what I want to show you.—*

—How long is this going to take?— I ask, falling back on the sofa so I don't have to see exploding brains or bloodthirsty cannibals. *—This is going to give me nightmares.—*

—I'm almost there— he assures me. *—I just have to stop in this store here and pick up a scuba tank.—* His character enters a store and

approaches another character. They have an entire dialogue about what he wants to purchase and for how much.

—*You buy things?*— I ask.

—*Yeah. And eat. And sleep. You can even get married*— he says. —*It's the most realistic game out there.*—

—*And you play it a lot?*—

Robbie gives me a guilty look when he says —*Hours every day.*—

I'm jealous when he says that. I wish I could make my dreams last for hours a day but they always seem to fade in and out. It doesn't seem fair somehow.

—*Okay, this is it.*— The part he wants to show me takes place underwater. His character dives below the surface of a virtual lake, swimming to the deepest part of the murky water and into a tunnel. —*This takes me to a secret place that's not even in the game map. I had to find out about it online*— Robbie explains.

He surfaces in a cave filled with glittering light. Silver flowers glow on the ground and music comes from their petals instead of scents. Robbie works the controller to spin slowly around, showing me the whole scene before coming around again to face a female character with illuminated fairy wings. I can tell she is naked but the light is so strong that none of her features are visible.

—*Cool, right?*—

—*Yes, definitely.*— I think about all the fairy coves I'd built as a child and how I used to sneak out at night to look at them. Just once, I wanted to see something like the image on the screen.

—*If I kiss her? She grants me full life energy*— Robbie says. —*She's like a guardian angel.*— I can see he's wondering what would happen if he kisses me—if I'm an angel too.

He's had a crush on me for years and I've always felt bad for not liking him back. He's always so nice about it—always nice to me, even when his friends give him a hard time. It's not my fault who I like. I've always tried to be friendly, careful not to lead him on. But when I hear him talk about angels and kisses of eternal life, it's like I'm seeing him for the first time—seeing that maybe our souls know each other better than we think.

—*Do you believe in that kind of stuff?*— I ask him. —*Like angels and fairies and everything?*—

Robbie shrugs. —*I don't know. I don't really think about it. I mean it's cool in the game and all. But for real? Nah, probably not.*—

The spark of love in my heart burns out as quickly as it flared up.

—*Oh*— I sigh.

I think he can tell right away that he's said the wrong thing. Before he has a chance to make up for it, Kayliegh and Thomas come back. Thomas takes over the room the way he always does. —*So? Did you ask her to the dance yet?*— he says, and Robbie's cheeks turn bright red. —*Guess that's a no.*—

Robbie stumbles to find something to say, but I let him off the hook. —*I'll go to the freshman dance with you*— I say without making him ask because I just can't stand the way Thomas acts as if he's so much better than anyone else. And who knows, maybe at the dance Robbie and I will kiss and in that moment maybe he will come to believe in all of the things I do. Sure, it's not likely—but I'm still allowed to believe in fairy-tale romances, love at first kiss, happily ever afters, and all that sort of stuff if I want to. If I keep believing, one of these days it might even come true.

My shoes sit beside me, full of sand. My socks are pushed up inside them leaving my feet bare. I bury my toes in the sand as the air turns cool and the tide moves in. Above our heads, electric light trickles down like liquid from the thin spaces between the boards of the pier. Alec and I are safe in the shadows.

The beach is nearly empty. The earlier crowds have evaporated as the sun sinks toward the water. Alec's head is resting in my lap. He's facing the ocean, waiting like me. —*I always hoped I'd meet someone like you. Like somebody who really gets me, you know*— he says. —*Before I saw you that day in the common room, I was beginning to wonder if a girl like you even existed.*—

—*I always knew I'd meet you . . . someday*— I say. —*I'm just glad it wasn't only in my dream.*— I watch a fleet of oil tankers traveling a straight line on the horizon. In just a little while, they will melt in the sun.

Somewhere in the back of my mind, I worry about spies. I worry about being watched and recorded by the crowds walking above our heads. I worry about the static eating away at the city like a swarm of insects that feeds off of concrete and metal. I worry about the noise becoming a weapon that destroys me. I worry that maybe everything I'm thinking and feeling is only taking place inside a computer while the body that used to be mine is back in Burbank becoming best friends with Skylar Atkins and sending text messages to broadcast all of the boring thoughts I have.

I worry about so many things it hardly feels like there's room enough to keep them all in. But somehow with Alec next to me, I'm able to manage.

—*Your doctor talked to me before I left, did they tell you that?*—

—*Dr. Richards? No, they didn't. Why? What did she say?*— I ask even though I doubt it matters much. Whatever it was she told him was probably a lie.

—*She said I was bad for you.*— He laughs. —*She said that I didn't understand how serious your condition was. That I encouraged you.*

214

Actually, I think the way she put it was that I fed you delusions, what-
ever that means.—

—No. That isn't true. You just . . . you believe me, that's all.—

—I know, that's what I told her— he says. *—I told her I was the*
only one helping you and what they were doing was wrong. You should
have seen her face! God, now I know why you hated her so much.—

—She can't understand— I say. *—She's not like us. She's not real.—*

—Well, real or not, she wants to get you away from me as bad as
anything— Alec says. *—But whatever. It's like you said, we'll be gone.*
Let them look for us all they want.—

Under the waves there is a tunnel. I can't see it yet, but I know it's
there. It shimmers under the surface. In the sky there are scribbled
stick figures of rabbits and spears and twisted tree branches. They are
hollering at the static storm behind me. The storm will battle them
with lightning but we'll escape long before that ever happens.

—No one will ever find us.—

_____

I'm staring out at the water when I feel Alec shift around. I don't know
how long we've been here waiting. I feel time slipping out of focus. I
know that means it's almost time for the world to end.

Alec has his head resting on my knee and his face is turned toward
mine now. *—You want to get out of here soon? Or stay for a while*
longer?—

The sky behind me lights up with a flash of white light that dupli-
cates the sun. It splits my head with a pain that makes me squint. This
is how the storm screams. Louder and closer than before.

I look at Alec, wondering why he would ever suggest leaving
when he knows we have to wait right here in this very spot. *—Go?—*
The word feels heavy in my mouth, sticking to my tongue like paste.

—Yeah, why not?— he says. *—We can't really go back to my house. I'm sure there'll be someone waiting for us, either looking for you or looking for me. But we could go to this fish taco place up on Pico. It's pretty good. I know this guy who works there and I'm sure we could eat for free, or cheap anyway.—*

—No.—

There's a swelling pain behind my eyes that blurs my vision. I try to squint it away. Shaking my head, I mumble *—no—* several times before Alec pays attention.

—That's cool. Forget tacos then. Are you hungry? We can get something else. We're in the city of endless possibilities after all.— He starts to mention other places to eat—places that have no part in our dream.

—Why are you saying these things?—

—I figure you haven't eaten all day, that's all— he says.

—I don't need food.—

—Okay. It was just an idea. We don't have to get something to eat— he says. *—We could do something else.—*

—We can't leave! We're supposed to be watching the sky.— My voice comes out rushed and frightened. I'm shouting at him even though I'm not trying to and don't want to. It's just happening. *—We have to stay right here! It's going to change soon and we have to be here for it! You know that!—*

Alec pushes himself up. I'm shivering now. He thinks it's because I'm cold and wraps both arms around me. I can feel his heart beating nervously against my shoulder blades. When I glance at him, I see that he's looking at me strange—like he's afraid. And I wonder why he's scared when I've told him how perfect it is going to be for us in our heaven.

I start to shake more violently and Alec rubs his hand up and down along my spine. —*Hey, it's okay*— he says softly. —*If that's what you want to do, we can stay here.*—

I take a deep breath. I start to count the seconds in my head until I stop shaking and then I nod. —*It's not going to take long*— I tell him. —*We just have to wait a little longer.*—

—*Sure . . . whatever. We can wait all night if you want*— he tells me, but he doesn't sound like his usual self when he says it.

I keep count in my head, trying to make time speed up. I squint at the sun, hoping to make it sink faster but it doesn't budge. Nothing is working anymore. Nothing is going the way I pictured. And then, when the noise beeps so near me that I feel it vibrate, I can't hold it back anymore and I scream.

—*It's okay. It's okay*— Alec says, digging in the pocket of his jeans. —*It's just my phone.*—

I watch as he stares at the screen—my heart ticking toward an explosion. I think of Thomas on the lawn behind the school. I wonder if Alec is going to film me—if he's here only to capture heaven the second it appears and erase all of the magic from it. But . . . no—Alec isn't Thomas. I have to remember these things. I squeeze the stone in my pocket until it hurts because the pain will help me to remember.

—*It's my dad*— Alec groans. —*I let it go to message. He's probably just freaking out, but what else is new. He went far out on a limb to get me that home-care deal. If they find out I left, they'll send me to juvy for sure. I imagine he had a coronary when he got home and saw that I wasn't there.*—

He's holding the phone in his palm as if it's always been there—as if it belongs. When he looks up at me, he notices I'm staring at it. —*You . . . didn't have one of those before*— I say accusingly. —*Where did you get that? Did somebody give it to you? Why do you have it? What are you going to do with it?*—

—It's just a phone, Sabrina— he says, making it sound harmless. *—It's not a gun . . . I'm not going to do anything with it.—*

—But you never said you had one— I say.

—This is L.A. . . . everyone has one— he says. *—I didn't have it at the hospital because we weren't allowed. You want to tell me what's going on? You're acting weird . . . did I do something?—*

He stands up and brushes the sand from his jeans. He turns his pockets inside out—shakes the last of the sand from his hair. As it rains to the ground, the lights on the pier catch Alec's hair and his hair is visible. It doesn't look bleached. It looks dark and there are dark shadows around his eyes. His tongue moves funny in his mouth like Thomas's tongue on my neck.

I scoot away a few feet in fear.

There is a whisper coming off the waves.

It says *—Alec is bad.—*

He wants me to get up and walk around. He tries to take my hand, but I shove them both deeper in my pockets. *—You're freezing—* he says. *—Let's get warm, okay? Come on, before the tide washes us away.—* He shuffles his feet in place, pretending to run. *—Up, soldier. Let's march.—*

—Who are you? Where is Alec?—

—What are you talking about?— He laughs again, but nervously like I've figured something out. Then his expression changes and I think I see him. I think I see my Alec as he leans closer. *—Sabrina, is something wrong? Just tell me what it is.—*

The last rays of the sunset crawl over the waves and shine on his face. In that one fragment of an instant, I swear that I see it—the small spark of static crackling in the center of his eyes.

—You're . . . you're not him, are you?— I crawl backward over the sand as he tries to get closer. He looks like Alec and sounds like him,

but it's not Alec. They let this Alec out of the hospital to trap me. This Alec is bad, that is what the waves are telling me, shouting it actually. —*Stay away from me*— I warn him.

—*What? You're kidding, right? This is a joke?*— He reaches toward me and wraps his fingers around my wrist. When he pulls my hand from my pocket, my palm is bleeding from where I've been squeezing the stone too tight. —*Jesus! What happened? Are you all right?*—

—*Stay away. I don't know who you are, but I want you to stay away.*—

—*Okay . . . just calm down.*—

—*No! I won't . . . not until you go*— I yell. —*I want Alec back. I want him now.*—

He stares at me with vacant eyes—eyes that look as if they could never have understood anything I told them. —*Sabrina . . . I think . . . maybe I need to call someone*— he says. —*It's going to be okay. I'm just . . . I'm going to call my dad, alright?*—

He takes out his phone again and I wait for the right moment.

As soon as he starts to dial, I lunge for it. My hands seize the phone and take it away from him. Before he can stop me, I throw it as far as I can into the water—then I run.

—*Sabrina! Stop! Let me help you*— Alec shouts as he chases me over the sand. The sun has gone under the water, but there is no hole in the center of the ocean. There is no safe place for me to watch the world end.

—*This isn't how it's supposed to happen*— I say, sucking on the sleeve of my shirt and searching desperately for stones that resemble fallen stars. There is only a screaming that soars through the landscape as the world spins out of control. —*It's not supposed to be like this!*—

He catches up with me. His arms trap my waist and we both fall in the sand. —*What's wrong? Just tell me.*—

—*Everything is wrong*— I scream at him. —*Everything we talked about.*—

—*What do you mean? This is exactly what we talked about . . . we're free. We can go anywhere, do anything. That was the whole point. It's everything we said we wanted.*—

I hear voices in the sky—they are laughing.

—*This isn't what we talked about at all!*—

Alec tries to kiss me but I turn away. —*Hey . . . it's okay*— he says calmly, but I cover my ears.

I feel myself breaking into a million pieces as I begin to cry.

—*I did everything I was supposed to*— I tell him. —*I stopped taking the medicine. I found you. I came here just like we planned. And you said you believed me. You said you saw it too. Why did you lie to me?*—

—*I didn't lie to you*— he swears, trying to smooth my hair from my face but I keep turning away from his touch. —*I meant everything I said. But I meant it in an idea sort of way, you know? Like a way to think about things. That's what you meant too, isn't it?*—

—*No*— I whisper. —*It's not what I meant at all.*—

There is a breeze rushing offshore—as warm as a thousand suns.

The sky is changing colors as fast as blinking lights and I know it is time. I also know he isn't coming with me. If I go, I'll be alone and I don't know what to do. Even the pen markings on my wrist begin to fade—only the grin remains of what once looked like a cat.

It occurs to me that I could stay.

I could let myself fall asleep and be like everybody else. All I'd need to do is let the static come inside. It would be as easy as anything. Maybe I'd even be happy. But I could never do that—somewhere deep inside I would know my life wasn't real.

I see the static gather in the sky. The birds are killed. They fall from the air as the sun is blocked out and slowly dissolves the way metal crumbles into rust.

I squirm out from under Alec. He stumbles to stand as I walk toward the waves. I unzip my sweatshirt and slip my arms from the sleeves, letting it fall to the sand. Alec stoops down to grab it, drapes it over his arm, and then hurries to close the gap between us. He stops again to collect the blue jeans that fall from my waist as easily as water. I hear him shouting my name but it's barely distinguishable from the rising noise.

He doesn't stop for my shirt.

My feet reach the edge of the waves and he runs.

—*Sabrina, what are you doing? You're freaking me out.*— I hear how fragile his words are and how desperate he is to keep me here. —*Will you stop, please?! You're acting crazy!*—

—*I'm not crazy*— I tell myself, slipping off the last of my clothing.

The water on my bare skin is cold and numbing but the tears on my face burn like fire. I let them stay though. I don't wipe them away because this is part of what's supposed to happen now. In a few moments, the sun will open up beneath my feet and I will slide away forever.

The first wave crashes over my head.

The tide pulls the sand out from under my feet.

I'm aware of the water in my lungs. My belly swells with an ocean of its own inside—pregnant with fish to keep me company. All around me is the comforting hum of the water and the noise from the sky goes quiet. In the watery light from the surface above, I see tiny air bubbles float off of me like countless twinkling stars and I surrender to the scenery.

Before my eyes, the murky water is swallowed by a brilliant light.

My heart glows.

There is a halo shining over my entire body and it keeps me warm. I breathe out water and breathe in air from heaven.

As if out of a dream, I see him dive toward me—his eyes glowing green through the water. The skinny muscles in his arms are the fins of a fish swimming to join me. He wraps his arms around me and I close my eyes.

Together we pass through the center of the sun.

TWENTY-ONE

Air chokes my lungs when I open my eyes.

My nostrils burn with the sterile scent of antiseptic bleach.

Sand crawls over every crevice of my body like fire insects.

I blink until the room comes into focus. There are machines beside the bed I'm strapped into. I can feel the tube in my vein and the dull pressure of liquid dripping into my bloodstream. There are all kinds of wires attached to my chest. I can't see them—a blanket is pulled over my body. I know that I'm naked under it. My brain tells me I should be freaking out, but for some reason I'm strangely calm.

I'm not in heaven.

There are no doctors in heaven and there is a swarm of doctors hovering around me. One of them pulls back my eyelids with icy fingers. She shines a bright light into my pupils—an intense white beam of light that makes me blind until she takes it away.

—*Did she take anything? Any drugs?*—

—*No.*—

I follow the sound of that voice. It's Alec. He's standing in the corner of the hospital room with a blanket around his shoulders like a superhero cape. His lips are pale blue. Water drips from his hair, which appears dark and brown when it's drenched—flat against his forehead. His clothes stick to his body. The shape of his rib cage shows through his T-shirt when he shivers.

—*You were with her before you pulled her ashore?*— the doctor asks, and Alec nods. —*And you're certain she didn't take anything? Tell me if she did. She won't get into trouble; I just need to know.*—

—*She didn't, I swear.*—

—*Any medications that you know of?*—

Alec's eyes meet mine and he hesitates. —*She's supposed to take something*— he says nervously —*but she hasn't been taking it.*—

A nurse enters the room and hands a clipboard to the doctor. —*We just spoke with the doctor who was treating her. Here's a list of her prescriptions.*—

The doctor looks over the list and raises her eyes up to Alec. —*She hasn't been taking any of these? Are you sure? For how long?*—

Alec shrugs. —*Awhile . . . I think.*—

The doctor shakes her head. —*No wonder*— she sighs, turning to the nurse. —*Okay, let's get these scripts filled. Let's get her on these as soon as possible.*—

There is a flurry of activity among the emergency room staff. The nurses adjust monitors, the doctor checks my eyes again and listens to my heart, and then they leave one by one. Alec stops the last nurse on the way out. —*Can I talk to her?*— he asks.

—*You can try*— she says, pulling back a curtain and disappearing behind it.

Alec glides over to my side. I can't see his feet. He could be flying, but I know that he isn't. This time is different from the last. This time I know that heaven is dead.

—*Hey there*— he says, sniffing the chill back inside of him. —*They said you're going to be okay.*— He takes my hand and holds it against his cheek, kissing my palm. There is a warmth in his blue lips that tingles like electricity.

—It wasn't real . . . was it?— I whisper, and he lowers his eyes. It's all the answer I need and my eyes tear up. *—When I was there . . . underwater . . . I almost thought I could see it, you know? It felt really close, but it wasn't. I knew . . . even as I wished so hard for it, I knew it wasn't going to come like I thought it would. And then . . . I saw you and I thought maybe . . .—*

Alec presses his lips to my face. There is a trace of my tears on his mouth when he pulls away. *—Sabrina, I was wrong—* he says. *—About the medicine . . . about everything. I didn't mean for any of this to happen.—*

—You never saw it, did you? Not for real?— I ask. *—You never saw heaven the way I did.—*

—No, I guess I didn't . . .—

—Does that mean that all of my dreams are wrong . . . that we don't belong together?— I stare at my hands as they fumble with the blanket's edge. I only force myself to look at him after to see if he's as broken as me.

Alec wipes at his eyes, pushing the hair out of his face. *—I think it means we belong together more than ever. You'll always have me, I promise.—*

We both go quiet and the only noise in the room is the beeping of the machines plugged into me. There is no static. There are no noises screaming in the air. There is only us.

—They are going to change me, aren't they?— I ask him.

Alec shakes his head. *—No . . . I think they are just going to help you. But they can't ever change you. No matter what they do . . . you'll always be perfect to me. Remember that, okay?—*

He leans over my bed and kisses me softly—his bottom lip against my upper one. There is a sound of footsteps coming in our direction and he backs away, still holding my hand. When my parents rush in, he gently lets my fingers fall to the bed and steps aside for them.

225

I look them both in the eyes—my mom and my dad. They are both clear and free of static and they have been crying. It hurts knowing that it's my fault and I tell them —*I'm sorry*— but it only makes them cry all over again.

I can't look at them anymore, and close my eyes.

———————

—*That's you*— I say, giggling as I point to a picture in my science book of a gorilla sitting in the jungle. My dad laughs too, curling one hand under his armpit and scratching the top of his head with the other as he makes grunting noises. —*That's you too!*—

My dad looks at the next picture. It shows a whale with mist shooting from its blowhole and he frowns. —*I may have put on a few pounds, but I would hardly consider myself a whale.*— He's only pretending to be offended though and I crack up even harder.

I turn to the next page.

There is a hummingbird pooping as it hovers.

Before I can put my finger on the photo, my dad beats me to it. —*That's you!*—

—*Gross! That's not me*— I shriek. A few specks of spit fly from my teeth when I laugh and hit the page. —*That's you!*— I tease, folding my arms on the kitchen table and resting my head down because I'm laughing so hard I can't breathe.

My mom is over by the sink preparing dinner. She rolls her eyes, but there is a smile on her face. —*Nice to see you're acting your age*— she says.

—*I'm only twelve, I'm still allowed to act silly for another year*— I say, sticking my tongue out at her. —*What about Dad? He's like a hundred.*—

—*That's who I was talking to*— my mom says.

—Busted!—

—Wait, no fair— my dad complains. *—I'm not nearly a hundred.—*

All three of us are laughing then.

I turn the page. My dad and I both spot the picture of a hornet. We touch it and point at my mom. *—That's you!—* we shout.

—Yeah, you got me— she says, acting completely uninterested. *—And if you've had your fun, it's time to take your schoolwork up-stairs and set the table.—*

I groan as I get up and stack my books into my backpack. I stomp away, but they both know I'm only faking. I'm not really mad or anything. In fact, I'm pretty certain I have the best parents in the world— even if they won't buy me everything my friends have.

As I go up the stairs to my room, I think about the boy at my school who lost his parents in a car accident last year. I don't know him or anything. He's a grade below me. But every time I see him in the hall, part of me wants to go up and give him a hug. I never want to lose my parents—I'd miss them too much.

———————————

As we're sitting in the hospital room, I'm remembering how things used to be with us as a family. There wasn't always tension between us. Things used to be good. I want it to be that way again. So when my mom tries to hold my hand, I don't pull it away like I did yesterday.

—We're so glad you're okay. We were so scared— she tells me.

Alec isn't in the room any longer. He left once my parents came. Nobody said he had to, but my dad glared at him and I thought for a minute he would kill Alec with his eyes. *—Don't hate him, please—* I say.

—Who, honey?— my mom asks.

—Alec— I say. *—I know you don't like him, but I do. And he likes me. He did save my life.—*

227

My dad grimaces. —*That's what they told us*— he says. —*I can't say that makes up for putting you in this position in the first place.*—

My mom is about to argue with him—about to beg him not to start this here. I don't want to see them fight. Not about me. Not again.

—*He didn't. I did*— I say. —*I made myself worse. I stopped taking the medicine because . . . I thought if I didn't, then I wouldn't be special anymore. I thought they were going to make me into someone boring and terrible.*—

I see my dad's heart break inside of him—I hear it in his voice. —*Oh, Sabrina . . . no, sweetie. Why didn't you tell us? If you didn't like it there, we could've found you someplace better.*—

—*I couldn't . . . I was too scared*— I say. My words almost get lost in the ache in my throat. —*But now, I'm more scared not to tell. I don't want to be like this anymore. It's too hard . . . when all of the things I believe stop being true . . . it just hurts too much.*—

My mom puts her hand on my forehead and runs her fingers through my hair before her palm comes to rest on the back of my neck. Then she pulls my face to her shoulder where I can cry as loud as I want and not have to worry about it. She taps me so lightly, making the kind of soothing sounds only a mother can make to her child. My dad has one arm around me and one around her. His strength is enough to hold us both and we are enough to hold him up too.

—*It's going to be okay*— he says, and I think for the first time, we all believe in the possibility of that phrase.

EPILOGUE

—How are you feeling today, Sabrina?—

I see Dr. Richards's reflection in the window. She strides over to the chair and sits down, but I don't go over to her right away. I want to look out at the trees just a little longer.

It's beautiful the way the leaves dance in the breeze. There's a blue jay sitting on one of the high branches. When it spots me staring out, it takes off—soaring over the building, the sunlight catches its wings. I'm somewhat relieved and sort of sad to see the bird remain the same color all through his flight.

—Everything okay?—

I turn away from the windows and smile at her.

—Everything's perfect— I say.

My stay at the Wellness Center has been different this time around. I know myself better.

It was my decision to come back. My parents were willing to send me anywhere I wanted or even have me stay home if I chose to. But I wanted to come back. I knew Dr. Richards was right the first time. I had been getting better before I stopped taking my medicine. I wanted to try again, and this time finish what I'd started.

When I sit down across from her, I notice that she doesn't have her notebook with her. We are only here to say good-bye.

—It's hard to believe that it's been four weeks— I say. Scenes from both of my stays here flash through my memory. The cafeteria and the common room with their brightly painted walls, group sessions and art class. The nurses who were always nice to me even when I got frustrated with them. I made some friends this time too—friends who get me. Like Amanda. There's so much more to her than I saw before. As much as I miss my friendship with Kayliegh, it's somehow easier talking to other kids with the same kinds of problems as me.

—You must be excited to finally be going home— Dr. Richards says.

—I am— I tell her. *—But this kind of feels like home too. I've been here so long.—* I laugh as I say it, but it's a nervous laugh. As always, she reads me like a book.

—It's normal to be a little scared.—

—I know— I sigh.

The warm glow from the afternoon sun is slowly taken over by the light from the fluorescent lamps in the ceiling above us. I know my parents will be here soon, if they aren't already filling out paperwork for my release. One of the nurses will be by any second to bring me to my room so I can collect any last things I may have forgotten to pack. But before any of that can happen, there is something I still need to ask.

I bring my sleeve up to my mouth out of habit. I leave it, but keep from putting my mouth on the fabric because it's a habit I'm trying to stop. *—Dr. Richards? Am I going to end up back here? Or some other place like it?—* I ask. I already know I'll never be cured. We've discussed it together every week. Not just in my sessions with Dr. Richards, but with Dr. Gysion as well. They both say the most important thing for me to keep in mind is that schizophrenia can't be cured—only treated.

—I'm not going to lie to you, Sabrina. There's a chance, yes— Dr. Richards says. Even though it's not the answer I want to hear, I'm

glad she's being honest. I would've been able to tell if she weren't. —*If you stop taking your meds again . . . or if your symptoms return and you decide to ignore them . . . then it's possible you'll end up right back where you started.*—

I take a deep breath and let it out slowly, feeling deflated. —*I don't want that.*—

—*Don't get discouraged*— Dr. Richards says, forcing a smile. —*I think you've learned to recognize what's happening, when it's happening.*—

—*And what if I don't notice it happening?*—

—*I think you'll do just fine*— she says. —*Besides, you're not alone in this, you have support.*—

My parents came to visit me last week. They were looking at some paintings I made and instead of simply saying *that's nice* like they used to, they were genuinely interested. They asked me how I made them and what I was thinking about when I did. But not in a bad way. Not like they're afraid of my answers. They weren't checking up on me. It gave me hope that we might become close like we used to be once upon a time.

—*You know . . . I think you're right*— I say. —*I think I am going to be fine.*—

There is always going to be a little voice in my head telling me that the static is still out there. I can't ever shut it off. All I can do is turn the volume way down. Most of the time, it'll be on mute. But once it starts to creep louder, I know I'll need to speak up.

Walking through the halls, I'm feeling anxious. I run my fingers along the smooth surface of the wall as I round the corner. My heart skips a beat, anticipating seeing my parents waiting outside my room, but the hallway is empty except for a nurse on the far end. My parents must not be here yet.

My pink bag leans against the side of the bed. It's not my bed anymore. I won't sleep in it again. It's already made up with new sheets, tucked tightly for the next person who will stay here—some other girl like me, as afraid as I was the first night I slept here. The memory of that night comes flooding back to me and I unclip the koala bear key chain from my bag. I slip it carefully under the pillow. Hopefully it can bring some secret comfort to the next guest.

When I turn around, my dad is standing behind me. He's smiling as he reaches out to place one hand on my shoulder. With his other hand, he fixes the corner of the pillow so that I know he saw me leave the tiny gift behind. Then we share a smile and it feels like before when we used to build fairy coves together. —*Ready to go home, Breen Bean?*— he asks.

I wrap my arms around him and bury my face against his chest. —*You bet*— I say. I still don't know what will happen with school, whether I'll transfer to another school or sit out the rest of this year. I don't know which of my friends are still my friends or if any of them are even friends I want any longer. Home is a place of questions for me now. Even so, a big part of me can't wait to get back.

—*Come on*— he says, putting his arm around me. —*Your mother's signing the last of the papers, let's go meet her.*—

The wheels squeak as I pull my bag through the hall to the hospital entrance. They get louder as I speed up around the last turn and see my mom waiting. She looks different than she has in a long time—she looks happy. She greets me with a hug before saying —*I think there's someone else who wants to say hello.*—

I think she means Nurse Abrams so I tell her —*I think you mean good-bye.*—

My mom shakes her head and laughs. I follow with my eyes as she turns her head. Alec steps out from around the corner, his eyes glowing as he grins. I'm so surprised to see him that the shock shows on my face. —*You act like you didn't expect to see me*— he teases, walking toward me. For a moment, we lose ourselves and become the only two people in the world. Not caring about anything or anyone, I fall into his arms and kiss him under the glare of the lobby lights.

—*I've missed you so much*— I whisper as he runs his hand through my hair. We've spoken on the phone, but I haven't seen him since I came back. Holding him now is like a dream only better because he's real.

—*It was your parents' idea*— he says with a smirk. —*I think I'm growing on them.*—

My dad rolls his eyes, but he's smiling. Maybe Alec really has grown on them. Maybe they've gotten to know him a little. Like me, Alec sees the world differently after what happened. He's seeing a doctor too. He doesn't belong in a place like the Wellness Center but he admits that maybe he's got some problems to work out.

—*Shall we hit the road?*— my mom asks, and I nod. On the way to the parking lot, she turns to my dad. —*Who's going to drive?*—

—*I'll drive*— Alec says.

—*That's not going to happen*— my dad says, and we laugh.

—*Can you believe they gave me a license?*— Alec says to me. —*The court says I'm too dangerous for public school but not for the highway.*— Even my dad laughs at this. It's nice to see his sense of humor has returned.

Moments later, we're in the car, racing down the highway. The air rushing through the car window is warm. The sun is hot enough to heat my skin. I hold my hand out of the window, letting it dance as the traffic speeds by in the other direction. I have a feeling in my heart like everything is perfect, but I'm trying to take things one day at a time like Dr. Richards told me. Today is perfect and that's something to remember. I can deal with tomorrow when it comes.

Alec's hand is resting on the seat next to me and I hold it in mine. I close my fingers around his and squeeze. I watch the sky as we drive. It doesn't change colors, but it's just as beautiful as ever.

ACKNOWLEDGMENTS

I'd like to thank the following people for their support during the writing of this novel. My amazing wife, for always being my first reader and biggest fan. My mother, for her valuable input. My wonderful editors, Kate and Jean, for their insightful thoughts and guidance. Everybody at Feiwel and Friends who cares so much about the books they publish. I'd also like to thank my fellow writers, Andrew Smith, Lewis Buzbee, Julie Halpern, Yvonne Prinz, and Damien Toman, for their conversation that keeps me inspired. Special thanks to Rossi, and especially Boo, for generously allowing me to borrow Fred; I hope you'll find he's in good hands. Thanks to the girl in Hannaford, lost in her own world, who momentarily left it in order to inspire me with a smile, and to the hitchhiker I picked up two winters ago, for being open with me about his own schizophrenia. Lastly, I'd like to thank Zoë, whose fairies ended up making it into a book after all.

Thank you for reading this FEIWEL AND FRIENDS book.
The Friends who made

life is but a dream

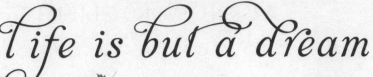

possible are:

Jean Feiwel
publisher

Liz Szabla
editor-in-chief

Rich Deas
creative director

Elizabeth Fithian
marketing director

Holly West
assistant to the publisher

Dave Barrett
managing editor

Nicole Liebowitz Moulaison
production manager

Lauren Burniac
associate editor

Ksenia Winnicki
publishing associate

Anna Roberto
editorial assistant

Find out more about our authors and artists
and our future publishing at macteenbooks.com.

OUR BOOKS ARE FRIENDS FOR LIFE